Welcome to Oakland

a novel

by

Eric Miles Williamson

Published by Raw Dog Screaming Press
Hyattsville, MD

First Edition

Cover photography: James F. Nelson
Cover design: Kevin Prufer
Book design: Jennifer Barnes

Portions of this book have appeared in the following journals:
Arroyo; Boulevard; The Chattahoochee Review; Rosebud; The Texas Review

Thanks to the Christopher Isherwood Foundation

Printed in the United States of America

ISBN: 978-1-933293-79-0

Library of Congress Control Number: 2009922633

www.rawdogscreaming.com

In Memoriam P.J. Rondinone

Nobody dast blame this man.

—Arthur Miller

Also by Eric Miles Williamson

Novels

East Bay Grease
Two-Up

Nonfiction / Criticism

Oakland, Jack London, and Me

Welcome to Oakland

I'M ALWAYS HAPPIEST WHEN I LIVE IN A DUMP, AND I'VE LIVED IN SOME serious shitholes.

I've lived in people's backyard sheds that stank of fertilizer and gas-powered lawnmowers, in the storage rooms of the construction companies and snorted diesel fumes all night, in garage apartments that haven't been converted into apartments, concrete floors and rickety wooden work benches against the walls, the stink of cat piss and dead possum. When I've found a place for my car where I don't get hassled by the cops or the neighbors or the business owners or the nightwatchmen, I've crashed in the back of my stationwagon.

Right now, I am one happy motherfucker.

I'm living in a garage, detached, single-car, in the middle of bumfuck Missouri. Warrensburg. Costs me $200 a month. The floor is concrete, stained with oil because the previous tenants have been Chevys and Fords. It's summer, a hundred and five degrees, and if I turn on a light at night-time the bugs stream through the holes in the walls and ceiling like some shit from a horror movie. Mornings I drink my coffee from a cup with a lid because if I don't I end up swallowing spiders and roaches and gnats and flies that swim in my cup. I wake with bugs in my mouth, in my ears. Until I started wearing sweatpants with elastic bands around the waist *and* ankles, they'd crawl right up my asshole.

For a shower there's a hose been run in from outside hanging from a hook on the ceiling, drain's a hole in the floor, and when water's not going down the hole, bugs crawl up it. These are some weird-ass bugs, too. I don't know what the fuck they are. Missouri designer bugs, is what. Winters I kick the snow off my shoes when I walk in and it stays there, doesn't melt, and I have to sweep it out. When I shower, the water turns the floor into a fucking ice-skating rink.

I'm sure as shit not living here for some *romantic* writerly reason, slumming with *the people* so I'll have something to write about, being some heartfeeling tourist in the intestines of the world. Dig: I'm not one of those trust fund art-fags who thinks it's fun to hang out with "the people," who does his sympathetic pity-essay for NPR on the weekend, cataloging the denizens of the student ghetto he lives in so as to preach art-Christianity to the other condescending snobs who listen to that crap, pretending that they *care* and *understand*, making like they do anything but sneer at the pregnant drug addict teenage whore who's weeping for the peppy yet *understanding and compassionate* interviewer. I'm not one of those wine-drinking sushi-eating faggots who takes up causes he's never had anything to do with (men who call themselves *feminists! Good God!*), who thinks it's groovy to wear work boots that have never stepped in concrete or hot asphalt, who *buys* faded and ripped up jeans, who drinks Bud because it's cool and not because it's the best they can afford. I'm not like those guys you see at the coffee shops pretending they have something to write in their *notebooks*, dressed in black like that makes them cool instead of dressed in black Ben Davis work duds so the grease don't show.

This book is not about my overcoming of *adversity* or about my *struggle against my environment*, because I *like* my environment and always have, excepting the time I got uppity and married into the suburbs. It's about people who *work* for a living, who not only get dirty but who never get clean, who wash their hands with Gunk and solvent and bleach and Lava soap, who scrub their skin with chemicals and the skin dries out and goes shiny as buffed leather, and when the skin finally peels like a molting snakeskin beneath is still grease and oil and permanent filth that goes down to the bone. They're characters—to *you*—but to me they're my *people*, the ones I grew up with, my father who beat truck tires with a sledge hammer until he worked himself to death, my brother who was killed by a gang on the Mexican streets of Oakland, my other brother dead wrapped around a lightpost in a night-drunk carheap, the men I worked with on construction sites and dozens of them now dead in needless and stupid accidents not of their making, the Hell's Angels who reared me and who threw me a party in Oakland at Dick's Restaurant and Cocktail Lounge after I wrote down the first part of this story, posting a guard at the door to keep out the non-smokers, at the party telling me the gory stuff I'd not remembered or not known or neglected to commit to the page for fear they *would not be flattered*, when in fact they *would have*.

Living in a trailer when I was growing up—a nineteen-footer—next to the Mohawk gas station where Pop worked, and then later living in the black ghettos of Oakland and having my white ass whomped at least once a month, and then being homeless while I had a job driving a dump truck because I couldn't afford the deposit and first-and-last-month's rent on an apartment, I got stupid and decided I wanted the good life, the *suburb* life, that I wanted to live where people mowed their lawns and washed their cars and drank water that didn't have flakes of rust settling to the bottom of the glass.

I wanted a family that wasn't fucked up like mine, a family in which the grandfather hadn't boned his daughter, in which the kids knew who their parents were, a family that didn't have to live in a trailer or move every year because they got evicted, a family that didn't have to wait reunions until people got out of jail or rehab. I wanted kids who didn't have to deal with over a dozen step-parents and countless ex-step siblings. I wanted to marry a woman who didn't have some other man's jism drooling down her jowls when I got home from busting my ass all day at work, a woman *not* like my mother who jumped the fence like a bitch-cat in heat every time there was a male neighbor under thirty in a two-mile radius, whose kids wouldn't walk in on her humping five or six dudes at a shot.

I wanted a *good wife* who smiled at me when I walked in the door at day's end and took my suit-jacket and handed me a glass of iced tea and asked me how my day was, and I'd say, "Just fine! Let's see if your parents want to have dinner with us," and she'd say, "I've already invited them, and they'll be here any minute!" and we'd both grin like idiots and look around our house at the clean, light-colored furniture and white shag carpet that had never been soiled by oil or grease or diesel or transmission fluid or the blood of family, friends, or enemies. I wanted it all: the house, the car, the kids, the in-laws, the retirement fund, the lawnmower, the washer and dryer and electric goddamn can opener.

I got married. I cleaned up and went white-collar, wore t-shirts with collars and pussy brown shoes with tassels like I was some fairy, gained fifty pounds and became a fatass like my new neighbors. Bitch went vegetarian on me after we were married half a year. *Organic tomatoes.* Shampoo, *not tested on animals.* Tofu hotdogs, for fuck's sake. What the fuck are those?

I'd had girlfriends from the suburbs before, and I didn't mind the way they covered up their vegetarian spice-stink with organic perfume and herbal deodorant. I slipped them the dick when they came slumming in my hood, cruised on over to Oakland's *nasty* to piss off their pasty parents, brought them home after their curfews to fancy houses with mowed lawns and garaged cars with barking curs that had more expensive haircuts than anyone in my family has ever had, ever. I've seen those freaked out porch lights come on and the mommies and daddies come to the door and scope my stationwagon and me, and I've seen the terror in their eyes when they've seen my "Yep, I screwed your little bitch" smile.

"She's spawned with the scum, Sir, Ma'am."

They made me want to puke, the pleat-slacked tassle-shoed satin-sheet penny-loafer alligator-shirt clean-shaven Gold's Gym American Express SUV blowjob at the strip-joint Starbuck's BMW crystal rocks glasses gas fireplace bottled water wine with a cork Heineken hot tub mowed lawn entertainment center waterbed fancy cracker twenty-dollar haircut mall-shopping black sock clipped fingernail nosehair-trimmed contact lens wearing mail-order catalog easy-listening ski slope Hawaii Holiday Inn flower garden brand name grocery fresh veggie only pussies, and their bitches squatted like fat bitch turkeys in their McMansions, inbred retarded poodles yapping and pissing on the Italian marble tiles. Those suburban runny little shits are insured against everything—fire, flood, earthquakes, bodily injury, bad husbands and wives, ingrate spawn. No amount of insurance, though, can take away their fears. Where I come from we don't need insurance because we're already at the bottom. *Sue me?* Right. What you going to take, my eight-track collection of Creedence and Santana and Tower of Power? Fuck you. Back home, we're not afraid of shit except not having enough loot to hold court on Friday night at Dick's Restaurant and Cocktail Lounge, ten whiskeys and gallons of beer and plastic baskets of fried zucchini and pretzels.

But they only made me want to puke because I knew they were so far out of reach, so way out there that I'd never be allowed into anything more than an occasional pair of non-skid-marked not-bought-at-Sears fancy silk lace-trimmed panties. I wanted an *address*, a *phone number*, a normal life that didn't surprise me at all. I wanted a *television* I watched night after night, a *bed*, and *curtains*. I wanted to be *happy*, like *they* were. Like they are.

Now I'm really fucking happy. I'm happy because the stink of my dump has replaced the stink of the suburbs I attained. Now I am wise. I'd rather smell like ghetto shit or country death-rot fertilizer and rotting deer carcass than suburban potpourri.

I am not a milkman, a postal worker, a cab driver, a ditchdigger. I've delivered newspapers, I've poured concrete, I've scrubbed the coffee stains from bosses' mahogany desks, from plush white carpet, I've had my skin burned off by hot tar and asphalt, I've manufactured healthfood, I've built freeway overpasses, I've mixed drinks at lonesome bars and at bars where I had to wear their starched uni-colored uniform. I was a caretaker in Marin County watching over private tennis courts, protecting nylon nets from theft in the night. I have trowelled the concrete slabs your glass and steel building rests upon.

I've done the shit work, the work the fat-faced red-neck whiskey-gutted blue-collar grunt has done. I've watched seven men die on construction sites, seen men flopping on the ground like fish in the dirt, their pants fouled, seen men with their skulls split and splattered like hammer-beaten watermelons, seen the way the corpses' eyes clouded and ceased to see. I've passed out from exhaustion before lunchtime. But I'm not a postal worker, I'm not a milkman, and as poor as I might be, as little money I might have to spend on VCR's and wristwatch-televisions and ice-making refrigerators, I still haven't become a bucket-headed middle-class television-stupored mat of toilet blood. The "I" of this story, this thing, is the most important character. That's me, T-Bird Murphy.

I called a chick poet—one of those baggy pants silver jewelry no make-up bumpersticker healthfood hairy-armpit types—and I read her what I've just written, and she got pissy and said, "People don't want to know the *truth*. That's why they read fiction. You're just telling the truth, and the people who read books are the very 'art fags' you're railing against."

The art fags didn't like my last book and they're going to like this one even less. I showed some of this book to my agent, and he fired me. He said, "I can't help feeling like one of the people that T-Bird would like to see dead." He was right. Art fag.

Big fuck. I'm not writing for art fags.

I write for the not yet born and the dead.

I don't write for you.

Or for the gang of housewives who invited me to a bar to talk to me the last time I wrote a book.

"How much of this really happened?" one asked.

"The editors made me cut the bad parts," I said. "It was much worse than I was allowed to write about."

That got them gooey. They bought me more drinks, which suited me fine, because I was broke. Then the good looking one, a woman maybe 35 years old, the most *promising writer in the writer's group* they all agreed and dressed in appropriate low-cut black, started telling about her new Winnebago that was being paid for with her ex-husband's child support money since she'd "married up" and gotten herself a plastic surgeon who specialized in fake titties for hags and strippers. Her ex, she chortled, was now mopping floors at the bar across town, paying sixty percent of his take-home pay in child support.

I knew him. I'd heard his story. I'd been to his trailer. I'd puked in his toilet. He was a good man. He gave me another beer. He told me the route to drive home so no cops would catch me. I've driven drunk exactly seven or eight thousand times. I've never been caught. I'm not stupid, after all.

She wasn't an art fag.

She was an art cunt. Art Cunts wear fancier clothes, and they're not drunk before they start drinking for the day. Art Cunts know who their parents are—or so they think. Art Cunts have for their dowries houses—wired with cable and automatic garage door openers and garbage disposals and ice-making frost-free refrigerators and Mexicans to mow the lawn neat as a carpet, underground sprinklers and grounded plug outlets—and they come equipped with cars and washing machines and promises that you don't have to worry about your retirement fund. Spend it now! My Art Cunt inheritance will take care of our Art Cunt retirement! We won't have to worry about a thing, *honey bunches*. Honey bunches. Honey *fucking* bunches.

Are you an Art Cunt?

By the way, the occasional "you" in this book isn't a stylistic tic. It's an implication, a chastisement, an insult. It's not addressed to some universal "You," no. It's addressed to you personally. Take it to heart, motherfucker or motherfuckerette. I don't want to hear about your pain. Fuck you. I've howled and cried until my eyes bled from salt. I got no sympathy for you. I eat my own shit every day.

Eat yours.

You might think it tastes better than mine, but I bet it don't. Sushi shitbag.

You want sympathy? Talk to your psychiatrist, your counselor, your guru, your swami, your fortune teller. Talk to your goddamn mommy. Talk to that wife or husband or yours who pretends they love you and who loathes the way you smell, the stink of your age. If I ever meet you, I'll probably not like you. I'll probably do my damnedest to make sure you don't like me. I sure as shit ain't going to comfort you, give you a story larded and stuffed with *redemption* and *hope*.

I'd kick you in the cunt, except it'd mess up my shine.

I've looked out of my window at night and seen the smog, I've breathed the same crud in the air that you have, I've walked out my door at three in the morning and smelled the stench of the great American armpit. I know it's there, and I don't claim to embrace it. I condemn it. And I condemn you.

Back in Oakland, in the *neighborhood*, I was one of the folk. I could walk down 98th Avenue and every other warehouse or shop was run by someone I'd known since I was a kid pumping their gas, back when I lived in the trailer next to the Mohawk with Pop. I'd been in their houses during holidays, and I'd sweated it out with their kids in school trying to learn how to read and shit like that. No matter what I did, no matter how many times I showed up to work hungover or stupid, no matter what kind of screwups I did on the job that cost the big man money, the foremen and managers were my *compadres*, and the job stayed or I got fired with the best refs you've ever seen ever. And the next boss understood the code and hired me and I got checks long enough until I could line up another job soldering or welding or laying brick or asphalt, busting tires or running fence or lumping crates at the docks, jackhammering or guniting or rip-rapping or pouring mud or sheetrocking or doing something really nasty. Those cool old dudes took us on knowing all along that they'd eventually have to fire us and send us to the next guy down the street, and that when they did, we'd get our shit together for six months or so, do a good job for long enough to make us worth the checks until we started on the skid.

Some advice for you: if you want to get a job, don't wear new work-boots when you meet the boss. Your boots need to be old and sucked dry by concrete, spotted with roofing tar, the laces tied back together where they've broken. You want your shirt to be torn and dirty, and you want the back pockets of your Ben Davises to have holes from carrying margin-trowels and pliers. You got to look strong, but you need to look tired too, like this is your first day off in a long time, like you've worked every damned day of your life until yesterday, like you woke up at four in the morning not because the alarm was set, but because you've been trained by years of busting your ass.

I've never filled out a job application and I've gotten damned near every job I've tried to get. If a company wants you to fill out an application, then you tell them to shove it up their ass and move on to the next company in the phone book. If they want you to fill out an application, that means they're so stupid that they can't tell whether or not you're working hard from watching you on the site. If they want you to fill out an application, then that's just the beginning of them nitpicking you to death like a bunch of persnickety faggots. First the application, and the next thing you know you'll have to wash your hands every time you take a leak.

The jobs, they were just to get by, because what I really wanted to do and what I was good at doing was playing my trumpet. I was the best second-rate trumpet player in Northern California, and there wasn't a merengue or salsa band I couldn't cut a chair with except the good ones. I could make forty bucks a night nearly every weekend, and if I played well, which I often did, I could get wasted on whiskey sent by the customers after my solos.

I mostly played Mexican bands, and I always felt ashamed of myself around those guys. There's nothing I'd rather *not be* than an American man, a man who by world standards is a eunuch, a dickless ball-less please-fuck-me-up-the-ass slob who stands in the doorway getting slapped around by his wife when he's late getting home because of a traffic jam or a subway stall, the bitch saying, "Who were you fucking, you bastard," who begs his wife not to divorce him because he knows damned well he's fucked forever and always if she does, she raping his retirement, getting his house, taking his children, and making him pay for the privilege of living beneath an underpass the rest of his numbered days while she lives into eternity, who comes home to find his woman become a Wiccan gathered with her cunt club and burning a straw effigy of Priapus in the backyard, the *ladies* dancing in joy at Priapus' flaming and shrinking cock, and while the Roman boner-god burns, the American man tells his wifey that he's *proud of her for asserting her female otherness*, who slaves like a pig on the assembly line or the construction site or driving a greasy semi or runs a jackhammer until his guts are Jell-O only to find himself called a *White Male Oppressor* and *Enemy*, who opens a door for a California *liberated* 300 pound disgusting zit-faced quarter-pounder-choked *lady* only to have the bitch turn to him and say, "I can open it myself, thank you, and don't think I'm impressed by your feigned chivalry because I know all you want to do is fuck me," who digs ditches and unplugs toilets and cleans carpets that have been shat upon by generations of feline and hound and then on the daily news finds himself deemed "advantaged," who, truly, would be better off without his balls and even better off if his balls were being served up on a Rocky Mountain Oyster Platter, barbecue sauce slathered and cole slaw on the side, gimme a fucking beer. An American man, shit. Why do you think whenever an American man goes overseas he comes back with a foreign wife? Because women in every other county know, from experience, that no man treats a female better than a sucker of an American man, a man who does not believe his woman farts or shits or wipes her menstrual slobber with her restaurant napkin. Navy men go overseas and come back with Asian spinners.

There's Norman Stephanski, a buddy of mine who was *in love* with a short-haired Jewish runt named Lisa with big lips and a mustache. He'd have done anything for her, and he did, the sap: he went to college where *she* wanted to go to college, lived in the apartment *she* chose even though he couldn't afford it and took out student loans to pay for it, never drank normal beers but always fancy imported shit in green bottles that *she liked* because it made her feel fucking special and better than the rest of us because we'd never even heard of the countries those fucking beers came from, let alone the beer brands themselves. Some African or South Pacific swill that tasted like a mowed lawn or the smoke from the Kellogg plant. Norman waited on that bitch hand and foot, put on a white shirt and tie when he met her Goldbergstein parents and they inspected his gentile ass, made the paycheck and did the laundry and dishes besides. She was a literature major, wanted to be a *literary critic* when she grew up. Didn't want to be a writer, because writers are just idiot savant chumps, genetic mutants who know not what they do, *emotional retards*, she once said, *unable to cope with the intellectual and psychological and sociological realities of life.* Critics, she said, are those who lend credence to the malconceived and accidental manifestations of those whom the white male patriarchy have deemed to be artists. The insane, she said. Critics, she said, are why artists exist, and without critics, she said, there would be no art. And then she'd go off on Norman, who had dreams of becoming a writer, pseudo-psycho-analyzing him, saying that the reason it took him so long to shit when he went to the pot was that he refused to let his bad *karma* go, that he was a typical male living on the bile of his testosterone, when, as Norman once told me, the truth of the matter was that she watched him like a hawk all the fucking time and he never got any pussy out of that cunt and the only place he could be alone enough to jack off was in the can, and so he spent half the day there pounding his pud until he jerked it ragged.

He said the few times she actually did let him fuck her the cunt squeaked, made a noise that sounded like one of those little toy mice you give your cat to play with, and in four years he never managed to get his dick all the way inside her, all fifteen times he double-condom boned the bitch. He'd go silly, semen making his eyes bulge and his speech go whack, staggering the dockside bars idiotized saying, "Squeak! Squeak! Squeeeeeeeeek!" and laughing like some deranged souse, Squeak! echoing off the warehouse walls. Well, three years they spent taking classes at the university *she chose*, and then she decided she didn't *like it* anymore, wanted to go to a university more befitting of her *specialness*, a *private* university that wasn't *attended* by riff-raff commoners, an *East Coast*, not an East Bay, *private institution of higher learning* that *only the best people* attended, and so off to Syracuse University, in *upstate* New York, they went.

Two torched credit cards of moving expenses and tuition later, that is, three months later, Norman's smelling something nasty about the bitch's behavior. She smells like sexing and he knows it's not his, and he breaks open the lock of her desk drawer and finds love letters, dozens of them, love letters from her Syracuse man dating back two years and begging her to move to Syracuse so they could fuck and fuck and fuck, and lovey-lovey and kissie-kissie and drink wine and eat some French-shit food Norman couldn't pronounce, huggie-huggie, huggie-fucking-huggie. The letters made Norman want to puke. He said they stank of some faggot cologne. He read them and read them and he got drunk, not on that fancy ass nigger gook beer, no. He went out and bought himself a bag full of Colt 45s, 40's, and he sat on the porch like an Oakland boy and watched the pale eastern sun slip away and gone into dark. And he got calm, calmer than he'd ever been, and when he was calmest, about five 40's into the night, he stood up and pulled out his dick and pissed, pissed standing there on the porch and it was a stupendous, a purifying piss, one that nearly reached the sidewalk, and, while he was standing there pissing and his groin tingling with the relief that only a good piss can bring, Lisa Goldbergstein, his *love*, his woman, cruised up on her stylish mo-ped and he swung the stream of his piss toward her and doused her, saying, "Hey hey! *This is not symbolic! This, bitch, is not symbolic! I'm pissing on you and you don't need to interpret this, bitch. What does it mean? What the fuck's it mean? It means, bitch, it means that I'm pissing on you. That's what the fuck it means.*"

A month later Norman was on a plane to Tokyo. I'd been married and divorced by the next time I heard from him, nearly a year later. I'd partied with the angels and then had the great asshole of life pucker up, build up pressure, and unload, dousing me with the shit and digested bile of the cosmos, and I was on a drunken spree, trying to find the merest of solace in the deep dry cavern of booze soaked cunt. The mornings I woke and was not alone I rolled away from whatever stinking cooze I'd harpooned the night before, some skanky love-desperate big-eyed whore just low enough to want *me*, to trust *me* with the remnants of her shat-upon hopes. Alone or not, mornings I woke and wished I hadn't. And before I began to cry I'd find some booze and swill, put a buzz on that would numb me from my own desolation. I was bad off after that wife was gone, couldn't shake the image of her, of Rhonda sitting in the corner with her panties down around her ankles, her heroin-silked eyes dilated like black hubcaps, saying, "Fuck you! I hate you! Fuck you! I hate you! Fuck you, I hate you!" and pissing. I couldn't close my eyes without hearing her and seeing her in a squat. And it was always a violent piss, a piss that said all she had to say about the world. She was more fucked up than me, and that was saying something, and I didn't find out why until many years later when I discovered that before she met me the man who'd been fucking her had been her father, and her mother had found out and instead of jailing the bastard, threw Rhonda out on her own. She'd fuck any man who'd give her a place to crash for the night, and eventually she fucked me.

It's funny, you know: no matter how many jobs you lose, no matter how broke you are, no matter if you have a place to live or if you're sleeping in the junkyard—no matter what there's always a way to cop a tumbler or a 40. Women, of course, can always use their cunts to get some hooch. But men? Men don't use their cunts. We come through for each other because we all secretly suspect that we'll be the next one broke and without a bed. We help each other because we like to have people in our debt, owing us a bender. You need a drink? Somebody will always come through, not out of love but out of hope that when they need their bottle someone else will cough up their debt. One day when I was pretty low, scrapping for meals and living in an ISO—one of those cargo containers they use for trains, semis, and ships—they have entire unpatrolled cities of them by the Oakland docks, and those ISOs are bigger than a single-wide and more rock solid, and the census takers never come around, but if they did, the populations of the seaside and railroad cities of America would grow by ten percent—one day I came back to my rusted ISO and found a case of Glenfiddich and a note: "Fuck You! No one should die on rotgut. The Lone Ranger Rides Again! –Love and Kisses, Duke." That case was gone in a week, and I never even got a hangover. No wonder rich fuckers drink expensive hooch. Duke's dead now, died a month after his wife of 35 years, Myrtle, divorced him. Died of despair. She'd gotten God on Duke, and hadn't fucked him in twenty years, and she'd finally decided that by being married to Duke she was being unfaithful to Jesus, and so she divorced Duke so she could suck the heavenly weenie without guilt. Duke was one of those men who knew everything, displacing his ridiculously constant and loyal wolfen love for his hateful wife with a voracious passion for acquiring knowledge. Myrtle's final act of spite was having his funeral service performed in *her* church, Jesus Fuckyourwife Christ officiating, *Jesu Cristo* grinning over the dead cuckold with bleeding hands and forehead that don't mean a fuck because he's God and can heal those hands right on up and shoot a game of pool anytime he fucking wants. That bitch hated Duke so much she had "Amazing Grace" played on the church organ as they hauled his methane farting carcass away to the dirt.

A year had passed since I'd heard from Tokyo Norman and when I finally did hear from him it was on Christmas when I was visiting Pop and his family at the trailer. The phone rang and all I could hear was a sloshing sound, and then Norman's voice came on and he said, "Hey, T-Bird, you know what that was?"

"Norman?"

"You know what that was?"

"Let me crack a beer," I said. It was early, but I was already pretty soaked.

"Phone sex," Norman said. "That was the sound of the phone up Kimoko's cunt. Want to hear it again?"

"Course I do," I said.

For two or three hours and two six packs of Oly Norman kept it up, jamming his phone in and out of Kimoko's cunt and then licking off the slobber and telling me his Tokyo stories, about the time he shat on some chick so drunk was he while he was fucking her and about how she got rags and cleaned him up and then fucked him again, about how he and his roommate Burlton boned some Jap girl who got drunk and thought she was a bunny-rabbit, hopping around the room and bouncing on their cocks bunny-style, she screaming ichi-mo! or something like that which means I'm cumming in Jap, about the Shinjuku district of Tokyo and how if you fuck chicks on stage at the sex shows you get to fuck them for free if you have a "Western-size" cock, drooling Jap businessmen as horny

to see a big white cock as they are watching that big white cock fucking
one of their women, somehow hating Yankees for torching their city to
cinders and getting stiffies thinking about us enslaving and humiliating
their females—like *they* do. Somehow people who've been truly fucked
want to keep on being fucked and fucked and fucked, Norman on the
subways surrounded every day by Jap girls jockeying for position to rub
their little asses against his cock while pretending they're not, reaching
around and tightening their little fists around his cock and through his
slacks and leading him off at the next subway stop like dragging a bull
by its ring to the nearest "Love Hotel," Jap no-tell-motels that don't have
rooms but instead have slots like filing cabinet drawers, fuck tubes you
rent by the hour. On and on he went, and then he hung up because the
phone cunt was about to cum, and I didn't talk to Norman again for about
another year, and this time I called him from a bar and this time his bitch
was Taeko of the Skies, a stewardess whore, his flying prostitute, who,
after describing all the noises she made when they fucked, he confessed
he *loved*. And so while she slept there on his futon, and he described her
beauty, and how she'd thank him after they fucked, and then she'd do the
dishes, and then she'd leave like a puff of cool mist into the dilapidated
and twisted streets of Tokyo, the subway rattling past and the sound of
sad shuffling hungover feet grinding the pavement into dust. He married
her. He's still married to her. He doesn't let her out of the house for fear
she'll become just another American cunt. It's working. It's been working
for a dozen years. They have kids. They have a house. They can't see their
neighbors. They don't want to. She still thanks him every time they make
love. And now, heart mended, he thanks her too.

Everywhere I looked I saw misery, destitution, hopelessness, rage,
filth. Everywhere but in *my* soul. Somehow I hadn't been touched, not in a
way that could shake my unalterable faith and optimism. I knew somehow
that humanity wasn't as ugly as the humanity I'd seen. I knew that the

festering rot and swamp of the hearts of man was not its natural condition but was born of disillusion, that the cannibal rending of man from man was a consequence, not a cause, was the desperate reaction of hearts shorn and devoured raw and still a-pumping. I'd seen the men I'd known—and sometimes the women—seen them destroyed into suicide, seen them reduced to the subhuman ugliness of Norman in Tokyo—despair turned into shitting on oneself and defiling all with whom he'd come in contact. I'd seen the sadness of Duke, on his knees every time he got drunk begging the hallucination of his wife to come home to him, to lay down with him, to love him as she had before she loved an ideal and perfect and snickering god. I'd seen my father, Pop, lose wife after wife, seen him lose his dignity and kill in rage, wanting to strike at something, at anything, to somehow heal the wounds that never heal, the cancerous sores of disappointed hope. There's P.J., who hanged himself after his wife dumped him and took his daughter, and Mike, whose wife dumped him and took his daughter and married a doctor and so he drank himself to diabetic death on a bottle of single-malt that I bought him, Antonio, whose wife kicked him out and took the sons and by the time this book sees print he'll be dead of drink, and on and on, so much sadness it's almost too much to bear.

The crowd at Dick's has a particular interest in The Case of Blaise, because no one knows if he's alive or dead. Blaise called himself a full-time alchemist and part-time composer. As far as I knew, he couldn't figure an A from a G on a banjo, probably couldn't play a goddamn throat warbler or a kazoo. No one ever heard him play a note, and no one ever saw a score he'd written, not until after he was taken out by a SWAT team. He told us he was a studio composer for TV commercials but wouldn't tell us which ones, and so even though he seemed to have some cash from those alleged commercials of his, and he didn't have to work like us, we suspicioned. He told us the jingles paid the bills while he performed alchemical experiments and composed *serious* music, that one day he would only experiment and create art. One of those guys who thinks *art* can replace *work*. Asshole. We loved him.

When he met Ashleigh, he didn't know that she'd been running all over the neighborhood telling everyone she was getting the hell out of Oakland, that she was going to get pregnant and marry a scientist, in that order. She couldn't tell a scientist from a bartender. She had no idea that alchemy was an art long abandoned and dead, a relic like human dignity. So when Blaise moved to town—he wasn't really one of us, but instead a *Southern Californian* who grew up living on a hill—and he'd been to a community college in L.A. for two years, the only guy in the neighborhood, excepting Shapiro, who'd ever set foot in a real *college* and not just a union hall training course or cop school or refer/a-c camp—he wasn't prepared for Oakland, and he sure as shit wasn't ready for Ashleigh.

Blaise moved to Oakland because his aunt died and left him her house. On 62nd Avenue, right in the heart of niggertown, much to his surprise. He used to come up from L.A. summers when he was a kid and the neighborhood was white, and that's what he remembered, not an ornamentally-ironed caged shack with fried chicken bones on the lawn and junkies on the run from the cops hopping his fence every night like Olympic hurdlers.

Someone told Ashleigh that Blaise was an alchemist, and she asked what an alchemist was. A scientist, is what she was told, and then Ashleigh went after Blaise balls out and titties turned upward. When Blaise met the guys at Dick's Restaurant and Cocktail Lounge, he told us he was getting married and he bought us drinks, and then he stood there smiling and telling us about how this woman, his *love*, his *angel*, his *mythological Celtic goddess*, made him shoot his wad *five times* the first night he boned her. Pregnant, we all thought. She milked him, and now he's had it, the poor son of a bitch.

We all knew better than to go near Ashleigh, and she'd at one time or another late at night howled at most of our windows—those of us who had good union jobs—and begged us for dick. She even called Ed the Jew and whispered to him, "Please, Eddie, please come fuck me. I'm so wet. Please fuck me, Eddie." And Ed the Jew, the ugliest of all of us, well, he was married to a beautiful sad woman, long dark hair and eyes that were older than the world, and he treated her like shit, threatening her all the time that he'd throw her out on her ass, telling her that she was lucky, bitch, that anyone would have her. And she believed him, even though any of us would have taken her in a flat second. Ed the Jew went and screwed old howler Ashleigh, not telling her—like he told us afterward—that his pecker shoots blanks, and so there was no way she was going to catch him in her baby-baking snatch.

It wasn't long before Ashleigh decided that she didn't like scientists after all, particularly scientists who are composers, and least of all those of the Blaise variety. Blaise was an Italian—Catholic, that is—and so *of course* he married her when, a few weeks after the five orgasm evening, she announced the pending arrival of the swelling zygote in her quim. Blaise *owned* the dead aunt's house, making him initially double desirable—a *landowner*—and making him an honorary citizen and another among the whitey minority, and therefore hated and fair and obligatory game for the blacks and Mexicans. Blaise became a local celebrity at Dick's, showing up at six in the morning when we were having our pre-work vodkas, except Blaise didn't leave. He'd still be there at noon when we came for our mid-day pop. The baby was almost due, and Ashleigh was going out of her mind because *she didn't want to live in Oakland*—as if any of us wanted to live in Oakland, for fuck's sake. *Why'd I marry a nerdy goofball scientist if I'm just going to have to live in this shithole!*

Blaise's science, she had discovered, wasn't the science you see on the TV, the Berkeley or Harvard dude in the white smock making a killing designing weapons that melt the eyeballs of billions of gooks and turn their bones into interstellar dust, then coming home to his swanky house with a dock and a rowboat where he stores a ukulele on which he plays *his honeypie* love songs while he paddles leisurely around at sunset. No, Blaise's alchemy consisted of a little shed about as big as an outhouse he'd built in the backyard, an ice-chest filled with cheap plastic-bottle vodka, a stack of paper, some pens, a port-a-potty so he didn't have to ever come out, and a door that locked from the inside so no one could bother him, especially his new bride. What he was working on? None of us knew, and when we'd ask him, he'd just say, "Yes." We'd push him, we'd buy him drinks, we'd try to get him drunker but he'd just smile, even when his head was hanging, and he'd say, "Yes." He *was* kind of fucked up, come to think of it.

The day after the baby was born, the blacks and Mexicans welcomed Blaise to the neighborhood, Oakland fashion. Some Mexicans stopped their low-rider in front of Blaise and Ashleigh's house. A black dude was walking past on the sidewalk and they opened fire, Mac-10s and pistols, the black dude a mess of meat strewn all over the yard and guts and blood splattered on the house's windows and porch. That wasn't the bad part, though, not for Blaise. The bad part, he told us, was that Ashleigh really hated him after the "multi-cultural exchange," as he called it. Ashleigh hated him because when the bullets started flying, when they came through the front of the house and peppered the walls, Blaise grabbed the baby out of Ashleigh's hands and dove, protecting himself and the baby, while Ashleigh, in some kind of chick state of shock, just stood there, motionless. Most of the bullets missed her, but one didn't. It went through a butt-cheek and lodged right in her asshole. She screamed, "They shot my ass! They shot my ass!" And Blaise laughed. He couldn't help it, he told us, it was just so fucking funny, at the time. Even at the hospital, when she came out of the anesthesia and asked Blaise if she was okay, if she'd live, Blaise laughed even then, and he said, "You had a bullet stuck in your asshole, but the good physicians have removed it, and someday you'll shit just fine again." Ashleigh never forgave him, didn't forgive him for not helping her out of harm's way, didn't forgive him for laughing when she got shot in the ass, and sure as shit never forgave him for making that crack about being able to shit fine again someday. The more pissed off she got at him, the less he gave a fuck. She'd be hobbling around complaining about her asshole, and he'd tell her that someday he'd have the money to buy her a laser-sight *bionic* asshole, one that would be able to shoot a turd three hundred yards with the accuracy to pop a Mexican square between his beady brown eyes.

Blaise went to work harder than ever at his alchemy, or his composing, or whatever the fuck he was up to, locking himself away in his shed for weeks at a time, never coming out except to sneak some food or dump his port-a-potty along the fence in the backyard, making a dash back into the shed before Ashleigh could catch him. She was still too fat from the baby and hobbling too much from her injured asshole to start screwing around on Blaise—Ed the Jew told us *he* wouldn't even fuck her anymore, not without her asshole, because Ashleigh's asshole, Ed the Jew assured us, was exactly fifty-one percent of what was interesting about Ashleigh—and so she'd stand in the backyard holding the baby in the air and yelling at Blaise, calling him every name she could think of, screeching, "This is your *baby*! Your *baby*, you motherfucker! Some fucking *father* you are!" One time she even wedged a two-by-four under Blaise's shed and tipped it over when he was inside.

She left him. She left him and took his baby, took his baby away, took away his child. They do that, our women. She left him, took the baby, and told him he was a *very bad father*, pointing and wagging her finger at him like she was scolding a naughty child, which, of course, is the worst thing you can tell or do to one of us. Christ, we know we're *bad men*—no one knows that better than us. Hell, we know we're *bad human beings*, but what we hope, what we *want*, is to make some goddamn babies and raise them better than we've been raised. We want to make up for our shittiness by producing people, kids, that are better than us, that have it better, that get the toys we did not get, desserts after every fucking meal.

When Ashleigh left, Blaise lost it. He sold the house and moved into a stucco apartment building that used to be a shitty motel just two doors down. He sold all his stuff. I bought his silverware. Louie, the bartender at Dick's Restaurant and Cocktail Lounge, bought his velvet Elvis. "She told me I'm a *bad father*. She took my baby. She took my *baby*," and that's all we ever heard before he stopped coming to Dick's. "She took my baby," he'd say. "My flesh and blood, my progeny, my *raison d'etre*, my soul. My *child* is going to be raised by that harpy."

When he stopped making forays into public, we'd send recon teams to check up on him, and Blaise would just be sitting in the little apartment he'd rented watching CNN, mesmerized, bottle of vodka in one hand and a cigar in the other. There was no furniture in his apartment, not a scrap, just a TV on the floor and a boom-box that played the classical station even while the TV was blaring. No food in the fridge. Not even beer. No dishes. A bar of soap in the bathroom, but no towels, no washrags. What was weird, though, was the floor of his bathroom. It was lined with row after row of bleach bottles, and each time anyone pissed or shat in his toilet, he'd dump in a bottle of bleach. That was one clean fucking toilet.

Everything that happened on the news was a sign from the gods for Blaise. A tornado would rip through some dipshit trailer park in Texas and Blaise would know, I mean he'd *know*, that the government was conducting secret weather-manipulating experiments that would eventually culminate in a cataclysmic weapon that would shear renegade neighborhoods from the map and spread them over the globe like confetti. Some carpet-pilot in the Middle East would mumble about Allah and then blow himself up in the market square in Jerusalem, and Blaise would have visions of angels warring in the heavens. A species of toad would go extinct in the rain forests of Brazil and Blaise would calculate the precise hour of mankind's final breath. If a sandstorm in Egypt burned a whisker off the Sphinx, a curse had been unleashed and punishment was coming, the wrath of ancient demons rolling across the planet in a wave of sulphurous fire.

Yeah, yeah. We'd seen this kind of shit before, so none of us was all too worried. It was a stage we all went through once in a while. That's just the way things work. Louie, the bartender, was used to us having the occasional vision of doom. "It's just the scaries," Louie would say. "We all get them, the scaries. But eventually the scaries go away." And he'd help whoever'd fallen off their stool, prop him back up at the bar, and pour him another cocktail. The scaries? No problem. That's why God invented booze.

Blaise's ravings about gods and goddesses, his references to stuff we didn't know shit about, his high-falutin cosmopolitical geoconspiratorial gulash—we chalked it up to all that education he'd got himself at his fancy community college, all the crap he'd been served by his goofball hippie professors with more degrees than common sense. Hell, Blaise didn't sound any more out there than the nutcases you could hear at any rally, in any bar, on any street corner in Berkeley, the Bay Area's no-man's hive of screwed-up whacked-out pot-head acid-freaked zombies with degrees that were good for nothing but rolling their marijuana cigarettes and wiping their educated assholes. The Berkeley freaks all sounded just like Blaise—everything was a conspiracy, the government was out to get them, the end of existence was coming. They were as goofy as the Jesus freaks, only they didn't believe in God, they believed in *all the gods*, and a bunch of other weird-ass shit besides. Berkeley is filled with faggots that don't even know they're faggots, that won't admit it. San Francisco faggots aren't so bad, really. They're smart as hell, and they run a good city, clean, tidy, and lots of good music. San Francisco faggots have good goddamn taste in lots of shit. Berkeley faggots, though, they're a different story. One time I was doing a construction job on the Berkeley campus, guniting a swimming pool, lining it with concrete, and at lunchtime I went outside and sat on the lawn with my can of raviolis to watch the college girls. First of all, that was a big mistake. They all wore baggy clothes, nerd glasses, and had hairy legs and armpits. Man, their legs were hairier than mine. But as I sat out there scooping raviolis with my fingers, my face crusted with concrete dust and my hardhat spackled and weighing a ton, I heard a bunch of chanting, and so I walked toward it to check things out. I went around a building and what I saw was a group of about fifty students, guys, sitting around in a circle and they weren't wearing shirts and they were beating their sunken pussy chests like gorillas, in rhythm, chanting and beating their chests. They were some weakling little shits, by the way, flabby and white, their hairless bony chests red from the beating. I watched for a while—there was a group of onlookers—and then I asked the chick next to me, a normal looking chick wearing a skirt and heels, what the hell these guys were doing. She had this look, watching them, this look in her eyes like those audiences in TV preachers' shows, those glazed eyes that stare like a pigeon in love. She told me they were *asserting their maleness.* What? They're asserting their *maleness,* their *gender identity.* Well, that was too many for me. "What time is it?" I said. She held out her arm to me and showed me her wrist. "Here," she said. "You *can* tell time, can't you?" Cooze. Berkeley. *Maleness.* You want to assert your *maleness,* you little faggots? Get a fucking job.

Blaise had always talked like one of them and when he flipped out, when he started up his own personal Church of Incomprehensible Bullshit, when he started sounding like he'd been sucking on an exhaust pipe, we still checked up on him. But when he went over the edge, when he lost it utterly and went beyond what any of us had ever seen, we said fuckit. What's the point? Not only was he gone into Berkeleyland, sailing away on some fumes none of us wanted to inhale, but instead of just floating away, he made a spectacle of himself, and even though we tried to bring him back down to earth, nothing we tried could tether him. He was gone.

At first, there were merely Blaise sightings. Someone would spot him wandering the neighborhood, shaking his fist at the sky and ranting lines from Shakespeare or the Bible or some shit like that. Glenn said he spotted Blaise one time on the top of the bleachers at Castlemont High School, a piece of re-bar ten feet long in his hand and pointed like a lightning rod, and it was raining and Blaise was laughing so loud Glenn could feel the laughter rumble his feet as if a train were going past. When Joey Polizzi spotted Blaise, Blaise was face down in the gutter on 98th street, right in the heart of darkest Oakland dark. Not that this was a big deal, someone face down in the gutter. Hell, we'd all been *there*. But on *that* street? Where the nearest white man was miles away and where even in daylight the blacks would gut you at a stoplight if your work truck's door was unlocked? What the fuck was Blaise doing there, anyway? Polizzi hoisted Blaise into his truck and started back toward Dick's, where people would take care of Blaise and Louie would pour him one of his fancy expensive vodkas, but when Polizzi got to the corner of 98th and East 14th Street, while the truck was moving, Blaise unlocked the door and tumbled himself out onto the street, rolling. Polizzi stopped his truck, but by then Blaise was off and running, howling and reciting some of that college shit of his, disappearing over barbed wire and into dark. After the Incident of 98th Street, we agreed to send Shapiro to Blaise's empty apartment to check up on him, because Shapiro had been to that fancy Jew college in New York City, and because Blaise was obviously *not right*. Shapiro wasn't right either, and so maybe they'd have some kind of college boy fucked up simpatico karma going on.

Shapiro heard classical music playing through Blaise's door. It was loud, as if Blaise had hired an entire symphony orchestra and all two hundred musicians were right there in his apartment. Who listens to classical music loud like that? Blaise was obviously a madman. Shapiro knocked and knocked, beat on that door, and a black chick came out into the hallway and said, "You go, boy. Shut that crazy-ass honky motherfuck the motherfuck up. He crazy," she said. "And shit." And Shapiro beat on that door, and finally Blaise answered and his eye was leaking, blood rolling down his cheek and neck and staining his shirt, not fast bleeding but a steady leak like a brake line, the red fluid oozing in visible pulses. Blaise held a 1.75er of vodka. He held it out to Shapiro, uncapped. "Have a drink, good sir?" he said. Blaise had jabbed his eye with an ice pick—Shapiro saw it on the floor, bloody—and when Shapiro took him to the hospital, dragged him there, actually, all Blaise would say was, "Mine eyes seeth not the evil of the world," over and over again.

After the Incident of the Eyeball, we knew things had gotten out of hand, so we decided to sic Owen Jorgensen on Blaise. Jorgensen was a retired Navy SEAL, and he was a serious person, Jorgensen. Jorg became one of the Dick's crowd after he got discharged on a psych for mowing down a dozen Columbians when on a special op. The SEALs were crawling through the jungle an inch an hour to avoid motion detectors and their C.O. told them they couldn't shoot back even when shot at—they weren't supposed to exist. The bullets were coming in, tracers like flares peppering all round them, and finally Jorgensen lost his nut and stood up like Rambo and mowed until the jungle was silent.

We always told him he'd done the right thing. Hey, someone's shooting at you. You're from Oakland. What the fuck you do? You shoot back at the fucks, that's what. Take the niggers out. Now Jorg worked for the Concrete Wall Sawing guys, demo—demolition. He loved blowing shit up, anything. Fourth of July he'd bring out all the stuff he'd swiped when he got discharged, his footlocker filled with sticks of dynamite and plastic explosives and detonators and all kinds of other goodies that made a statement, and he'd dance in the alley and we'd drink beers and duck for cover and laugh hysterical when he blasted a tricycle into the air or blew a crater into the asphalt. Buildings, though, buildings were his favorites, tearing them into rubble. There'd been half a dozen houses filled with Mexican gangs that'd been mysteriously blown to smithereens since Jorgensen came home to the neighborhood. None of us minded, because those scumbags were nothing but trouble anyway, pothead lowrider fucks. Jorgensen was the Concrete Wall Sawing metal and explosives man, doing what he loved best, running the torches to cut the iron, and, when not showered in sparks and fire, destroying. "It's better to destroy than to create," he'd say. "And the effects are more permanent and more sublime. Eternal."

Every time one of us had a problem, every time someone at Dick's got fucked over by his boss, every time someone's wife was fucking some Mexican or San Francisco lawyer faggot, Jorgensen would practically *beg* us to let him take care of *the problem*. "Address," Jorgensen would say, and he'd put on his sunglasses and stare at us through them, expressionless.

And we knew Jorg was absolutely serious, that if we would just give him that address, our problem would be solved, and solved utterly—utterly and without repercussions. We loved him, and he loved us all, Jorgensen. He'd do anything for us, and he'd be able to take care of our problems without getting caught, because that's what he'd done for a living. We needed someone tougher and smarter than us to get Blaise straightened out, and Jorgensen was the man for the Blaise problem. He'd been asking us to send him all along, telling us that he could take care of this shit, but we'd not wanted to send him, for obvious reasons. Now, though, now it was time for Jorgensen, and so we assigned him to the case of Blaise.

When we asked Jorgensen to take care of Blaise's problem, of course the first thing Jorgensen thought was that we were putting a hit on Ashleigh. "About damned time," Jorgensen said. He took his sunglasses from the pocket of his pea-coat and put them on. Jorgensen said, "Address." Then he smiled. No, we said, this time it's not an ex. It's Blaise. Jorgensen stopped smiling. "Look," he said, "Blaise isn't my best buddy in the world, but he's a buddy. I drink vodka with him right here in this bar. I have no problem with bitch exes, or with their new lover-boys, but I draw a line.

No one I drink with is a potential target."

We were relieved to hear this, and I bought a round for everyone, and we drank together, us and Jorgensen.

We took turns telling Jorgensen what we knew of the Blaise situation. I said, "Blaise bleaches the toilet after every piss and every turd, a gallon of bleach for every pint of piss." Shapiro told of the Incident of the Eyeball, Polizzi recounted the 98th Street Occurrence. Glenn explained the Castlemont High Bleachers Improper Laughter Event.

Jorgensen shook his head. "Bleach?" Jorgensen said.

"Every time."

Jorgensen said, "Something must be done."

Jorgensen told us that he'd do it right. He told us that first he'd cover the necessary intelligence, find out everything he could about the target. He led us outside to his F-150 and opened his tool boxes. They were filled with all kinds of stuff, boxes of ammo, pistols, disassembled automatic weapons, Tommy-gun shotgun cartridges to make streetsweepers with, plastic explosives and detonators we'd seen him fart around with every Fourth of July, sticks of dynamite. He pulled a cammie combat vest from the top of the pile and put it on. He checked it—pistols strapped to the inside, knives in a dozen pockets, metal Chinese stars that looked like they could mow down telephone poles, grenades.

"Knee pads," he said. "For CQB, Close Quarters Battle. A Super Lite bullet proof vest. Classified—you tell, you die."

He looked at us. We nodded.

"First-aid kit for self-surgery, claymores, frag-grenades, Blackhawk assault vest, 40 millimeter grenade launcher. A Surefire flash light with visible laser-sight mechanism—hey, put the red dot on what you want to kill, maim, or destroy. Pop goes the weasel!"

"But Jorgensen," I said. "We just want you to take *care* of him, not take *care* of him."

Jorgensen jerked his head toward me. He stared. His eyes twitched. "You," he said. He looked at all of us. "You, my *friends*, are sending me on a *mission*. Do you understand."

I said, "We understand, but."

"But nothing," Jorgensen said. "You are sending me on *a mission*. On a mission a man must be prepared. If you shits understood this basic principle of survival, if *Blaise* understood this most elementary aspect of the nature of the way things work, he wouldn't need *me*," Jorgensen said. "And neither would you."

We looked at the ground.

"Any more dumb-ass comments?" Jorgensen said. "No? Good. Now," he said. "Multiban-inter/intra team radio specific for spec-ops coms known as the AN/PRC-148, alternatively as the 'lash' which is the unit mounted around the neck and larynx throat operated mike, the MSHR encrypted coms unit. I can whisper and my team will hear me like the voice of God. Flotation flak jacket configured as a raid vest with D-rings mag-pouches and accessory pouches strategically located. An LBV, Load Bearing Vest, will carry from 125 to 200 pounds of equipment. I carry one whole hell of a lot of shit."

He tossed a grenade to Shapiro. "Don't drop that flash-banger," Jorgensen said. He looked at Shapiro serious behind those sunglasses of his. He lifted a box and opened it and it was filled with electronic equipment. "Wiretaps," he said, "to discern the nature of his communications and the possible effects of hostile incoming, namely, *The Ex*."

He lifted another box and opened it. "Night vision," he said, patting the goggles with love. "An AN/PVS-7 *and* the new AN/PVS-21 see-through NVG, strobe light. If the target leaves under cover of darkness, tracking him will be as easy as trailing a semi in the desert."

From the same box he pulled a mini radar looking thing. "Ears," he said. "His mutterings will be known."

He looked at Shapiro. "I'm counting on you to translate that college boy bullshit. I'll provide tapes, you transcribe them, and then they must be destroyed. Audio recordings, unlike video impressions, are illegal unless proper consent is secured. That's the law."

It wasn't quite what we wanted of Jorgensen. All we really wanted was for Jorgensen to stop Blaise from destroying himself, scare the living shit out of him enough to make him stop acting stupid over a cunt and her deviously conceived progeny, because though we'd all been down, and were sure to go down again, we'd not seen anyone down as far as Blaise without rubbing himself out, shooting himself or gutting himself or drinking himself to death or just plain losing the will to live and letting his heart stop beating. Fucking *alto*, amigo. *No mas, adios.*

We just wanted Jorgensen to slap some sense into the boy. Sure, Blaise was kind of weird, fucked up in ways we didn't really understand, way out there because of all his college and books and big goddamn words, but Blaise was one of *us*, and any time one of us went down, in a way we all did, we all dropped yet another rung down into the shitpile of life, and although none of us ever entertained any hopes of climbing any higher out of the shitpile, none of us for damn fuck's sake wanted to go any lower. We were all way too close to the bottom, and we knew it. Lose Blaise, and the next thing you know you can't even afford Olympia beer. Lose Blaise, like we'd already lost Mike, Duke, P.J., George, Andrew, Joey Corollo, Clyde Lee, Bill Ware, Antonio—shit, lose Blaise, and it would take a lot of beers to get over it.

Blaise wasn't even bad off. He still had some money coming in from his jingles, Blaise. He'd been to college. He was nowhere *near* the bottom. He scrubbed toilets not because he *had to*, but because he *wanted to*, for fuck's sake.

We didn't see or hear from either Blaise or Jorgensen for about two weeks, but one day, Jorgensen walked into Dick's with scrolls of paper tucked beneath his arms. He was wearing his sunglasses and his combat vest. He looked bigger than usual. Really big. His chest looked like a 55 gallon oil drum, full.

"Non-regulars," he said. "Out," he said. "Now."

Jorgensen looked at the new guy. The new guy left. I finished his Scotch. It was some of that expensive shit Louie keeps only for show.

Jorgensen said, "Clear the bar." What, we said. "Clear. A clean bar is necessary." And we took our beers and drinks and cleared the way. He set the scrolls on the bar and began unrolling them, grabbing cocktail glasses to hold the paper down. We sidled up to the bar to see what was the what.

Blueprints, is what. Schematics. Detailed studies of all Blaise's comings and goings, of every movement he'd made in the past two weeks. Arrows, dotted lines, stick figures, special symbols, skulls and crossbones, Spy-v-Spy little black bombs sparkling and ready to explode, color-coded indexed dated timed and stamped, notary-public. He'd coded a legend at the bottom of each scroll as if each were an atlas. "The life of Blaise," Jorgensen said.

We drank.

"Blaise is a consistent person," Jorgensen said. "Every day he does the same things at the same times in the same ways. As far as targets go, he gives any professional a hard dick. O-four hundred hours, Blaise leans out of bed, left hand on the floor followed by left foot and then right hand and foot, resulting in a four-point position resembling either a baby or a soldier, depending on one's perspective and personal opinion. Soldier, in my opinion." He gave us that look of his. He said, "Soldier."

There was a reverence in Jorgensen's voice I'd not before heard. It was as if he were way too commiserate with psycho Blaise. Jorgensen understood something about Blaise that we didn't, and I could tell the rest of the guys felt as funny about it as I did. Somehow I felt really small, like some fucking dwarf that didn't understand the world of *great men*.

"Purification," Jorgensen said. "He crawls to the toilet, vomits, then pours a gallon of Clorox bleach into the toilet and scrubs with his hands, wiping the random splatters with bleach soaked toilet tissue, Charmin. After clearing of the stomach, emptying of the intestines and bladder, followed by Clorox and toilet tissue spot check. Sweat, the color and texture of cooled bacon grease, oozes slowly from temples, brow, neck, armpits, and groin."

"Jorgensen," I said.

"O-four thirteen, to the kitchen, clad in boxer shorts, plain white and uncannily sanitary. Open freezer. Withdraw Absolut vodka bottle, 1.75 liter, four gulps, Adam's apple clicking once per gulp. Cap rescrewed, bottle reinstalled."

"Jorgensen," I said. "We don't need all the details."

He gave me another one of those looks of his.

I think I might have sighed or something like that, an outsuck of breath or a shoulder-slump of desperation or resignation. "Jorgensen."

He, though, he, Jorgensen, he gave me a look like no one's ever given me before or since, a look not of disappointment or sadness, no, a look of some kind of shock or disappointment or incomprehension. It was as if I'd said something or done something utterly unutterable, something so *wrong* that no human being, and certainly no one at Dick's Restaurant and Cocktail Lounge would ever say, something so *bad* that somehow Jorgensen's *faith*, his belief in humanity, had been shaken, had been rended and ripped and torn and shredded and stomped upon. It was as if I'd told Owen Jorgensen that *his work* didn't matter, and there's nothing worse you can tell a man who's having a beer at Dick's.

He told Louie to bring him a glass of bottled water.

"Not a beer?" Louie said.

"A soldier," he said, "a *man*," he said, "does not compromise his clarity," Jorgensen said.

"What?"

"*Water*," Jorgensen said.

"Water," Shapiro said.

Jorgensen cut Shapiro a look.

"What?" Shapiro said. "What? What? What."

Jorgensen bowed his head as if in prayer, then slowly raised it. He looked creepy, like someone truly serious. His head looked fucking huge. He took off his cap. He'd shaved it. His skull looked like someone had pounded it with a ball-peen hammer. You could see dents and craters. Fucked up, that head of his.

"You boys have called on *me*," Jorgensen said. "And do you know why? Why is this. Why is because I know the difference between that which is clear and that which is not, and these two things can be predetermined by he who nourishes clarity." Jorg looked at me. "*You* taught me this, T-Bird. When we were kids. *Know the other*," Jorgensen said. "Know *yourself*, and victory will not be at risk. Know the ground, know the conditions of nature. The victory will be utter—if we know the face of the enemy. If you intend to win the war, it is proper to continue fighting. If loss is imminent, it is prudent to quit. If you do not know—well gentlemen, if you don't know, you're fucked."

Jorgensen took a sip of water. "I never fight," Jorgensen said, "if I don't know. In order to know, one must gather, one must ingest, one must *become details*."

He looked around the room. "Details," he said. "Details, gentlemen. If you'd paid heed to details, you wouldn't be here with the likes of me. Fuckup motherfuckers."

Someone bought Jorgensen a drink.

Jorgensen pushed the drink aside and took another sip of his water. "To continue," he said. "The target then returns to his bedroom, attires himself in unfashionable straight-legged jeans, Puritan label—Wal-Mart—and denim button-up shirt. Florsheim wing-tips, black. Returns to refrigerator, four more generous gulps of Absolut vodka. He then makes phone calls. It is these phone calls that pose the most interesting question concerning the target and his behavior."

Jorgensen reached into his ruck-sack and pulled out a small plastic box. Inside were a dozen cassette tapes, each labeled. He handed the tapes to Shapiro. "A transcript, accompanied by a translation of his psycho-babble. By seventeen hundred hours. Return the tapes to me so that I can destroy them with acid."

Jorgensen looked at us hard. "The case of Blaise is perhaps more serious and sinister than any of us had suspected. This is not merely a matter of Clorox."

"He's that fucked up?"

"You gentlemen remember the Chavez girls?"

We remembered. They were two of the sexiest girls in Oakland. They were legendary. When one of them came into the Mohawk station, every-body fought for the chance to fill her tank, to, as we'd say, give them the hose. Their cars always left with the air pressure exactly on target, the oil, water, transmission oil, brake fluid, and windshield wipers checked. We'd be readjusting our dicks for an hour after one of them came in. About six months before the case of Blaise someone had killed both of them, raped them, chopped their heads off, and, according to Eddie Martino the cop, each of them had something jammed up between their legs. Martino wouldn't tell us what it was. "Pretty nasty is what it was," he said.

"Blaise may be the killer," Jorgensen said.

We laughed and tipped one.

"His phone calls," Jorgensen said, "are to the coroner, the police, the morgue, the cemetery, the Chavez parents, and the girls' friends. In that order, every day. He wants all the details, and he's writing them down, copiously and with method. The tapes will tell."

Jorgensen directed us to his scrolls, and he told us the rest, indicating Blaise's movements with his finger moving along carefully drawn and color-coded lines on the schematic. Every day Blaise would leave his apartment and walk to Ashleigh's house across town, a seven mile trek, and he'd just sit on the curb across the street staring, sometimes crying when he caught a glimpse of his kid. Then he'd pull a little notebook out of his pocket and retrace the steps of the Chavez girls' last day alive, starting at their parents' house, going to their boyfriends' houses, on to Castlemont High, from class to class and Blaise would walk the halls—he'd convinced the guards that he was on the school board—and then to the Mac's Lounge where they'd had lunch together, back to school, to the football field where they'd had cheerleader practice.

Jorgensen paused. He knitted his brow and said, "Here the target deviates from the Chavez girls' last day. He drives to Medeiros Liquors and purchases a 1.75 liter bottle of Absolut vodka, opens the bottle, takes four gulps, caps the bottle and places it in the trunk of his car. He then resumes the day of the girls—to their boyfriends' houses, each in turn, as the target could not be in two places at once."

At nightfall, Blaise would sit in front of the house until the time when they'd gone on their dates, Lucy and her boy to Skyline Boulevard to make out with a view of Oakland and San Francisco spreading out like a miracle and looking beautiful instead of ugly, Maria and her boy to the San Leandro Marina, the Oakland dumps where I ended up living to one side, San Mateo across the water of the bay, the Tony Lema landfill golf course behind them, the smell of methane rising like a fog as they fucked in the car. And Blaise went to each place, squatted and with his chin cupped in his hands, and he stared and he cried. The Chavez girls met up at midnight in Berkeley to see *The Rocky Horror Picture Show*, and after the show they went to the bathroom and that was the last time anybody saw them, except, evidently, the guy who chopped their heads off and shoved something really nasty up their twats. Every night Blaise would go to the theater, and the nights *The Rocky Horror Picture Show* wasn't play-ing, he'd watch whatever was, then go into the ladies' restroom at the exact time the Chavez girls would have.

We shook our heads. We drank.

"The ladies' restroom excursions are not the fucked up part, nor are they the most incriminating," Jorgensen said. "What's fucked up is this. After the target emerges from the ladies' room, he gets into his car and drives to Mountain View Cemetery, locates the graves of the Chavez girls—section one hundred sixty-six, row forty-five, lot thirteen, Lucy, and fourteen, Maria—and he lies down, alternately, for one hour sixteen to one hour twenty-two minutes, on their graves. After which he returns home and drinks most of the bottle of Absolut purchased during the day, leaving enough to drink in the morning, the ritual of which I have conveyed."

"Fuck," someone said.

"Yes," Jorgensen said. "Fuck."

"The fuck," someone said.

"The fuck," Jorgensen agreed.

"What the fuck," someone said.

"I'm not the only professional on this case," Jorgensen said. "The FBI and the local authorities are both very interested. Very interested indeed. Do you know how difficult it is to tap a wire that is already tapped? Do you know? Do you? No," Jorgensen said. "No you don't."

"Fuck," someone said.

"The target has an alibi. The night of the Chavez double murder, he was in the hospital with his wife, who had a bullet lodged in her anus. However, the anus alibi may be a cover for the crime. At least that is the suspicion of the law enforcement agencies interested in the case. They suspect."

Jorgensen pointed to his maps, took a pencil from one of his vest pockets, and drew an X over Blaise's apartment. "The target must be silenced," Jorgensen said. "He may be silenced through removal, relocation, or means more sure." Jorgensen said, "In any event, the target must be silenced. Promptly, and permanently. For the sake of the neighborhood. For the sake of Blaise the Suffering Soldier."

He slammed his water back like it was a shot of Beam. "This briefing has concluded," he said.

He snapped his sunglasses to his face, rolled up his scrolls, and marched on out of Dick's. He had to turn sideways to walk out the door, so big were his shoulders, and so much equipment he bore beneath his vest.

We didn't see Jorgensen for two more weeks, and so we figured that nothing had changed, or would. At Dick's things stayed the same. I kept playing Cumbias and Rancheras and Merengue with Los Asesinos at the Mexican nightclubs and weddings and quinceaneras and parties while working days as a laborer, my most recent gig running the tar mop on commercial roofs, warehouses mostly, nasty rusted oversized corrugated tin sheds, sweating my ass off in the crude oil steam, actually getting to like the smell. I didn't ever get any nookie, but I'd come not to care, and I didn't have the time anyway, because nights I'd read, hoping that in a year or two I'd have enough money to go to college and get some job like Blaise's, some job I didn't have to do shit for and get paid lots to not do it. I worked as an investment in future screwing off, delayed and splendid sloth. I wanted to lay around picking my ass, wearing boxer shorts and eating tortilla chips and chile con queso, drinking Olympia beers, eating linguisca, and, basically, living the high life. I'd seen enough of this life to know that everything ended in a big pile of shit, that marriages resulted in either divorce or enduring hatred, that children despised their parents forever and for good, that white people had committed such atrocities that there was no way the Mexicans and niggers would ever forget about it, that no matter what I did in life it wouldn't matter, that, even if I were to become a fucking saint, canonized by the Italians as an honorary WASP degenerate who'd never been to a church of his own volition, that even if canonized I'd still be one dead and miserable motherfucker even after I'd done whatever ridiculous altruistic act of stupidity I'd done, saving some goddamn bunch of starving Aboes or some such shit—I'd seen enough of this life to know that I didn't matter, and, somehow, somehow and oddly, this put me at ease. Knowing that *I* didn't matter one fuck, that no matter what *I* did, no matter how hard *I* tried, no matter what *I* might accomplish, *I* was fucked and so was everyone around me—knowing all this somehow liberated me to be the selfish, narcissistic, self-deprecating, egotistical, ridiculous, venerable, and badass pathetic demon angel that I was and just might be and become. I was going to go to college and get myself educated someday, learn all the shit the rich people knew so that I could use it against them, annihilate them with their own crap, bury them in knowledge of their own researches and experiences but with my own special Oakland recipe and blend. When the revolution came, I was going to be at the front of the rabble wielding a flamethrower and a mace, my face contorted in sincerity.

And so when I wasn't working, I wasn't chasing pussy, no. And not just because I thought I couldn't get any, which I probably couldn't have. There's something about a nerdy ghetto boy that don't get the chicks gooey. When I wasn't working, I was—and I never let this on to anybody—I was *reading.* The librarian at Oakland Public Library was Mrs. Weismann, and I'd known her since I was in grade school. Even then she'd be shoving the right books my way, Jack London, Theodore Dreiser, John Dos Passos, Upton Sinclair, Twain. She gave me Marx, Nietzsche, Herbert Spencer, Walter Lippman, Sartre, Camus, Trotsky, and a bunch of people you wouldn't have heard of because Mrs. Weismann knew some really cool books, she did.

I never told anyone I was reading all those books. That's not the kind of thing you admit in my neighborhood. You tell people that instead of watching the Raiders, instead of drinking beers, you're reading *books*, and shit, you're a faggot no one will ever talk to again, and sure as shit no one will ever *trust* you again, not with a head full of fancy commie artsy horseshit and floating around in the clouds looking down on everyone. You read books, you keep it to yourself.

What kind of fucked with my head is that I worshipped both Nietzsche and Marx, and as far as I could tell, their ideas didn't jive together. Marx was all for the working man, the guy on the construction site, the man working like a pig for the rich motherfuckers, for all the guys at Dick's, for *me*. Marx was all about ripping the guts out of the swine like our bosses, like every one of the rich sons of bitches sitting on their fat asses up on their swank mansions in the Oakland hills. Marx, like us, wanted them dead. And Nietzsche, Nietzsche thought that the weak, the sniveling simps who were at the bottom of the social ladder, the downtrodden, the hopeless and the retarded and the maimed and the idiots who were waiting for rewards in some fantasy afterlife in which the rich and powerful were punished for eternity for being rotten to the weak—Nietzsche thought the lame got what they deserved, because the *strong* would always and eventually rise, would conquer and find themselves at the top of the heap, ruling the roost. Of course that's where I thought I'd be some day. I'd outwork the weak, I'd outsmart them, I'd grind them into the dust. So reading both of these Krauts messed me up. I couldn't figure out whether I wanted to lead the greatest worldwide union mankind's ever known, or become supreme dictator of Oakland, the *Bossman*. And if I ever became Bossman, what would I think of the *workers*? And if I stayed a worker, what would I think of the Boss? Reading books was some tough shit.

The day Jorgensen resurfaced was not a good day. Louie, the bartender, had discovered that not only had some chick he'd banged twenty years before given him a child, but that she'd popped out a set of triplets. Three boys, now men, and they all hated him, because all the mother had done for twenty years, twenty pissed off Italian Catholic years, is train them, train them to hate the motherfucker who fucked her and left her pregnant in the Bronx, where Louie was from, left her knocked up in a roach infested walk-up, and then blew out of town to *California*, where all the *pretty people* lived. Louie the deadbeat, Louie the louse, Louie the no-child-support no-Christmas-present no-christening-card no-gradua-tion-present no-college-fund no-count piece of human shit.

The triplets had come in at lunchtime, and Louie didn't know at first who they were, and then the awful fact began to dawn on him, the fact that there were *three*, that he'd knocked up a Maria and she'd had not one child but *triplets*. They'd come into Dick's Restaurant and Cocktail Lounge and bought a bottle of whiskey, bought the whole bottle, and told Louie they wanted three shotglasses. Louie looked at them, the three of them, huge Bronx men dressed in black tee shirts, muscles bulging, black Ben Davis work pants and even the baggy Ben's weren't enough to hide the huge thighs—these sons of bitches looked like they'd been working out their entire lives just for this meeting—and speaking in the old neighborhood accent and sounding exactly like him, looking exactly like him, four Louies at the bar all looking at each other, three Louies looking at Louie like they were going to kill him, talking about their deadbeat motherfucker father and how they were going to take care of his sorry ass, and just how they were going to do it, in great detail. They nailed that bottle, and they left Louie a c-note for a tip, the last tip Louie thought he was ever going to get, and he was sure that's what the triplets had intended him to think.

Louie was not in good shape. His hands shook when he poured our beers. And then, to ice it, Jorgensen walked in, and Jorgensen was excited, something we all thought impossible for Jorgensen, the levelest head of us all. His face was painted green and black. He was wearing his sunglasses. Sweat dripped down his face and smeared his warpaint. He had a big manila folder in his hand. He looked very serious.

"Hey Louie," Carlo Mendez said. "Hey, the scaries always go away."

Dave Campos said, "A triple-shot for Louie!"

Jorgensen looked at Campos and Mendez with contempt. He said, "Non-regulars, *out*."

No one moved.

"*Now*," Jorgensen said. And he meant it truly. Something was up. Something was very wrong.

The non-regulars were women. One of them ugly, the other a porky two o'clock special.

"Don't send out the beautiful ladies," Shapiro said.

Jorgensen said, "I will tell *your* tales first." He said, "Would you like that, Shylock?"

Shapiro turned to the women. "You have to leave," he said.

He tried to get the non-ugly's phone number while he was helping her on with her sweater, but she'd have none of it. "Assholes," she said as she stood. The porker was cool about the expulsion. She acted like it happened all the time.

Jorgensen said, "The mission is complete."

He killed Blaise, what I thought. He tried to reason with the crazed alchemist composer, a struggle ensued because Blaise doesn't have the common sense of a turnip, and Blaise lashed out, and Jorgensen, trained to react and to kill before being killed, Jorgensen whipped out some knife or pistol or grenade and stuffed it down crazy Blaise's throat and that was that, end of Blaise. And now Jorgensen was human. Jorgensen needed help because he'd murdered someone without the sanction of the U.S. of A. Jorgensen never understood that you don't get medals for killing people unless you're killing people you don't know and who've never done a fucking thing to you. Half of us had either killed someone, had someone killed, or had someone in the family do one or the other. Killing people—that was what you did when the cops you knew couldn't do it for you. But you don't get caught doing it. It's always funny, that. Kill a burglar, kill a junkie, kill a fucking hobo child molesting shitbag, kill someone who stole the car stereo that took you six months of eating cheap to save up for—take five hundred bucks' worth out of his esophagus—and you go to jail if they catch you. Kill some sandnigger riding his camel across the desert because some bucketheaded moron following orders and giving orders tells you to do so, you're a hero. Whatever it was Jorgensen had done, he wasn't happy about it. Not at all.

"Blaise is gone," Jorgensen said.

He took off his sunglasses, and he looked at us, and the look was one of shame.

He said, "I have failed."

If I hadn't have known better, known it was sweat trickling from his forehead, I'd have sworn I saw a tear.

He set the manila folder down on the bar and sat on a stool. The Raiders were not winning, Louie was a mess, Shapiro's wife had given him "one year's notice" again, threatened to leave him again and for good this time, told him that if he didn't shape up and start making more money like a *man*, if he didn't give her a real *home*, she was going to dump him. "And then she went shopping," Shapiro said, "bought a bunch of expensive *organic* vegetables and fruits. Do you know how much that stuff costs?" It was shaping up to be a pretty rotten day.

"Jack Daniels," Jorgensen said, and we all knew that something was seriously wrong. No one ever ordered stuff like that except non-regulars. Why buy Jack when Beam gets you just as drunk and costs half as much? Sure, you get a hangover, but hell, if you haven't had much to eat, you can even get a hangover from beers if you drink enough.

Louie lined him up. Jorgensen tossed it back. "Another," he said. Louie poured. Jorgensen drank. "Bottle," Jorgensen said. Louie slid the bottle in front of him. Jorgensen drank.

We just watched him, sat quiet and sipping. We knew eventually, when he'd had enough, he'd cue us in to the score.

Jorgensen drunk is not a good thing, usually. It doesn't happen often, because Jorgensen doesn't like the mop-up work afterwards, retracing his steps and fixing the shit he's fucked up, making all those phone calls. That can be some real work. Sure, when there's women and when he's happy, he's a good drunk, like anyone is when he's got a woman wants to go home with him. But when he's going to go home alone, and when he's not happy to start with, and when he gets drunk, and especially when someone messes with him, then, then Jorgensen drunk is not a good thing. He's pretty quick with those knives of his, Jorgensen. He could be just sitting there at his stool, calm as ditch water, and if he's had enough to drink, and if someone crosses one of his lines—and still no one is quite sure of what those lines are—they shift around all the time—once Polizzi ended up with a broken finger for having coffee with cream instead of tough-guy black—if someone crosses the line the next thing you know Jorgensen has one of us on the ground, three or four knives in his hands, one of them at our throat.

"I was posted in the park, approximately two hundred yards from the residence of the target," Jorgensen said. "In a redwood tree."

And he told us what happened. "Feds," Jorgensen said. "Stupid fuck started making house calls at the homes of kidnapped girls. Kidnapping, federal. Not good."

Jorgensen said he was perched in the redwood, binoculars trained on Blaise, when he saw the vans and unmarkeds silently coast to stops to either side of Blaise's, engines turned off, vehicles in neutral, stealth mode. Two SWAT teams in full combat gear and two carloads of COs emptied onto the street and fanned out, surrounding Blaise's apartment building. The exterior units used ropes to scale the walls, the interior units poised at the rear and front entrances. Then they stormed, crashing through Blaise's door and windows. They trained their weapons on Blaise, smashed his face down on his manuscript, manacled his wrists and ankles, and carried him down the stairs, depositing him in the back seat of one of the unmarked cars. Blaise was limp, as if he hadn't a muscle in his body, and he didn't say a word. Jorgensen said he thought he saw Blaise smile.

Jorgensen looked at me. "T-Bird, I give you the remains of Blaise." And he handed me the manila folder.

It was Blaise's symphony, scored, eighty pages, stopped mid-phrase in the ninth movement.

Jorg said, "Is it any good, or is it as insane as Blaise?"

Everybody knew I played trumpet in the Mexican bands around the Bay Area, and they thought I was pretty damn good, too. But I knew I was only good enough to sound badass at a wedding or a bar, far from being good enough to play with the pros. I stopped practicing hard when I went to a concert one time at Cal State Hayward and heard a dude, a *kid*, a kid still in high school at Castro Valley High named Jeff Farrington. This pimple-faced nerd-glasses wearing little shit was still in high school and he was playing with the university jazz band, and when he soloed, it was like nothing I'd ever heard except when I heard Wynton Marsalis playing with Art Blakey and the Jazz Messengers at the Keystone corner in San Francisco. Marsalis was nineteen years old, and so was I, and he played so fast and so perfectly, and the fucker played with *Art Blakey*, holy *shit*. He was late for the concert, Marsalis, and when he came in, Julliard buttwipe, it was like some god had descended, some god in diapers. It made me ashamed of myself, and I got really drunk and smoked the pot that was being passed around.

But Farrington, Farrington was another story. This guy was *white*, and he was a nerd like me. He was white and a nerd and he played like he had the wisdom of some biblical character burned into his bones, coursing through his veins. Marsalis played like someone who would be good someday, someone technically perfect with no soul, even though he was black and their soul-quotients are supposedly exponentially larger than those of us whiteys. Marsalis played like he'd never taken a lesson from Miles Davis or Clifford Brown, like he'd never considered not filling space with sound, like he *had to hear himself* and didn't give a shit about the music of the world, the music of the air, of the clinking of the cocktail tumblers.

But Farrington, Farrington playing in the sterile and snotty atmosphere of a university auditorium, Farrington knew about the music of the spheres, and he used the music to his advantage, playing only when he needed to, pausing sometimes to let the greatness of what he'd just blown sink into the ears and bones of the audience. When I heard a white boy, one of *mine*, when I heard a white boy doing these things that at the time I'd never considered, it put me in my place. It let me know that there are some things about creating art that cannot be learned, that either you got or you don't. And I knew I didn't. And on the construction sites, I worked harder and with more seriousness, because I knew that I wasn't a trumpet player because of gift, but because of inclination. My only gift was that I could *labor* for sixteen hours straight, keep up with the best of the Mexicans, and not pass out. My gift was that I was born to build pyramids, and if I couldn't build them, I'd grease their stones with my guts.

Blaise's score? I couldn't read that motherfucker. I could read treble clef, and only in the key of B-flat, the key of the trumpet, which meant that I could read music written for tenor sax and for trumpet, and that's it, *no mas.* All that other shit, the key of E-flat, the key of what the fuck ever, bass clef, pentatonic this and mixolydian that, it was all a foreign tongue to me. I couldn't even play chopsticks on a piano without fucking it up, and plenty of times I'd tried.

Some guys, they can look at a score and actually *hear* the music, hear all the instruments playing, hear what the piece would sound like in a concert hall. They can look at the notes on the page scattered all over the place like some spattering of ink drops and they can see the mess and their brains instantaneously translate the medieval secret code gibberish into a hundred and twenty musicians moaning a note, moving through a phrase, swelling to a crescendo, banging the muse. Not me. I see that shit and all I can do is peck out the trumpet line, my eyes only seeing two measures ahead. With jazz and improv it's different. You follow the pulse of what's being pumped into your balls because your fluids are flowing, because there's this stuff in you while you're playing that isn't there when you're not playing that you can tap when you're playing and spill out into the bar. When you're playing jazz, it's like being drunk out of your mind and babbling to your favorite woman, trying to convince her of how sexy you are. And you're succeeding. As a legit musician, though, as a legit straight up tux-wearing soldier, as one of those guys who knows the ins and outs of how all this stuff theoretically works, as one of those guys I suck.

So here's this score in front of me, and all the guys are there, Campos, Polizzi, Shapiro, Jorgensen, Louie. To make things even more fucked up, Pop, my *father* Pop, walked in. And Pop was a real musician. He'd played in the Oakland Symphony. He could play "Carnival of Venice" on his trumpet and he knew his way around the piano's ivories. He wasn't a bar bum like me, Pop. He walked in and his arms were slick with grease and motor oil and his knuckles leaked from banging around under the hood of some fucked up Plymouth or Rambler. Pop walked in and saw the bunch of us sitting there in confused gloom and he said, "What the fuck?"

"Blaise," I said.

"That *bitch*," he said. "What she do to him now? Fucking bitches. Why can't they just steal our souls and leave us the fuck alone? What she do this time, the bitch?"

"He's in jail," I said.

Pop looked at Jorgensen. "He pop her one? About damn time," Pop said. "I thought you were his friend. Bail him out. When you pop a bitch, especially an ex bitch, it's only a couple grand bail. Judges understand what a man's got to do sometimes."

Jorgensen, steroid pumped Navy SEAL wide as a lube bay solid as a girder Jorgensen, he broke down. He choked, and then he sobbed, and his eyes glazed and got water. We looked away, but Pop didn't. Pop stared at him. He gave him that look none of us ever want to get, that look that says, You're a piece of shit, asshole, and you know what? You, amigo, are not a man to be counted on. You are someone I will not call when the hour is late and the situation is critical. You, fuckup, are on the B list.

"Well?" Pop said.

"You want me to kill myself now?" Jorgensen said. "I'll fucking do it," he said. "*I will.*" And he flipped out some big knife from somewhere in his vest and held it at his gut. "I don't care. Just give me the nod."

"Hold off, Hoss," Pop said.

"Pop," I said. "Jorg tried his best. The feds got Blaise. He's gone. Adios motherfucker gone, bye-bye," I said. I said, "But he left this." And I handed Pop Blaise's score.

We all looked at Pop, watched him flip through the pages, watched the expression on his face. He first looked at the pages with scrutiny, brows knit. He pulled a Roi-Tan from his coveralls and lit it and puffed hard. Then he raised his eyebrows, and he looked at us over his plastic Clark Kent black-rimmed glasses, looked at us like he'd heard something we'd said but wasn't sure exactly what it was, like he was checking on us, looked at us as if we'd done something questionable and a bit on the shady.

He took his time. We drank some cocktails. It was getting on in the day. Louie's triplets walked in.

"Out," Jorgensen said.

"They stay," Louie said.

Jorgensen gave Louie the look.

"They're my sons," Louie said.

They looked mean as shit. Two of them were packing—you could see the bulges under their arms. They ordered cocktails, and Ed the Jew paid. Then he bought a round for the house, un-Ed-like. Since cheap-ass Ed the Jew bought a round, so did Shapiro, not to be out-Jewed by Ed the Jew. And since the Jews were buying, shit, all the Catholic WOPs and the Portugees and Swedish Jorg and Heinz-57 me, we all bought rounds, and hell, we each had a dozen drinks lined up and Louie's boys kind of liked that and so did we.

We were getting pretty jolly. The triplets joshed at Louie.

"Fucked our mama and left," they said. "Made some triplets. Triple shot. Think you have one big-ass dick, don't you?"

"You little wops haven't seen a dick till you've seen mine, boys," Louie said. "You think you got dicks like your daddy? Triplets. Each one a third of Big Papa."

Louie slammed one back—he was drinking his chick nigger Crown Royals—and then he said, "So let's see them, boys. Let's see."

And Louie asked them if their dicks were as big as his, his big dick triplet-making Italian baby-maker. "You think you're the only kids I have out there? I probably got fifty or sixty of youse."

The triplets stood up, all three of them and all at once and they dropped their pants and even though they all looked exactly the same in every way we could tell, drawers down they didn't, and everybody started chanting, "Louie, Louie, Louie," and Campos chanted a little too enthusiastically and when he saw us look at him he toned *that* shit down is what he did. We don't need none of that shit at Dick's, not even when we're drunk. We chanted "Louie Louie Louie" until finally Louie stood on the bar and dropped his drawers and flopped it out, and holy shit. No question about Louie, no way. It was so big we probably all wanted to see him bone a woman we knew. He said, "That puppy's how you make triplets, boys," and we cheered and the triplets looked sheepy at first, because they knew it took a dick that big to leave a woman and her triplets and make a man's life for himself, and then they looked really proud. They wanted to buy Louie a drink and they wanted to buy us drinks too and we let them.

Pop said, "Trumpet."

"What," I said.

"You got your horn?"

"In my car," I said.

"Get it."

"My drink," I said. "After."

"Get it," Pop said, and he meant now.

When I walked outside my eyes blinded white. It was near sunset and the fog had curdled in and the fuzzed air was electric. Birds flopped and fell through the mist like dark ashes from a big burn. You could hear the trains, their whistles and their wheels grinding on the iron rails, the crunch and slide of metal on metal. Somewhere a pile-driver slammed rhythmic and sure against concrete, breaking the foundation of a building that once served a purpose. Something burned and smelled like rotted dog. You couldn't make out the writing on the billboards on the other side of the street, but you could see the beer bottles and the bikinis and big sweaty tits. Warning buoys on the bay sounded low and plaintive, and they sounded more like they'd lure sailors than avert them. Sure as shit I'd go *toward* those bouys, so beautiful and *home* did they sound. *Come home, T-Bird,* they called. *Come home.* On the Nimitz Freeway the semis slicked across the asphalt and circulated the air, and birds and crickets and frogs—*frogs in Oakland?*—even frogs belched a song in the drape of fog.

Oakland is at its best, at its most beautiful, when you can only see twenty feet of it. Oakland is the most beautiful place on the planet, and I know, because I am a tuning fork over the asshole of beauty. Every note the city makes is tested by *me*, tuned by *me*, translated by *me*. I see it, the beauty, everywhere, in the dandelions on the lawn being poisoned by the suburban lawn fanatic, in the rust on the wall of the warehouse graffitied by the home boys, in the dead duck hanging by its ankles in the Chinese grocery, in the fat roll of the retard Martinez boy who sacks my groceries at Pete's Market in the hood, in the drool that hangs perpetually from the dwarf Tony Costello's chin because his brain is so fucked up he can't even breathe without his sister Maria alongside him saying, "In, out, in

Tony, out Tony, in Tony, out." I see the beauty of slathering Dobermans and Pit Bulls ripping apart trespassing children, of bloodslicked sidewalks, of pools of beer vomit and hurled vital organs in alleys behind bars, of mounds of dogshit wiggling with worms like living beings, those shitpiles brooding like unfathomable heaps of intent lurking over an unknowable primal cause, of lecherous teenage girls licking their lips on streetcorners for pervert Midwestern military boys on their first trips away from their small town shitholes, of old ladies lifting their dresses and pissing in the gutters and smiling all the while, as they should. Nothing is more beautiful than the will to live amid absolute desperation. Hope is for assholes. Only the most sublime of souls can know the beauty of despair.

Our beauty, our beauty in my neighborhood is this: the world, *asshole*, is only what you can see of it. When you can see only very little, you see it better, you see it more true. We're cloaked in a shroud of fog in Oakland, smothered. Choked. We can't see the next street corner. And so we *examine* what we *can* see, and we *know* it. We know the cracks on our sidewalks. We know who lives in what apartment. We know the other senses—we know what it *smells* like when we pass the Borges house, when we walk past the GE plant. We know what the asphalt *feels* like under our work boots and our out-on-the-town Florsheim wingtips. We feel the acrid tingle of scorch and burn chemical plant burnoff in the morning hours before the inspectors and OSHA druids crawl out of their suburban huts to tell us what to do and when. When the refineries overfill and resort to burnoff our skins wrinkle with petrochemical joy and familiar dread and relief. We are alive.

If the shit we see is shit outsiders think ugly, it's because outsiders are used to the shit *they* think is beautiful and don't realize the ugliness of their own digs, the ugliness of their maids, their antiseptic European and Japanese cars which have never been stained with sex or shame, the ugliness of their perfectly squared bricks and their steamcleaned tiles, their gardeners, their plumbers, the people who work for them, *us*. But since we *are us*, we can see beautiful shit they cannot see. We can see the beauty in a well-made fence, a properly poured driveway, a pregnant and fat and sad Mexican thirteen year old angel, a well demolished building. We, we who live *in the ugly*, we know beauty that doesn't get into fancy magazines in the offices of doctors and divorce lawyers.

And while I stood outside Dick's, fetching from my car the family trumpet I'd been to some debasing but to me honoring by playing it in Mexican nightclubs and bars instead of in symphony halls and recording studios making money for fat fuck white shirt sweat face no counts, when I stood outside it came to me that my place, my home, my Oakland, my Dick's filled with drunken maniacal *loyal and good men*, my place on this planet was a good place, a *good* place that even though rough and harsh and miserable and awful was nonetheless sacred. My *Oakland* was mine, and it was Louie's, and Jorgensen's, and Shapiro's, and the Oakland of every other Oaklander that mattered, and we worked and we worked and in Oakland we would die and we would die beautifully and fulfilled, having done everything we were meant to do.

When I walked back inside, I couldn't see a thing except the bar lights, neon. The guys were quiet, working their drinks.

"Give me the horn," Pop said.

He oiled up the valves and he looked at me as if I'd just handed him a turd. "You ever polish this thing?" he said. "You ever grease the fucking slides? You ever empty the spit-valves? You ever fucking *play* it?"

I looked at the ground his barstool rested on. "Day job," I said.

"Day job what?"

"Day job keeps me busy."

Pop shook his head slow and with a combination of sadness, loathing, and repulsion. Nobody worth a shit ever let his *day job* get in the way of what he was really all about. *Day job.* If you can't do what you want *after work*, then the awful truth is *you don't want anything*. Drink a goddamn beer, fuck your depressed fat wife, and sleep the good hours away, slob.

Louie poured me another Scotch, and Pop flipped through Blaise's folder once more, studying certain pages, whipping through others. He drank water.

Jorgensen sat staring at himself in the mirror behind the bar, looking through the bottles and post-it notes. The triplets were pretty hammered now, and they giggled like girls. The phone rang and no one picked it up. A wife, probably. They do that, even though they know where the hell we are. Shapiro and Ed the Jew were talking about money. No shit. That's all they ever talked about, as if they'd invented it. Otherwise, they hated each other, called each other kikes and Shylocks and fuckwads. But when they were both at Dick's, they talked cash, even though neither of them really had any. Otherwise, they'd be drinking somewhere else and not hanging out with us. Some non-regulars walked in but Jorgensen didn't notice. They walked back out anyway. If I walked into a bar like ours that wasn't mine, I'd walk out too.

"Percussion is important," Pop said. "In this piece."

I nodded.

"Who else here reads music?"

I said I didn't know.

"Any of you morons read music," Pop said.

One of the triplets did. So did Ed the Jew and Shapiro. Jorgensen said he was a mean drummer, played in the military band before he wised up to the action and became a SEAL. Weapons make their own sweet tune, he said.

Pop said, "Make yourselves useful."

"I can play the trumpet line," I said.

Pop sneered at me. Tires squealed and someone screamed loud enough outside to make everyone look at the door.

"Jazz," Pop said.

"Sorry," I said. And I was.

Pop gathered us around, and he made us rehearse, telling us what lines to read. The triplet used a spoon and a half-full water glass. Ed the Jew and Shapiro, they volunteered to play the call-drink bottles with their porcelain fountain pens, lining up the bottles in ascending order of volume and therefore pitch like beautiful and expensive booze marimbas or xylophones. Pop told Jorgensen to use coffee cans and tomato cans and a barstool, beat upon by a spoon, but Jorg said no fucking way, he was all about the body, and would only use his hands and fingers and fists against his body, and Pop said Sure Jorg without missing a beat.

"How about me?" I said.

"You turn pages."

I said, "Give me a break."

Pop said, "Someone who knows how to read music has to turn the pages." He said, "This piece calls for a musician, not a jazz player. I'm on horn."

Louie poured another round. We drank it. Pop said it was time. And we played.

It was the most strange and weird and sweet and horrible depressing thing any of us had ever heard. We smiled, even though we thought we didn't want to and knew we shouldn't. Sometimes sad shit does that to you.

It started out with just the Jews clinking away on their marimba/xylophone booze bottles, fast and frantic, some kind of jungle melody, running up and down the bottles, the notes jumping across each other, not chromatic but instead in thirds and fourths and sixths and octaves, low-high high-low, clinking and the notes banging against the mirrors and against the linoleum floor, an echo but not a deep one, an instantaneous reverberation that ricocheted against the notes and created a shrill harmony like the way sometimes the sound of a jackhammer meshes with the sound of the traffic. Then while the Jews were playing, and they were truly playing those Jews, playing as if they were telling us the parts of Exodus that we never hear about in the Bible, telling us about the angst and joy of Biblical Hebrew party-your-ass-off drinking and fucking and praying to a God that had the power to wipe out the Gentiles with a breath and *would*, while the Jews were summoning up their ancient Jew-god of vengeance and laughter and justice, the triplet Italian Catholic joined in, and he wanted to show that even though his dick wasn't as big as Papa Louie's his soul was bigger, and because Louie had abandoned him and fucked him over and made him a bastard forever, he might not have had as big a dick but he had bigger *balls*, a louder and more resonant *howl*, a howl that would call forth the bestial demons of all the yet known hells and all the hells to be for eternity and after that too and it would be a howl that redeemed. That little shit played a water-glass like he was knocking on the doors of a heaven made just for bastards, and he was going to be let in, he was.

When Jorgensen's part came in he peeled off his vest and his shirt and his pants and Jorg stood there in his military issue tightie-whities. None of us had ever seen him in anything but a long sleeved shirt, protective cover since he worked as not only an assassin but a demo-man and steel-worker, when not blowing up buildings, welding, showered by sparks and flame, Vulcan at his forge.

First of all, Jorg was one big sonbitch, but we'd all seen big mother-fuckers before. I'd worked with a construction worker just out of Quentin, a black dude named Fish who was three hundred fifty pounds of iron, veins bulging through his skin like cables. Hell, Rich Kuam, who didn't come around much anymore because he'd finally met a hooker he liked and married her and now he was in some kind of domestic lockup, Kuam was big enough to carry a hooker on each shoulder, and we'd seen him walk into Dick's plenty of times like that. Kuam would save his money up instead of going out on dates, and twice a year he'd drive up to the Mustang Ranch just outside of Reno and he'd get two hotties, bring them back to Oakland for the whole week, and they'd play house. He never shared.

He was never broke. He always had something to look forward to. He was always happy. Kuam, he had the right fucking idea.

So when Jorg took off his shirt we were impressed but not shocked. What curioused us was that he was covered, I mean *covered*, with tattoos. No skin showed that wasn't inked. And you see the shadows of tattoos through his shorts, too, like bruises. All the way up to his neck, down to his wrists, his entire feet, excepting toenails. I bet the flats of his feet were artworked.

There was nothing trendy about Jorgensen's tattoos. They were battle scenes, kills. None of that skull and crossbones dragon big-tittied women Celtic weave scorpion cartoon character Harley Davidson I'm tough because I wear leather and drive a motorized bicycle horseshit. Jorgensen's tattoos featured himself, sunglasses and all, Jorg in the jungle breaking a drug lord's guard's neck barehanded, Jorg in a warehouse scoping a suit-wearing diplomat in the high-rise across the street, Jorg on his belly in the sand taking out a sheik with some kind of telescope machine gun rifle, Jorg in D.C., the capitol in the distance, slitting the throat of a businessman right there on the mall, a crowd strolling past oblivious, Jorg in scuba gear attaching a mine to a yacht, the water clear and the fish sparkled with color. Hundreds of tattoos Jorg had. We were glad he was our friend.

His tympani part came, and Jorg was not only the best killer we'd ever known, but as he stood there in his underwear his hands became a blur, open-palmed at first then high notes slap-clapping cup-handed against his inner thighs. He must have been one hell of a drummer before he found other trades more spiritually satisfying. Then his hands flashed faster and higher, Jorg tightening the cup of his hand and moving down his leg along his calves, p'pop pap, p'pop pap p'pop pap, cracking like gunshot and gattling crossfire.

This was preamble, prelude, the foreground noise of some Los Angeles Oakland Sacramento Lodi Watts Modesto San Diego Compton Fresno San Francisco Los Banos static of Blaise's mind. The frenzy and rhythm of

Blaise's deliberate suck-ass life—and all of our lives suck because we *want them to*, no other reason—the nicotine and narcotic haze of vodka and bliss, of hopes unfulfilled and a baby ripped from his womb and umbilical chord trailing along the asphalt, a bloody line purpled with vein and white with curd as he watched the bitch-driven car slide away and gone and gone forever-fucking-ever and more and more permanent and ongoing, perpetual, done: the frenzy of Blaise's life he'd claim unwanted but desired sure, the mess that was his life scratched onto the symphonic page, and us playing it.

And I turned those pages, what I did. I turned them and with each turned page I felt my heart speed. My heart sped and raced and the reason it went fast was because I was jealous. I was jealous and envious of the accomplishment of Blaise: he'd *done* something. He was somewhere off in Fed land jailed and manacled and probably getting cornholed by some FBI faggot in a suit but we were playing the work he left behind. When you die, will you have left anything behind but your genetic filth? Ask yourself.

I had a stomach urge to kill Blaise, to eradicate him, to erase him from neighborhood and personal memory. We all want to kill people we envy, don't we? And we would, too, if we weren't all chickenshits, scared of *the law* since there's no need to fear someone's friends and family. Most people can't get pissed off enough to kick the neighborhood's nasty and barking dog. Most don't even have the guts to bitch-slap someone who's fucking his wife, or his cheating wife, for that matter.

It sucked to be turning the pages for Blaise, for Pop, for Jorg and the Jews and the triplet. They were *playing* something, and I was spectating, onlooking the place from which I'd sprung, *watching* my Oakland instead of being part of it. I'd always felt this way, as if I somehow did not belong there, as if somehow even though Oakland was the only thing I knew, nonetheless I was not *of Oakland*. And this fucked me up sure. Fucked me up in ways that I don't think I can even explain here, here where I'm telling everything I think because I truly don't give a shit about your opinion of me, you fuck. I never felt part of Oakland because I thought I was way too smart to be bred of that shithole, and I *knew I lived in a shithole*, but at the same time I could never live up to what was good about *my Oakland*, the Oakland of Pop and Grandpop Murphy, the Oakland of Shapiro and the retard Martinez, the Oakland that no matter what was my home. Here they were all playing, and I was turning pages.

Pop's line didn't sound like that of a trumpet, and I looked at the score and saw it wasn't. He was playing the flute's riff, whistling plaintive through the percussive jackhammer airgun glim and scint. Pop played and more air came through the horn than note, a high note above the clink, a stream of precious metal, a wiggle cutting through sound like something sharp and narrow and tinsel through a vibrating wall of iron. He played, and I listened, not only to Pop but to all of them, even to the New York boy, and while listening a wash of contentment came over me like the cum of a woman, a gush. It was not my job to participate in this. It was not my job to *be* this. It was my job—and this job had been conferred on me by powers distant and serious—it was my job to *understand* this, and to make *you* understand it.

So get this: we were at Dick's Restaurant and Cocktail Lounge, Oakland, California, warehouses surrounding our bar, docks in the distance, cranes groaning back and forth across tracks and dropping ISOs from ships to trains that would take them to trucks and to your fucking grocery store. We were at Dick's and our friend Blaise, our *friend*, had been lost, and he'd left us something. He'd lost his baby, his wife, his perspective, his *will*, but unlike you, unlike what you'll do when *you* vanish, he'd left something behind for *us*, something of *substance*, not just some photo album or his great-grandmother's fucking China. No, Blaise had not left us a trust fund or a coin collection or some piece of dirt we didn't want and wouldn't know how to farm. Blaise had left us what obsessed him, what made him Blaise, the reason he was willing, maybe eager, to lose that kid and that wife. What kind of man is this? This is the kind of man I want to call late at night, when I know no one else will answer the phone. This is the kind of man I want to get hammered with. This is the kind of man I want to be.

Pop, bearded greased coveralled Pop, his note was not just what there was of that symphony of Blaise's, of ours. No. There was more, and there was more beauty and more disdain. Blaise had it nailed, hammered to the subfloor. He somehow knew us better that we did. He knew something about us that all of us suspected, that all of us might have been able to say in a small hours drunk flicker. He knew it, and we'd never heard it said. Not to ourselves nor to anyone else. But Blaise was saying it, and he was saying it without words, without all the bullshit innuendo of language. He might have been a genius, Blaise, if genius is the ability to tell us in words of our own, in expressions of our experience, in tones and hushes of our recognition, that which we know when we hear or see or feel it but which we have not expressed ourselves. This is why Mozart and Miles Davis and Shakespeare and Leonardo make us cry, or at least forget ourselves and our bullshit for an instant, even the most brute and flat-headed among us. Genius echoes the best in us, calls back our howls to us with something even *we* can understand and with the grandeur each of us knows some instant in our lives to be the essence of what we *could have been*. It lets us know that even though we're as shitty as we suspect, we entail the greatness of all that is full and human. Genius is some cool shit.

That's what we were getting from Crazy Blaise. We felt pretty damned good. Like we were part of something we didn't deserve and yet absolutely did.

The men of Dick's didn't make it through the symphony. Louie's boy broke his tumbler and booze splintered glass exploded over the bar. Jorgensen got goofy crazy, beating on his back and the soles of his feet, and he scrambled some phrases and couldn't focus on the sheet music and find his place again. He'd been doing some weird shit anyway, not really reading the music but instead playing his own personal version of Blaise's symphony. Shapiro and Ed the Jew stopped playing the bottles and started taking turns popping shots, since Louie didn't care about anything but seeing to it his boys had a good time and didn't decide to kill him. And Pop's lip was giving out because it had been a long time since he'd played horn. Blood spittled out the bell and hung at its lip like pink drool.

Louie poured a round of shots, Blaise's Absolut. We lifted a drink in toast, but none of us clinked glasses.

We didn't say anything. We didn't look at each other. We drank.

Dick's is the vortex of the sadness of the world, and sometimes it's almost too much to bear, and since I'll always be considered a Dick's regular, sometimes I think there's something *wrong* about me. But then again maybe, just maybe there's something *absolutely right*, something pure and transcendent, something that was meant to see and to feel the pain of the world and take it all in and process the raw horror into a thing crystalline and beautiful, crushing garbage into fine gems. I'll always end up living a dump of my own and I'll always be damned happy about it, happy because I know, I mean *I know*, that someday things are going to change. Sound ridiculous? Oh, yes, it is, and I know it, but I am by nature ridiculous. I am the Absurd made flesh. And I will endure. And I will prevail. One fine morning I'll wake up and look out over the wasteland of pickled and shredded souls and my vision will transform the bile of the world into nectar. And I will not be alone.

Before I went into hiding in Missouri, the Hell's Angels threw a party in my honor at Dick's, and this was a big deal. Some people go their whole lives without being thrown a party at Dick's, Rich Kuam, for instance. Why throw him a party when all he did was save his money to rent whores, while the rest of us actually *married* them and had to own up to the consequences of cuntery. Jorgensen?—throw a party for Jorg after he'd taken care of *a problem*, make his victory public, and *we* might become his *next* problem. Some things you celebrate, and some you just tip a toast. But they were throwing me a bona-fide *party*, no bitches allowed, as is right and proper. Bring a bitch into a mix of men and we get distracted even if her fat rolls flop over her knees while she's bent over at her barstool and her halter-topped titties wag over her belly button like water balloons. And if we're not distracted, we don't talk right. We either censor or we pump it up. We call them "ladies," because they don't (or pretend they don't) understand that "lady" means "cunt" at Dick's restaurant and Cocktail Lounge.

The party was after the California No Smoking law was passed, which forbade smoking in public places, bars included. What the fuck is that, anyway? Cops learned the trick about that real quick, too. In California smokers step outside the bar for a smoke, since they can't fire up inside, and when they do, the cops throw them against the walls, give them the drunk tests, the breathalyzer, the walk, the fingertip to nose, the flashlight in the eyes, and then they haul them all away in the paddy wagon for public intox. The Angels fixed that. First of all, in our neighborhood, the cops come *from* the neighborhood. No one else will or *can* work there. So cops? No problem. Shit, most of the neighborhood cops were all at my party, anyway. But what the Angels did, just in case some non-regular got some idea in his noggin to wander in on the party, find us smoking, and call cops that weren't *our* cops, some California Non-Smoking SWAT Task Force or some shit, was they posted two guards at the door. The guards would say, "Regular, or non-regular?" The unsuspecting non-regular would then take stock of the situation, look around and see parked on the sidestreet fifty or sixty Harley choppers and another thirty or forty pickup trucks, women standing around in the street and smoking cigarettes and passing around bottles of wine and waiting on their men so they could get home without getting DWIs, and they'd just turn and walk away. I got to stand guard with Charlie for a while and play like I was one tough dude, interrogating.

They were all there—not only all the regulars from the neighborhood but all the bikers from my youth, Fat Fred, Domer, Uncle Ray, Budley Johnson, the Flynn brothers Jimmy and John and Ricky and Chuck, Sonny, Dodge, Bingo. Some of the old bikers had beer bellies now, some wore button-up shirts with their names embroidered in red. Most had gray hair or were shiny-head bald. Budley wore overalls and walked with a cane and looked like a dignitary, some kind of Hell's Angel Oakland blue-blood aristocrat, and when he spoke, everyone around him went quiet and listened up. They recognized me from my author photograph, even though that picture doesn't look like I do now. In that photo, my hair is greased back, I'm not wearing my black plastic nerd glasses, my eyes are glazed with drink. Ok, well, my eyes are usually like that sometimes. In the picture I was two hundred twenty pounds, but by the time my suburban divorce was complete I'd lost sixty pounds and looked like a holocaust survivor, hair gone gray, veins mapping my forehead, cheeks sunken and even my fucking hat size shrunken half an inch. I was so loony the Dick's crew once sent Jorgensen to look after me, sent Jorgensen to make sure I didn't go on a murder spree and ruin the glorious fucking life I had ahead of me.

The party was as much for them as it was for me. They wanted me there as much to tell me *their* stories as to celebrate *my* version of their stories. They crowded around me like I was some celebrity, like I was a hero. They bought me drinks, told me to have whatever I wanted, and I knew enough to order well drinks, not call drinks like some asshole. Louie would slip me a Jack or a Chivas once in a while, and he'd just nod and pour himself one too, tipping it back with me. And man, they told me some stories.

They told me stories about the biker days, about the glory of the sixties and the early seventies, about Livermore and Altamont Pass and why the Stones were sniveling shits and why the Angels were right. Every time Sonny would walk away they'd tell me Barger stories, about how he'd taken care of them all, and they asked me if I remembered the collections he'd taken for groceries for me and my brothers and my mother, how Sonny Barger would bring home an Impala full of Safeway to feed not only us but all of them, how he fed my mother and us kids and how anyone who fucked with any one of us was meat, and how, folks, to this day, even though Sonny might not deliver the order, I the only remaining Murphy boy am immune from harm, how if anyone fucks with me they not only have the Oakland Chapter to answer to but Sonny himself, because he loved my mother, like they all did and will always. They told me stories about the time my mother got pitched from the three-wheeler, and how I'd gotten it wrong in *East Bay Grease*, how it was actually Budley, not Fat Fred, who was at the wheel and how when my mother's head hit the barbed-wire fence-post it split open and her brains wormed out and Budley pushed her cracked skull back together with his hands and held her brains in, riding in the rumble seat of a three-wheeler all the way to the hospital in Modesto—50 miles—her brains *trying* to squeeze through the cracked skull as if to spill onto the dust on purpose, like the brains themselves did not want to be in the skull but wanted to escape, wanted to be *free*. They told me that the accident made the papers because a hundred Hell's Angels lined the entrance to the hospital where they were stapling my mother's skull back together, and the Angels wouldn't let the cops into the building, or the press, because Budley had had a few to drink and it was bad enough that he'd wrecked and split my mother's skull like a coconut, he didn't need to go to jail to boot. He loved her, and fucking her up was punishment enough. They told me about how, shit, I thought my father was really the McClellan's Air Force Base fuckwad my mother had claimed to be my father but that the fact was that I could really be any of theirs, because they'd had some wild orgies—Jimmie Flynn said of all the chicks my mom was his favorite—and there was a chance that I could be any of theirs, that any of them could be my father, and that's why they all loved me. *Kid, you didn't think your mother wanted to buy the house on*

62nd Avenue, right behind the National Headquarters of the Hell's Angels, just because she thought it was a groovy neighborhood? Oh, I think I'll move right into the center of black degradation and horror, right into Oakland's war-zone where being the wrong color gets you diced! Oh, Bud Murphy, baby, let's move into the heart of white trash nigger cross-the-line bullshit and get ourselves killed! I didn't think she wanted to move there just because it was swank, did I? I wasn't that fucking stupid, was I, college boy?

The Angels told me stories, and I listened, and I got drunk as shit is what I did. It was a night of the long knives at Dick's Restaurant and Cocktail Lounge.

There's something *authentic* about men who love you even when you're at your worst, because *ladies* don't. When you're at your worst, *ladies* jump ship. *Ladies* think, Shit, I can get a better man than this man I've broken, than this sniveling heap of knee-begging weeping simpering child-support-paying alimony-doomed piece of faggotry. *Ladies* compare notes about how *bad* we are and use their cunts to get themselves some lawyer or doctor or real-estate agent or some fucker with a GTO or some house on Skyline he inherited from his bloated fatass parents who inherited it from *their* fatass parents and on and on all the way back to Adam and fucking Eve, the original capitalist land-owning gin-rickey drinking on the porch while the niggers work slavelords of all, especially of men from Oakland.

Things went pretty great until I got more drunk than usual and started whining about my divorce, and I whined a lot. Then I started breaking things, bottles and chairs and probably a couple fingers that were purple for months afterwards. Jorgensen's eyes got wide. Sonny talked low with people. The Flynn brothers walked off to conversation. Someone bought me a drink. Someone threw a bottle against the wall.

Someone bought me another drink. I had a lot of fucking drinks in front of me. I drank them best I could. I did a pretty fucking good job.

Jorg and Sonny pulled me aside with serious intent.

I can't remember what they said, not exactly. I've spent a lot of time like that, not remembering what people said, not exactly. Someone started playing pinball, and the jukebox played Creedence Clearwater Revival, our band. Listen to those guys some time. They're from Oakland, too. They know the score. Fogerty got jacked out of his royalties by the record companies, of course—he was an *artist* not some business fuck—and ended up broke and playing motels on I-5 while gray-hairs and sweaty businessmen and road-whores danced and drank watered-down cocktails and pretended like they were fuckable, when John Fogarty should have been President of the United fucking States of fucking America. Creedence was on the jukebox, someone played pinball, someone yelled something really loud and a cue-ball slammed into the wall like a cannon blast, broke a mirror and Louie shrugged. "Bad place for a mirror," he said. I remember that. Bad place for a mirror. Most places are.

Another cue ball sailed past. The mirror was already broken, so it didn't break this time.

Someone kicked the jukebox because the record was skipping. The Flynn brothers lit some joints.

"Address," Jorgensen said.

I shook my head no. My head was hanging, my head.

"Three hundred Angels mobilized in two days," Sonny said. "On the street in front of her place."

"Her father's place," I said. "Gardeners. Witnesses. You can't get all of them," I said. "Can you?"

Sonny stared at me.

Jorgensen pulled his sunglasses from his vest and snapped them on. He smiled slow.

"Mission?" Jorg said.

I tell people I said no.

My first job was shoveling shit at the Mohawk station, Snookie the dog's. I didn't get my allowance, a buck a week, until I'd shoveled the Snookie Cookies. During the rainy season, I followed Snookie around with the shit-shovel and waited until he squatted. You ever tried shoveling rained-on shit off asphalt? It's damn near impossible, and the shit sticks to the shovel, gets down between the oiled gravel and you shove the runny shit around the lot. Catch it fresh, though, and you can scoop it just like you'd scoop any other shit. The entire alley behind the Mohawk and Webb's Painting was a smear of dogfood light brown shit, and when you walked across it, your feet slid like you were on oil. Our trailer was at the end of the runway, like Snookie'd crapped out a brown carpet for us. The dry season was better. Let the shit sit for a week, it turns into white powdered shit, like chalk. You can sweep that shit with the push-broom right into the shovel in five minutes flat—a whole week's worth—collect your buck from Pop and go buy 20 packs of baseball cards.

My next job, when I turned ten, was manning the islands, pumping gas and checking the air pressure in the tires and checking the oil and transmission fluid and radiator and wiper fluid and air filter and washing windshields and handling the cash and running the credit cards through the press, access to the till, trusted. I had my own blue shirt, button-up, nametag. T-Bird, stitched in red, white background, red stitched circle around it, same as Pop and Joe and Steve Bolero. I was really good at my job. Once I even got a tip from a customer.

"Look, Pop," I said. "That guy gave me a dollar. A tip."

At first Pop looked pissed. Then he looked sad. He lit a cigar and leaned back in his chair. Snookie curled around his feet. "I never got a tip," he said. "Put the money in the till."

"Why?"

"Because you need to start paying back the money you steal."

"I don't steal."

"You think I can't add?" he said. "You don't get fifty packs of cards on a buck," he said. "The till."

"Has Joe noticed?" Joe owned the Mohawk.

"Joe can't count except on payday," Pop said. "I can. And I'm your father. And you're so fucking stupid that you got caught. If you're going to steal, don't get caught."

"Sorry."

His face got serious. "Don't be sorry," he said. "Just stop getting caught, for fuck's sake. I'm not going to bail you out."

"What?"

"The reason so many niggers are in jail is because they're so stupid they get caught. If you're going to steal, and *everyone* steals, steal like a Mexican."

"Mexicans go to jail too," I said.

"Not as much," Pop said. "Not as much as the niggers."

Early on I figured out how cool and how awful jobs were. Jobs were cool because you got paid, that's why. There are other reasons why jobs were cool, but I couldn't think of them.

I could think of lots of reasons why jobs sucked, though. Someone telling you what to do, someone criticizing you after you've busted your ass and done your best and telling you that you, not the job, suck, you don't cut it, you're lucky you're not fired. I started mowing lawns, pushmower, as a side job from my regular job at the Mohawk. A buck a yard, front and back. Took me about three hours to do both yards, so I was making pretty good cash. Mrs. Couto brought me a pitcher of iced tea one time. Mr. Goulart, Tony Goulart's father who had a milk-route in San Francisco and one time took me on his route delivering wire racks of glass milk bottles to Chinese restaurants and old people's porches, Goulart's father once gave me two bottles of chocolate milk while I was mowing his yard. But FatDaddy Slattern, one of the only blue-eyed white guys in the neighborhood, and he had a daughter who though she'd hump all the teenagers wouldn't talk to any of us so stuck up a little bitch was she—what the fuck they were doing in our neighborhood we never figured out but what we suspected was that the fat fuck didn't care about his family so cheap was he and all he cared about was packing his fat bank account with the money he made owning his custom toilet seat factory—Slattern's Designer Johns—Slattern gave me my first lesson on how shitty bosses can and are likely to be, because that's how they end up bosses. What FatDaddy Slattern did was when I asked him if I could mow his lawn he said yes, sure, you can mow my lawn, but I can only pay you seventy-five cents. A dollar is too steep. Front and back, seventy-five.

It was hard to see inside FatDaddy's house, he was so wide. But when he turned to the side I caught a glimpse. His daughter sat on the couch watching TV. One of her eyes was fucked up, just rolled around like a frog's. She was a teenager, and her face had so many pimples you couldn't tell she had pimples. Her skin was flaming red and crusted yellow from pus, and it was a face no one would want to touch. You wouldn't want her to leak on your hand. Everyone knew she'd do coke with anyone who had it, and anyone who had coke could fuck her. The trick was porking her without touching that face of hers.

Next to her and eating ice cream from a bucket and smoking cigarettes was Mama FatDaddy. She scooped a glob of ice cream with one hand, and before she finished chewing she brought her cigarette to her mouth. Her cigarette was stuck in a silver cigarette holder, and the way she held it let you know that somewhere in another universe she was a movie star. Not in this one, though. In this one she was as big and round as FatDaddy himself. Her face was always burnt red in the shape of a mustache and beard from where she waxed every morning. Sometimes the wax wouldn't get all the hairs and there'd be stray black wires pointing out like miniature pieces of rebar.

FatDaddy's walls were lined with his custom toilet seats used as picture frames. A zebra fur seat hung over his fireplace, Slattern family portrait behind glass framed by the ring. They looked like yokels trying to pretend they weren't, fat toothless farmers and their horsey wives (a Jew in the mix, most likely, though FatDaddy was the kind of man who'd never admit it) wearing their home-sewn Sunday best, the babies wall-eyed and drooling. An Oakland A's toilet seat hung next to a Raiders seat, pictures of Elvis grinning. Two oversized toilet seats, one decorated with teddy bears the other with ducks and both big as car tires and made for asses like FatDaddy's, framed pictures of his zit-faced horse-nose daughter when she was a baby. It looked like she had zits even then. They were pretty cool toilet seats, actually. I wished I had one.

For me, money was money, and I'd rather be making it than not making it, and so I shook his hand.

Shaking someone's hand in my neighborhood is not a thing lightly done, not when you're a grown up, and moreso not when you're a kid. When you're an adult, a handshake can be negated by a lawyer, or an ex-wife, or by having had too many to drink at Dick's. But when you're a kid, a handshake is your only currency, it's all you got, and in my neighborhood we remember every childhood handshake that was ever true, and we remember every one that ever was bullshit, that was a lie. And in my neighborhood we do not forget. *Ever.*

I shook FatDaddy Slattern's chicken-fat slimy hand, and the four-hundred pound toad-face *crushed* my hand when he clasped it, to show me what a *man* he was. "It's a deal, then," he said. "Seventy-five cents for the yard, front and back." He smiled big. He'd made a deal. My hand hurt like fuck, but I wasn't about to let him know.

And a deal that fat fuck had made, too. The front yard, the yard people saw when they drove past his peeling paint dump, plaster Jesuses littered around the lot to show how God and all his soldiers protected him from the likes of us, one Jesus holding a Bible opened to the Ten Commandments, plaster Jesuses and birdbaths that had so much birdshit they looked like melted candles, his fancy yard's lawn wasn't that bad except for the maneuvering around the Jesuses and the birdshit birdbaths. That took some work, but that was part of the job. Fine. When I finished FatDaddy Slattern's front yard, though, after four hours, I tried to push open the side gate, and what I found out after trying to push open that gate let me know the difference between FatDaddy and me. Me? What you see is what you get. I wear jeans and tee shirts. I own one tie, and every motherfucker in the neighborhood has seen it, because it's the one I wear at funerals. Me? I'm the kid who shovels dogshit at the Mohawk station and lives in the trailer next to it. I'm the kid who empties the trailer's toilet tank once a week one bucket at a time into the station's women's room pot. I'm the kid who fills your tank and checks the air in your tires. I get straight A's and I play trumpet and my trumpet is held together with rubber bands and solder joints. I once won a golf tournament with a 3-iron, a putter I'd found on the green, and sand-wedge. Whopped some rich boy ass. When I won by six strokes, the rich fuck clone-kid fancy haircut golf-cart button-up collar tee-shirt pussy from the other side of town, the hills, broke all his clubs over his knees, his fancy cleats a-sparkling in the sun-glint. He wore one of those hats that doesn't even cover your head, that only has a visor. I gloated and danced on the green, an Irish jig I'd seen Pop dance at the Elk's lodge when something he'd done but couldn't talk about outside of the lodge had made him really, *really* happy. I'm T-Bird Murphy and I'm named after the man who bought my mother cartons of cigarettes when she was pregnant with me, pregnant not by the man who raised me, Pop "Bud" Murphy, but by party-boy Cigogne perhaps unless my mother had just fingered him because his family had more cash than the Hell's Angels who were boinking her too and at the same time and all at once, by the fuckdog boy who schtupped my mama, and I'm blind in one eye, I have bowed legs, and my nose is Jew, my hair blond, eyes the color of wet concrete. Look at me: I'm T-Bird Murphy. The iron-on patches on the knees of my jeans cut into my skin and when I take off my pants there's red marks to prove. My clothes are second-hand, and the kids make fun of me for it because they've caught me wearing clothes their parents have donated to Goodwill. You fuck, FatDaddy Slattern: take a motherfucking look, if you care about the future of your family, your useless progeny. I am what I appear to be. That's what I fucking am.

But not you. Check out your yard. Your yard, your front yard, the one people *see*, is just like the other people in the neighborhood. You have plaster Jesii, weeds, maybe a fountain. You're pretty special for your ornamental iron over the door and the windows, but you know the iron don't make you safe against us, not *much*. Your ornamental iron might keep us from taking your television *out*, but the iron don't keep us from getting *in* with a flaming cocktail. What happens to you if your house catches fire and you can't get through your barred windows and doors? Your bars keep you *in* as much as they keep us *out*. And if you don't think so, think a-fucking-gain.

Your back yard isn't what you want people to see. But it's what you *are*, and what we all suspect people like you to be but we rarely get verification. Your back yard is what you are, and you don't want us to see it, but you're so greedy and slovenly and indolent that you can't help revealing it to us when there's a profit of cash in it for you, even though, and you never realize this, cash profit doesn't wash for much in the long run, not when there's more of us than you. When I pushed the redwood gate that led to the backyard, it wouldn't open. I pushed and pushed, tried jiggling the latch, but no go. I leaned into that gate with all my weight. Nothing.

Finally I knocked on FatDaddy's door and told him about the problem of the gate. He smiled. One of his teeth was green. He was eating a rack of spareribs, and juice lined the creases in his chins and dripped on his fancy button-up shirt, pink. "Can't get the gate open, little man?" he said. "How you going to do the job, how you going to get *paid*, you can't open the gate? You out of your league, *boy?*"

"I just can't figure out the trick," I said.

"There's no *trick*," FatDaddy Slattern said. "It's a matter of playing in the big leagues. Boy."

He led me to the gate, yawned, bit off a strip of sparerib. "Ribs smell good?" he said.

I said yes.

"Pretty good ribs," he said. He tore into one. "Damn good ribs," he said. "Big league ribs."

FatDaddy ripped another strip with his teeth and then he threw the rest of the rack down in the flowerbed dirt. He smiled when I looked at them, those ribs in the dirt. Some meat still hung on them. He turned around and pushed his ass into the gate and bucked backward. One of the redwood boards cracked. The gate opened.

"That's how we do things in the big leagues," he said.

I saw the problem with the gate. Problem was the weeds were taller than me. And not just regular weeds, foxtails and dandelions, no. These were serious weeds. Thorned blackberry bushes, sticker bushes, vines. The yard was a primordial tangle, four feet tall and buzzing with yellow-jackets and bumble bees, feeding. It was the kind of thing you see growing against the warehouses, lining the railroad tracks. It was the kind of thing you could see from the BART train's elevated lines in the nigger neighborhoods. The yard didn't need a lawnmower. Not even a bulldozer. That yard needed fire.

FatDaddy's teeth glowed red with barbecued crud. He laughed. Juice sprayed. I ducked but he still got some in my hair. He laughed again. "You look," he said, and he laughed and then he laughed so hard he coughed. He bent over a little, and juice spilled out of his mouth and he choked and then he laughed and he choked again. "You look surprised!" he said, and he just kept laughing.

He said, "Welcome to the big leagues! Seventy-five cents for the job," he said. "And the job's half done!"

He was right. I'd made a deal, and I was going to follow up on my end, do the job. I'd shaken hands. But I'd learned a lesson, too. Watch out for the fuckers. I'd been treated pretty shitty in my time already. I was in fifth grade, after all, and I'd seen shit already that even I knew wasn't shit like *normal* shit, but was *special* shit that only I had borne witness to. I'd seen Hell's Angels gut Black Panthers. I'd seen Hell's Angels beat the fuck out of a cop who'd come to break up a party at our house, beat him into burger and haul the mess off in the back of a pickup truck. I'd seen Hell's Angels beat the fuck out of *each other*, for fuck's sake. I'd seen some harsh shit in my time. My mother took me to the Berkeley riots so I could *experience the expression of the people.* Pop took me to James Jones' church in San Francisco where I got to see naked pregnant ladies giving blowjobs while The Doors played on the PA and a movie screen showed slides of someone swirling ink and oil around on glass. I wasn't all the way innocent. I'd seen what knives could do, and I'd hidden in my bedroom closet during fights and heard gunshot and the scuffle and shuffle and removal. I'd had the shit beat out of me by some badass hungover motherfuckers, and I'd been violated in every way a boy can be violated, but I'd never, *never* before been *betrayed*. This was something new. This was something fucked up. This was something I had to think about.

I'd learned a *lesson*. Watch out for the fuckers. But in order to watch out for the fuckers, you got to know how to pick them out, how to spot a fucker in a crowd. It's not always that easy. Fuckers are some of the best around at disguising their fuckerness. That's part of what makes them fuckers. I'd been conned by a fucker, and I took stock. It wasn't going to happen again. Some ways to spot them, that's what I needed. I made some.

Thirty-two aspects of Fuckers, Qualities of and How to Identify:

1. If they're fat, if they don't work as hard as the rest of us, they're probably a fucker.

2. If they're fat and they wear nice clothes, have a nice car, or live in a house they don't rent, they're probably *serious* fuckers.

3. Fuckers don't have breakfast at Dick's, and when they have drinks after work, they drink alone.

4. Fuckers have British last names.

5. Sometimes Mexican.

6. Fuckers make you check the air in their tires. They make you wash their back windshields.

7. Fuckers don't watch football, usually, but if they do, they don't root for the Raiders.

8. If you're a fucker, your wife has the kids and you don't pay child support.

9. Good men with ex-wives live in trailers, garages, and if they're really lucky, apartments.

10. They don't live in the house they bought.

11. When a fucker buys groceries, he doesn't even make an attempt to bag.

12. Fuckers don't eat linguisca. They eat steak. They eat steak at breakfast, steak and eggs. They eat steak at lunch, Philly. They eat steak at dinner, steak and lobster. They like cows a whole fucking lot.

13. It's part of their fucker genetic makeup.

14. When you've finally spotted a car in the junkyard the same year as yours, the same model, with all the same options, the same color with the same interior, a fucker will have spotted the same car

and instead of inspecting the car for which parts he wants, he'll wobble back when you're not looking to the office and buy the whole fucking car, just to be sure you don't get a single part you need. He'll junk his leftover parts, leave them for the monthly hard-trash pick-up just to spite you.

15. Never raid a fucker's trash.

16. A fucker will tell everyone in the neighborhood he saw you at his curb raiding his *garbage*.

17. Fuckers file taxes using the long form.

18. Fuckers wear cowboy hats and don't ride horses or tractors.

19. Fuckers don't make their kids work.

20. Fuckers let their kids be fuckers.

21. They encourage them to be fuckers.

22. Have kids who are fuckers.

23. Are glad they have fucker kids.

24. To be a fucker, you have to believe in God.

25. God is the ultimate fucker.

26. Fuckers don't think God is a fucker.

27. The haircut of a fucker: over ten dollars and done by a woman.

28. When fuckers fuck women over, they think they're doing something really fucking funny.

29. When fuckers fuck men over, they think they're doing something really fucking funny.

30. In my neighborhood, fuckers fuck, but eventually they get fucked.

31. Eventually they get fucked like they never imagined a person could be fucked.

32. Fuck fuckers.

FatDaddy stuck his hand out again, to reaffirm the handshake, and I put my hand into his sauce-clotted mitt, and he crushed it again, squeezed so hard I thought he'd broken bones, and he might have. Three of my fingers were purple for months after that handshake. They're crooked even today from that oath. Fucker.

I went home and told Pop.

"You made your bed," he said. "Lie in it."

I went to the back of the trailer and sat on my bed. I sat there a long time. My brothers fell asleep before me. Pop was on his kitchen-table foldout bed watching the news. He got up and stood. The trailer rocked. He opened the refrigerator. He handed me an open beer and sat down on the edge of my bed. "He's a fucker," Pop said. "And you're not the first one he's fucked."

I took a swig.

"You don't like the deal he made with you?" Pop said.

I shook my head no.

"Why not?" Pop said. "Why the fuck don't you like the deal? You made it, didn't you?"

I told Pop why I didn't like the deal. I didn't like it because I'd been deceived. I didn't like it because FatDaddy Slattern had *betrayed* me. He lived in the neighborhood—wasn't he one of *us*? Didn't FatDaddy Slattern understand that none of us wanted to live there, in shithole Oakland, and that for some reason he was living there *too*, for some reason he, FatDaddy, was such a fuckup that he'd landed on our turf? By definition he was a loser, and the only thing losers can do to exert power over their lives, to have some semblance of control, is treat their fellow losers as they'd have themselves treated. I didn't understand, at the time, that losers, sometimes, *true losers*, are different from regular losers, losers who've lost their children and homes and incomes to cunts and their lawyers. Some losers are such losers that they want to exert their loserness over others, to bring them down to depths of loserness most losers could not conceive of. The losers of the losers crave only this: they want others to lose more than they've lost, to lose worse. The worst of the losers, people like FatDaddy

Slattern, hate their lives, hate their fatness, hate their children, hate the wives who've spawned their disgusting progeny who hate them and keep living only because they hope they'll outlive their loser parents so's they can enjoy their inheritances. True losers hate everyone because they know they've never done anything in their lives worthy of *love*, of respect that is not born of fear or greed. They'll get theirs, of course, their non-taxed inheritances of money made on the blood and sweat of my Oakland people losing limbs in factories and dropping dead making aqueducts and falling off bridges they're constructing over ravines. They'll get all their parents wanted for them. Their parents were prefuckers, antefuckers, the fuckers of precedence. *Fuckers originales.* But the worst of the losers have no one who will come to bat for them when things get bad, and that's why they spend their whole lives trying to make money, trying to accumulate power, *capital*, to insulate themselves from the world. People where I come from insulate themselves from the fuckness of the world by being *loyal* to the people they love and who love them back. Can't fuck with a loved man, or woman, in my neighborhood. Can't fuck with someone who's loved, and that's a fucking fact. Try it, shitbag, and just you see what happens.

I didn't like what FatDaddy had done to me because he was rich and lived in a house and had a yard and I was only trying to do an honest day's work for an honest day's pay and he'd fucked me, the fucker. He had the money to do me right, and he didn't.

"Let people know."

"Who?"

"Let people know," Pop said. "You got friends. Use them."

I swigged again. "Who," I said.

"Everyone in the neighborhood, everyone in the town who pulls up to the pump. You tell every motherfucker you ever come in contact with," Pop said. "*Spread the word.*"

"What do I say?"

"You say the truth," Pop said. "Try it. See what happens."

So that's what I did. I'd be pumping gas and a customer would say, "Hey hey, T-Bird, how they hanging?" and I'd say, "Not good," and I'd put on the face like I'd been beaten and bitch-slapped and tossed in the dumpster with the Snookie cookies. "What?" they'd say. "Whassup?"

"FatDaddy," I'd say. "He conned me. Seventy-five cents," and I'd tell them the story.

I told the story to everyone, and not only that, I told the story to everyone who *counted* in the neighborhood. When Joe and Frank Camozzi of Camozzi Carpets needed fleet work done on tires, I told them the tale of FatDaddy Slattern. When the Yandell Trucking Company guys fueled up, hey, FatDaddy Slattern took me for a ride. The Concrete Wall Sawing men, all ex-marines running jackhammers and blowing C-40 and taking down buildings, when they came in I told them of the FatDaddy Slattern adolescent labor rape. Frank Carlito needed five old inner-tubes so his kids could ride the Sacramento River and I told him about my summer of bushwacking and mowing. Sometimes Pop would help out. "Hey, you know what that fuck Slattern did to my boy? My boy who was making a buck a yard, a yard a day? He fucked my boy is what. His yard is nigger, twelve feet high and nothing but vine and empties. My boy's been mowing and chopping and sawing and bee-stung for a month now, lost thirty bucks or maybe more while he's doing FatDaddy's yard instead of moving on to other yards. FatDaddy Slattern is a nigger, and a nigger fucked my boy, right up the ass, the nigger. What you think of that? You think that's right? You think that ought to go unnoticed? You think this isn't something the neighborhood needs to look after, to *settle?*"

And Pop meant it as a question, too. He wanted them to answer, and he wanted them to answer, "Kill." He wanted them to answer, "Kill the fucker," but in Oakland-speak. He wanted them to say, "No problema."

And a whole hell of a lot of them did. They said no problema without saying a word, Oakland style, a bit lower lip, a nod, a slow close of the eyes, a stone stare.

Pop told some shit to the men, and he crossed the line and talked to the women too, told all of them and every one. When someone's wife would pull up at the pump, Mama Fernandez who might have been related to all of us, or Mrs. Flynn who worked for the phone company and who was probably mother to the rest of us, when one of them would pull in, Mama Fernandez who ran the firehouse dispatcher and Mrs. Flynn whose sons, all eleven of them, represented the most terrifying posse in Oakland other than the unnamed nigger posses that couldn't be identified because they didn't have fathers but were instead born of virgin nigger birth, their mothers fucked by angels of God, usually whitey shitbags if we tell the truth which we usually don't in matters like this, Mrs. Flynn with her eleven sons and still more beautiful than any woman alive even though she had the eleven kid fat, her face shimmering like a moon hubcap in the lights of a gas station canopy, brilliant, Mrs. Flynn whose sons kept killing themselves when they were just on the verge of getting out of the neighborhood, one son a concert pianist who offed himself the morning of his first San Francisco solo concert with the symphony, another son bullet in the head before the California Demolition Derby Championship with his '56 Chevy Mauler Special, Mrs. Flynn long-suffering and tough as rebar and who knew how to take care of a drunken man, Pop told Mrs. Flynn. And telling Mrs. Flynn had some repercussions. She was a Swede, Mrs. Flynn, and Swedes aren't like the rest of us Mexicans, Italians, niggers, Irish, Spics, Portugees, and shit like that. Swedes have a sense of not only loyalty, like all of us have, but they have a sense of *justice*, of what not only is right in terms of our families and our neighborhoods, but of some kind of right that isn't like right we know. It's a *right*, a *this is the way the world should fucking work*, that is way more serious than any of us ever even consider. The long white beards of old Swedes are "Fuck you" to not only the hippies and the rednecks but to every one and all of us. No one but a fucking Swede can wear a beard like that and get a drink at Dick's. No one but a Swede can wear a beard like that and walk into someone's home and sit quiet during the conversation while the folk talk shit about their family, about other people's families, about politics and movie stars and physics and theories of existential import and sit there quiet and somehow be right about everything even though they've said nothing. Those beards command respect that none of us can ever have, because those old Swedes *care less* about shit than we do. They've got some old world shit in them that is immune to our American pretend-we'll-kick-your-ass shit bullshit. They are not people to be messed with, Swedes. Or Norwegians, or Hollanders, or swamp-true Germans, or any of those white-haired psychos. And don't you try to mess with a true-bred nigger, either. Those purple motherfuckers have the same attitude: you mess with one of me or mine, you're gone. No questions, no negotiation, adios kimosabe. You don't very often meet a pure-bred nigger in Oakland, but when you do, he's got a face that lets you know who he is and where he came from, and where *he* came from is a lot fucking worse than were *you* came from, because he's not a slave nigger sold off by some two-bit chieftain, but he's a *real* nigger blue-blood sonbitch who'll just as soon slice you and drink your blood from your skull as talk to you, because you're a *lower* life form, some kind of devolved un-human less-than piece of shit that doesn't rank higher than a yak. You can't kill an old nigger, and you can't kill an old Swede, because not only has the old Swede, like the old nigger, been dead since he sprouted pubic hair, but he's been alive longer than anyone you know. Those crusty motherfuckers—and they're all crusty motherfuckers, even if they're only twelve—those crusty motherfuckers do shit calm. You never hear of a Swede gang-war, but you think they don't have them? What kind of stupid fuck are *you*? They rumble over turf just like the rest of us. But they rumble serious. Think about it: Jorgensen's a Swede. And Pop, he enlisted Mrs. Flynn and all her boys that were alive. "My boy's a lawn-mower, and he's been fucked with. Slattern. FatDaddy. You know him."

We all do.

Pop had them all on the case, Joey Medieros the carpenter who'd finally finished doing his time for accidentally killing a wife with a nail-gun, Big-Bob Jones who'd made the papers when his ex left him and he'd dumped fifty ISOs into the bay, all their cargo sunk to the bottom and Big-Bob laughing when they hauled him away not to jail but to the loony-bin where he got to fuck the loony girls, all of them. Flann O'Shaunessey, the precinct's Fire Chief, one of the semi-regulars at Dick's and who Pop had gone to Oakland High with back in the days—Mr. O'Shaunessey came into the Mohawk station and Pop pulled from the filing cabinet a bottle of Jameson's he'd bought special to share. That bottle went empty and Pop had to break into the storage room fridge for the Oly. Before O'Shaunessey got into his red Fire-Chief Impala, he handed me a beer. "It's the last one," he said, "and you need to be the one to drink it." He started his engine, but he didn't put his car in gear until he saw me polish that can off.

Pop called the Corollo family to duty, seven brothers strong and beautiful and evil to the right people, who'd take care of any business they thought needed just treatment. The Corollo brothers were serious people, Joe most of all, Joe whose face was expressionless wax and though Italian his hair blond and eyes pale blue. Joe never said much, never more than a yes or a no, but somehow everyone wanted his opinion about matters of import. Someone would unravel their tale, their problem, their dilemma, and after a longwind hour of spilling would look to Joe and he'd just say, "Yes," and the seeker of counsel would nod and do according to Joe's bidding. You didn't want to mess with the Corollo brothers, nope. One of them, the eighth brother, had been killed by a crew of Mexicans, dragged the way my brother was dragged, it being a traditional method of whacking someone in the neighborhood. The crew was all minors, and when they got out of juvy, one at a time when they turned eighteen, they didn't come back to the neighborhood, didn't *disappear* like what usually happens in our neighborhood when we wait for fuckers to get out of juvy. What they did was *appear*, one body part at a time, all around town, a finger—middle—on the steps of City Hall, a tongue on the porch of a Chinese fish market, eyeballs in a bucket of bait at the pier. One of the Mexicans' mothers found ears with her morning milk delivery. One of the fathers found a shriveled bloodless dick in his lunchbox next to his twin-pack of Twinkies at work at the docks. Parts were abundant. It's really creepy when you think about it, how many parts of a person you can spread around a town. Lungs, testicles, noses, bones, carefully brain-scooped sawed-up skulls, toes, ankles. Each of the Mexicans was scalped, and each of the scalps ended up in fancy-schmancy shops specializing in shit for trendy people who worshipped ancient cultures, turquoise, skin drums and stretched animal hides imitating some kind of divine talisman and drums made from logs, as if the niggers and the Indians and the Pacific Islanders were some kinds of Bachs and Mozarts and goddamn fucking Mahlers. The scalps were works of art, according to Joseph Pappas the cop. He said that he'd get a call every time one of the Mexicans was let out of juvy, and the call wouldn't be that something was stolen, but that something had mysteriously appeared in the shop, some work of art, a hair-piece of some sort dried and stretched across a hubcap. "They're really quite original, actually. But we'd really prefer to deal with an agent than with the artist directly, especially in this fashion. It's a bit like, like *extortion?* We can't sell something on commission unless we know who we're selling it for. You know, whoever is making these is an artist of the first order, tapped into the primal instincts of man, into our purest soul." Pappas would say, "You got that right, lady." When ears were found they were always nailed to the wall of Club 17, the Mexican salsa and merengue nightclub, ears hanging from the wall bloody and listening.

When the main man of the town, Mr. Brown, pulled up to the pump, Pop whispered. He whispered a long time, and then he called me to Mr. Brown's car window. "This is the boy," Pop said. "My *son*. FatDaddy Slattern did that to this boy, this boy *my son*." Mr. Brown shook my hand. I tried to pull my hand away, but Brown held my hand close. "My shake counts," he said. And I believed him. And in retrospect, I was right to do so. We all suspected Jerry would be mayor of Oakland someday, even though he was white. Nut-case Brown, who thought everything could work out. He was rich but he drove a four-cylinder rice-banger and he wasn't afraid to come into Dick's once in a while and tip one with the likes of us. When Daddy Borges pulled up at the pump, Daddy Safeway Manager Borges who could cut you a break anytime if he was checking the groceries, mis-add your bill and give you a steak or two blocks of fancy cheese, Pop let Daddy Borges know the score on FatDaddy Slattern.

FatDaddy Slattern was getting to be really well known.

And I mowed. I chopped. I swathed. I cut and I ripped and tore and yanked and tore and tugged and bled. I leaked more blood into FatDaddy Slattern's yard than I had in my body. Every day I worked on that yard of his, sun-up sun-down. I'd shove into the briar, and the blades, spinning, would jam. Alto, motherfucker. Every shove I'd have to untangle. And with every shove bugs from some fancy designer continent would get pissed off and fly in my face, green and shiny roaches, golden gnats, grasshoppers as big as my fist and in every weird not-Oakland color you can imagine, pink and shit like that, purple. And while I mowed, while I sweated 10-30, FatDaddy Slattern, who didn't seem to have any job other than watching me and getting his money's worth, watched. He watched, and he liked it. He watched me, seventy-five cent little loser white-trash shit. He liked watching the grandson and the son and the boy of his lessers schlog it out in the fields, in his home, in his back yard, he the nigger overlord, me the nigger. He liked to watch. He'd sit on his back porch drinking gin, fat and sweating and bits of lawn and weed and thorn ground into lawnmower dust crusting the crevices of his chins. He'd sit there smiling and drinking cool iced drinks and telling me, "Hey, there," he'd say. "You missed a spot. There."

For some reason, things started going wrong around the Slattern house. I always started work at seven in the morning, and each morning FatDaddy Slattern would hear me on the pushmower and he'd open the back door and stand there in his boxer shorts that he must've had to buy at some kind of fatass specialty shop or had made for him. He'd stand there picking his ass, really rooting around like he was ripping something from his insides, and drinking a cup of coffee. Sometimes Mama FatDaddy would join him and she'd watch me, too. She'd stand there in a tee-shirt that was supposed to be a nightshirt but because she was so fat didn't even cover her baggy white panties. She'd stand there eating ice cream and smoking and farting, and you could hear those farts, and, worse, you could smell them, awful beef and pork farts that smelled like the animals weren't yet dead when she ate them, and you could actually *smell* the pig, *smell* the cow, as if somehow the whole animal she'd consumed, and the smell of a Mama FatDaddy Slattern fart was the smell of a refrigerator in the backyard that's been there for three months and you've just opened it up, summer, and someone left eight pounds of bologna and burger and bratwurst and when you open that door you're hit with the black and green fog of moldering death. That's what a Mama FatDaddy fart smelled like, and that's the smell I began work to every day, death and rot. You know what I'm talking about. And if you don't, you're one lucky mother-fucker. I'd tell you to hang out with Mama FatDaddy Slattern sometime, morning, but these days we don't know where the family FatDaddy is.

Mornings at seven I'd begin work on my only job, my seventy-five cent pushmower lawn job going to make a living as a hardworking Oak-land boy what I'm going to do. I'd be a-mowing and the sweat started quick, and then something would happen. One morning a pipe burst and FatDaddy heard it go and his toilet overflowed, the gigantic FatDaddy-sized shit he'd taken before coming to watch me work spread out over carpet and his hardwood floor and flavored with pork scent piss.

He looked at me and yelled. "Where's the main?"

"What?"

"The fucking main. Where's the water main in these shitty little houses?"

"I wouldn't know," I said. "I don't live in a *house*," I said. "Sir," I said. "We get our water from the gas station. Through a hose."

Shit oozed. It rolled slow across the floor like lava from a shit-volcano. FatDaddy got on the phone and called Jay Ellis, the neighborhood plumber. About a week before, Ellis had fixed the float on FatDaddy's tank. Ellis was famous because whenever he showed up on a toilet job, before he even talked to anyone he'd just march into the bathroom and barehanded stick his fist into the toilet and feel around. Pop once asked him about his method. "Two reasons," said Ellis. "Reason one—the homeowner is usually so sicked out that they go away and let me do my job without standing over me like a foreman. Reason two—you can find things with your fingers that you can't find with a tool." Ellis winked at Pop. Pop said, "Reason three—you're a sick fuck and you like the feel of shit between your fingers." Ellis permanently smelled like shit, and he tried always to cover it up with Old Spice, but all that happened was that he smelled like Old Spice and shit. To this day, I still can't smell Old Spice without a whiff of shitstink somehow wafting into my nose.

I smell Old Spice, I smell shit, and I think of Jay Ellis.

Ellis showed up on the scene and said, "Hey hey, T-Bird. What you got here. Still at work on that lawn job of yours?"

FatDaddy said, "I'm paying for you to fix my plumbing. You talk to me, plumber. Shit boy."

Ellis said, "I've unplugged a lot of your toilets, toilet guy! My favorite was the Nixon. And do I have an idea for you! What you need to do is make decals to stick to the bottom of the can. Targets. Imagine, politicians, ex-wives, ex-husbands, the Kansas City Chiefs logo, the democrat elephant, the republican donkey, a Mexican flag, Martin Luther King, a plain old bull's eye—what the hell. After the Nixon I liked the Confederate flag theme. I've been meaning to buy one of those." Ellis started whistling Dixie and doing a little dance. "You have a hell of a business going there."

"You're fucking A," FatDaddy said. "I own it. I make the money. I design the toilet seats, and my crew of hired apes makes them. Need a job?"

Ellis walked into the bathroom, FatDaddy following, their feet slopping around in the curd, and Ellis did his toilet-fisting trick, the water splashing onto the bathroom walls and onto FatDaddy's chest when Ellis' fist hit the light brown pool. FatDaddy gagged and slopped out of the room. "Hey you, you little shit," he said.

I looked at him.

"Yes, you. Aren't you supposed to be mowing my yard? I'm paying you good money to mow my yard, and you're just standing around with your finger up your ass. You're as bad as the apes at the plant. You're probably related to them, aren't you. Inbred Catholics. Get to work."

The briar patch awaited. It was a month into the job, and I'd cleared about a quarter of the yard. Summer jobs sucked.

Ellis came outside and crawled under the house. When he came out, he was covered with cobwebs. He looked at me and smiled. Then he winked. He told FatDaddy the pipes were rotted and that he was lucky it was only the toilet and not something worse.

"Worse?" FatDaddy said.

Ellis said, "It can always be worse."

"Just fix it."

"Will do," Ellis said. "You'll need to take out that carpet and get someone in here with a wet-vac or else the wood will buckle and you'll lose your floor. I recommend Camozzi Carpets. They do insurance jobs. And you should probably call your adjuster."

When Camozzi Bill showed up in his white van he'd brought Dan the Dope Man, the biggest stoner in the neighborhood, wild curly red hair and standing about eight feet tall, sunglasses always. I'd told Dan the Dope man about FatDaddy's deal with me when I was filling the Camozzi truck.

FatDaddy sat stewing on the back porch, watching me work while the Camozzi men rolled up the shit-sopped carpet and lugged it into the back of their truck. When they plugged the wet-vac in and flipped the switch, something exploded beneath the house and everything electric went dead.

FatDaddy said, "What the fuck."

"Can't vac the place without power," Dan the Dope Man said.

"Fix the power, then," FatDaddy said.

"Don't mess with electric," Camozzi Bill said. Dan the Dope Man nodded. He wore those sunglasses, but I could tell he was looking at me with an eye-smile. Dan said, "Probably best to call Gutierrez. He's the best electrician in town, and he works cheap. No green card. If he doesn't do a good job, you can just call la migra, get him deported."

"Call him. Goddamn it, call the wetback. Shit. Who built this crap-for-house?"

Camozzi Bill said, "That would be Mr. Williams."

Bill's last name was Williams. His father was the contractor, and anyone who counted in the neighborhood would have known at least that, if nothing else. The Williams family built the community center, the Elks Lodge, most of the houses in a twelve block radius, and Old Bob's Harley Davidson dealership. They built the park.

"Someone needs to tell *Mr. Williams* he builds shitty houses."

"I'll make sure he gets the message," Bill said.

"You do that. Now call that beaner and get him over here to fix my electricity so you can vacuum up that lake of shit."

"Will do," Bill said. "Sir."

Bill and Dan the Dope Man lit smokes and Bill said, "Take a break, kid."

"I can't." I was sweating like a baker.

"I'll mow," said Camozzi Bill, and he took the mower and cracked it into the berry bushes.

Dan the Dope Man took his leathers from his back pocket and bent over and started yanking bushes at the roots, throwing tangles of vine and thorn on the porch at FatDaddy's feet.

"That's the boy's work," FatDaddy said. "I'm paying *him*, not you."

"Nothing for us to do," Bill said. "And we're on the clock, by the way. You want us to go? We can go, sir, but I'd advise against cutting us off. Floor's more expensive than our time."

"Thieves," FatDaddy said.

Gutierrez showed up and went under the house. He came back with a fistful of wires melted together and scorched.

"The wiring it's fine," Gutierrez said. "No problema with the wiring of this house. The problem is this, Senor, Senor Slattern. You have too many bugs. The bugs, the termites and the other bugses eat through the wires and the wood and I think you have a big problema, my friend."

Things got rough on FatDaddy Slattern, and no one could quite figure out why. We racked our brains and none of us could make any sense of it. It was as if some biblical curse had been visited on the poor son of a bitch. It was like everything that *could* go wrong for him *did* go wrong. The bugs? Termite infested, his house. And then a plague of ants after the carpet was reinstalled, almost as if the Camozzis had treated the carpet with sugared water, which, of course, was such a mean trick that no one would hardly ever do such a thing. The house's wiring turned out to be much worse than initially anticipated by Gutierrez. It seemed like every time FatDaddy flipped a light switch, something shorted or caught fire. FatDaddy had to buy a new fire extinguisher every week. His phone bill included calls to Cambodia that he swore he didn't make but that he had to pay for because when they called the Cambodia number to verify, the guy who answered the phone said he'd talked with Mr. Slattern often, that Slattern was always calling, actually, that their conversations were about designer toilet seat design. He racked up thirty-three traffic tickets in a six day stretch, getting pulled over every time he put his car in gear and sometimes getting tickets when he wasn't even driving. He got a ticket for parking within five feet of his own driveway. Unsafe lane change. Failure to signal. Chickenshit tickets galore. At restaurants his food always tasted like someone had pissed on it. One time he bit into a sandwich and the deli worker had accidentally used gobs of killer Chinese mustard instead of a thin spread of American yellow. Somehow his mail stopped coming, and when he tried to track it down, he found it'd been forwarded, and not just forwarded, but forwarded first to another address in Oakland, then to Sacramento, to North Highlands, Elverta, Rio Linda, to San Leandro, then re-forwarded to San Lorenzo, then to Hayward, to Boulder, Colorado, seven consecutive addresses in Houston, Cypress, Texas, two different addresses in New York City, Queens, Freeland, Washington on Whidbey Island, Boulder Creek, California, Salem, Oregon, back to Houston, to Knob Noster, Missouri, to McAllen, Texas. He went for a haircut and ended up having to get a crew-cut, so screwed-up a job Joannie did, and she was really sorry about it and promised to do a better job the next time he came in. Joannie would have her mother, Mama Hernandez herself and in the flesh, do the job, and do it right.

Now the fire, the fire was a bad thing. The family FatDaddy was sleeping—around three in the afternoon they took family naps—and I was mowing. In Oakland it doesn't rain between May and October, and when it's hot you can hear the weeds crackle and snap when the oxygen in the plants' cells explodes. Stand in a field in California summer and it's like you're in a bowl of Rice Krispies, as if billions of microscopic firecrackers are exploding, as if the earth is burning itself alive. And you don't just hear the fire, you can *feel* it, you can feel the heat, feel it torch. FatDaddy Slattern's yard sang with fire. That it would catch was inevitable. It wasn't my fault. The mower did it. I got a running start on a bad patch of weeds and the blade hit a rock, part of a buried granite fountain. The blades made a spark, the spark caught the weeds, and before I knew it the yard was afire, and the house caught, and I tried to let the family FatDaddy Slattern know their house was on fire, really I did, but they were sleeping too hard and I couldn't wake them up by yelling and the doors were locked so I couldn't get in and they didn't hear me knocking and I knocked as hard as I could but I had to get out of there or else I'd have been burned alive.

"That's how it happened," Mr. O'Shaunessey said. "Right?"

I said, "Right. Right," I said. "That's what happened."

FatDaddy stood there in his shorts, rolls of blubber white and jiggling as he shook his fist at me. The Sanchez brothers, firemen, held him back. "Arson!" FatDaddy yelled. "The little Mick white-trash piece of shit burned my house down. I'm pressing charges. You're out of your league, boys." Fat Daddy laughed, and his laugh was kind of spooky. "Do you know who I *am? Do you?*"

"I believe everyone here knows who you are," said O'Shaunessey. "And yes, perhaps, Mr. Slattern, we are out of our league. Have you ever considered that there could be more than one league? That the league you're now playing in is not *your* league, but *ours?*"

"*Do you know who I am?*"

"I don't claim to know much," O'Shaunessey said. "But I *do* know who you are. Do you know who *I* am? I am the Fire Chief," O'Shaunessey said. "Mower blades set off the blaze. Your yard was a fire hazard. That is my official and legal forensic opinion."

"He hasn't paid me yet," I said. "There's nothing left for me to mow. My job's done. He owes me seventy-five cents."

Everyone looked at him with eyes that said, Pay the boy.

"Fuck you!" Fat Daddy said. "Fuck you!"

Mama FatDaddy joined in. "Yeah, fuck you. Do you know who my husband is? Fuck you all."

It wasn't a very dignified thing for them to say, not for people of their position and social standing.

"Fuck you!" FatDaddy said. "You're all in it together! Micks, WOPS, wetbacks, niggers, chinks, hairdressers, niggers, Portugees, niggers and niggers and goddamn niggers, all of you. Fuck you! You're all a bunch of Mick WOP wetback niggers. All of you. Niggers."

Somehow FatDaddy tripped, and he lay face down in the burnt and now hose-watered lawn. When he stood up, he dripped black char sludge, his face slick. The char smelled good. It made the factory stink go away. Oakland could smell a whole lot of a fucking better if something was always *always* burning, instead of only burning once in a while.

Everyone was still looking at him hard. Pay the boy.

FatDaddy walked into his charred house. He sifted through the smoking cinders and found his pair of pants and lifted them like he was hoisting a burned up tent. Coins dropped into the ashes and black sludge. He threw some change at me. I leaned to get the quarters, and O'Shaunessey said, "No, son. Mr. Slattern will hand you your pay."

FatDaddy just stood there. "Pay the boy," O'Shaunessey said.

FatDaddy looked at O'Shaunessey, and then you could see FatDaddy look around at everyone else. There were probably a hundred of us now, and FatDaddy first tried to look at people's eyes, but pretty soon he was just looking at something on the ground in front of each of us. Without looking up he trudged through the slosh and cinder toward me. He stooped. He picked up the coins and counted out three quarters. He handed them to me.

"Thank you Mr. Slattern," I said.

I didn't want to, but I smiled at him. It was one of those smiles I get when I'm really happy or I'm really guilty or when someone thinks I'm guilty and I'm not or there's something I want to say but I can't get up the balls to say it.

FatDaddy didn't say anything.

Mr. Slattern decided to move away from the neighborhood. He closed his shop, and moved his designer toilet business to another town, a town in *Southern California*, he said, somewhere where people would appreciate his artistic contribution to culture, he said, to shitting, we said. His daughter made her parting rounds, boning everyone who'd cut her a line. People made jokes about her huge nose, about how she could snort more than a horse through that schnoz.

FatDaddy tried every moving company in Oakland, Mayflower, Berkins, the Carlisle Brothers, even Yandell, who didn't do private moves. They were all tire accounts at the shop, and for some reason they were all booked, booked for a long time. He tried Perkins Movers, he tried Schlimsky's, Flores Home Movers, Fernandez Trucking. Everyone was booked solid for the foreseeable future. Finally Mr. Slattern had to call Manero U-Haul. They had a truck, but the problem with U-Haul was that you had to haul it, which meant that FatDaddy would have to load his own truck, load his fire-scorched furniture and custom toilet-seats himself. That FatDaddy didn't want to do, so he called everyone in the neighborhood looking for manpower. We were all busy. Business had really picked up, it being the end of summer and all. It was amazing how much work everyone in the neighborhood had all of a sudden.

He got his truck, and he pulled it up to the heap of black ashes that was once his house. He made his coke-slut frog-eyed zit-faced daughter do most of the work, picking through the ashes for family portraits and toilet seats of note, the especial ones, specially the Elvises, FatDaddy's favorites. When your house burns, there are some things you just don't want to lose, some things you just can't replace.

We watched. We sat on lawns across the street from FatDaddy and his daughter and Mama FatDaddy. We sat on folding chairs with jugs of lemonade and Spanada and more cigarettes than a human being could ever smoke in a lifetime. The women sat with packs of Pall Mall's at their sides, the men with cases of Oly. The Costello brothers brought fireworks, and we had Fourth of July again.

When FatDaddy and his daughter were loading their couch, he looked over at us. Mama FatDaddy sat in the cab of the truck sweating. Pop was standing up and making a speech. He did that sometimes, Pop. He made speeches about the bourgeois and the proletariats, about the chains that shackled the workers and about the revolution that would someday come and torch the fortresses of the oppressors. Pop was always talking some big words shit none of us understood but all of us agreed with. He pulled a plaster bucket from the side of the Couto house and he stood on it, and he said, "The sovereignty of the worker is his birthright. The infrastructure of the rich is mounted on the backs of the poor. We must control the means of production. The factories belong to us! We produced the capital. We built their houses. We unstop their toilets. We," Pop said, and he looked at Fat-Daddy Slattern and his chest swelled with air, "we mow their fucking lawns!"

No one understood a word Pop said, but we all cheered, and the people who had beers downed them and cracked some more.

FatDaddy sweated, and his daughter shook with coke need. She wasn't getting any better looking. She looked better when she was watching television. Her eye wandered less, and her nose didn't get the noontime shadow like a giant sundial.

Manny U-Haul Manero said something to Pop, and Pop smiled kind of small and sly. FatDaddy's truck was finally loaded. Mama FatDaddy looked like she was ready to pass out sitting there in the cab. She hadn't waxed in a few days, and the red beard was replaced with a black shadow. The daughter sat in the passenger seat and she looked at us. Some of the guys who'd fucked her were sad to see her going. The ones who hadn't fucked her wished they had, of course, because everyone wanted to fuck and fuck and fuck, but they didn't wish too much that they'd fucked her since there were other coke whores around who had smaller noses and had lesser snort quotients. Hell, Laureen Moone would fuck anyone for a line, and she was pretty good looking to boot, twelve years old and not only ready to rock but rocking away, and even though everyone said she had some weird kind of smell, not crustacean but instead mollusk, like an abalone, the smell didn't stop anyone from doing the boink with Laureen. The San Leandro Marina was her favorite spot, and Jeff Carlson had a van that all the teenagers and some of their fathers would line up behind waiting their turns. Laureen was really popular, and everyone liked her. They didn't get much better than Laureen, is what people said when they came into the Mohawk station.

Mr. Slattern pulled down the sliding door of the U-Haul and he didn't look at us as he walked alongside the truck to the cab. He had some kind of FatDaddy Slattern radar going that was honed in on that cab, as if he didn't have a hundred people lining the street in lawnchairs smoking and drinking beers and watching every slug move of his sweat blubber body lumbering. He was focused.

I felt kind of sorry for him, actually. He didn't really need to pack up and move. He just needed to admit what he'd done. He just needed to apologize to us instead of calling us niggers and wetbacks and WOPS and gooks and Micks and niggers some more. It was OK for us to call each other those things, because we were all in it together, all of us at the bottom of the cesspool of Oakland and slugging it out *together*. Those nasty names, when we used them, were us calling each other the names we *knew* the *rich* people called us, us calling each other those names in contempt not of each other but of those who would belittle and befuck us. My buddy Jim Johnston, half nigger, can call me a white trash Mick piece of shit, and that's OK, because I'm white trash and he's a nigger, so it kind of evens out. But if you're in a business suit, and you're driving a fancy car, and you call Pop white trash, you're liable to have some get-back visited upon your ass, if not then and there eventually, and with interest on the wait. If FatDaddy Slattern would have just apologized like a man, come into Dick's Restaurant and Cocktail Lounge and bought a round for everyone and a soda for me, maybe a linguisca sandwich, if he'd have come in, bought that round and said, "Gentlemen, ladies, I'm really sorry. That was no way to behave," then he would have had most of us helping him rebuild his house and even buying those fancy toilet seats of his, which actually were pretty cool. Man, he had one that was all baseball cards, laminated to the seat, Willie Mays and Sandy Koufax and even Vida Blue. I wanted that one bad, but even though the fire had boiled the lacquer, he packed it into the U-Haul. A lot of people were sad to see his daughter in the U-Haul and going away forever, and I was sad to see that toilet seat go.

He wasn't a man to apologize, though. Not FatDaddy. It wasn't about to happen. He'd schlepp along the side of his truck like a snail with his head hung as low as his fat chins would let it hang, but he'd never, *never* apologize to a bunch of niggers and Portugees and wetbacks and white trash like me and Pop.

He climbed in, clicked the door shut gently, and started the motor. He put the truck in gear, and when he did, something whined metallic and harsh, and then the engine started a-clacking, and it sounded like not only the transmission went but like the lifters were banging up against the hood. He gunned the engine and then something kind of whistled. A cloud of white smoke came from the exhaust pipe, and then black smoke curled from beneath the wheel wells, and then from under the hood, and finally into the cab and out the windows. FatDaddy and his daughter got out of the truck. His daughter came around to the driver's side and stood next to him. They looked at us. You could hear Mama FatDaddy cough or choke or gag. Nobody said anything. We looked at them. We went home. You could hear lawnchairs folding, beer cans crumpling, ice-chests rattling like pots filled with gravel, bottles dropping into garbage cans and some of them breaking, screen doors snapping gently shut and then their doors squeaking slow and sure after them, locks clicking home. The sun was setting, and the night was without fog or cloud, the hills where the rich people lived to the East glowing orange and the windows like stars burning out of the blackening mounds of ease. I wish I could say we heard the trains and the tugboats that night, that the train whistles lowed soft like moose and wild cattle, like buffalo, that the tugboats hooted calls that reminded us of the days when our grandparents had come to nearly virgin territory and heard those same tugboat horns and heard not labor and corporate drool but instead *opportunity* and *food* and *shelter*, that dogs instead of howling and fighting barked a symphony of primordial satisfaction. I'd really like to say that's what it sounded like, but it wasn't. There was no sound except the sound of us going home and to sleep. The sound of light dying.

I'd seen prettier nights, and have since, but not many. Not many at all.

I showed what I've written to my bartender, Dennis Rich, whose wife just left him here in Warrensburg, Missouri. She took the kid and the house and now he works three jobs instead of one. I slipped him a few bags of Wal-Mart a few weeks ago. I didn't have the cash to do it, so I put it on a credit card. Hell, lots of people have done the same for me.

"Too much cursing," Dennis said.

This far:

456 fucks and variants thereof

34 cunts

73 dicks (many of them the restaurant and cocktail lounge)

32 cocks

274 asses

270 shits

4 quims

6 coozes

9 pussies

29 fags

63 niggers

19 cums

79 bitches

16 whores

and 4 sluts.

I went through and cut some niggers. How many niggers does a man need?

I started this chapter just wanting to tell you about *work*, and so I told you about my first job—shoveling Snookie cookies for Pop at the Mohawk station. Then I decided to tell you some of the early shit-history of my life of labor, and so of course I had to tell you about the first crappy boss I had, my first direct experience as a prole with the evils of capitalism, mowing the lawn of FatDaddy Slattern. I could have just given you a couple of sentences, told you this: "I once spent two months mowing a lawn for seventy-five cents because the guy who hired me tricked me and I was brought up to honor a deal struck." Instead, it took me thirty pages, two bottles of whiskey, three cases of Busch, two cartons of generic cigarettes and a week and a half of time to write about FatDaddy Slattern and the ways of my neighborhood because I realized while I was writing the section that people and their neighborhoods, people and their jobs, are inseparable. You can't tell your own story without telling the story of your people, and so everything a narrator experiences becomes a universal, becomes a symbol whether or not the writer intends to do that kind of crap or not.

And if everything is a symbol, if every person I describe becomes a *type*, a representative of something *large*, then my responsibility becomes and is and remains always heavy.

I don't just have a charge from Pop and the Corollo brothers and the men of Camozzi Carpets and Johnson Western Gunite Company and Concrete Wall Sawing, but to all the men doing like labor living in like neighborhoods and having bosses like FatDaddy Slattern. You've had a boss like FatDaddy Slattern, haven't you? And can't you transfer your disgust for FatDaddy to your disgust for the boss who fucked with you, who might be fucking with you this instant as you hide from your work on the toilet, pretending to be taking a good long shit-break but instead reading this book while you're supposed to be at your desk or on the line? Haven't you at one time or another had your crew, your posse, your family, lay plans against, execute, and feel sad and satisfied at the same time, justice not always a pleasant but most certainly a necessary thing, the cosmos *right* just once? Chapter Two was supposed to very quickly (economically is the word I'm *supposed* to use here) tell my work story—shit-shoveler to lawn-mower to trumpet-player/construction worker and finally land on the time when I had to live in a garbage truck at the dumps, sleeping in the cab nights and running a route days.

Everyone I've ever shown my shit to tells me not to *explain*, not to tell what I want to say. Hide what you really *think* about things, and instead show events in a neutral and nondescript way. *Never* comment, *never* let the reader know that you feel *anything* about anything. Your narrator should be a cold *observer*, a camera that does not comment and that is just as electronic, passive, *unhuman*.

If you really want to say something, let one of your characters say it for you. Otherwise the reader will think it's you saying and thinking those awful naughty offensive things, and if the reader doesn't like what you have to say, the reader might not like you, might not like You the Author, and that could harm your sales.

What a fucking shame—you mean someone *might not agree with me?* So few people will ever read my book anyway that it doesn't really matter much to me if I piss a few off. Hell, I'd like to piss a fucking lot of people off. At least I'd be making the assholes feel *something. People might not like you, The Author.* Shit. My heart is all broken up about this. Honest. The real-life human being Blaise is based on read what I wrote about his crack up, and he wrote this to me: "You run the risk of the reader not liking the narrator." Evidently what I'm supposed to do is write a riskless novel. Well folks, I think we have enough of those already. Hell, Updike's written twenty or thirty of them all by his ownself. Add in the gutless nutless cuntless minimalists—Ann Beattie, Mary Robison, Frederick Barthelme, Jamica Kincaid, and the rest of their spineless inbred crew—toss in a crate or two of books by Ivy League pussies and award-winning jack-off artists writing about their European vacations and their days at the prep school and the times they've been slumming with people from my neighborhood and had an affair with one of us blue collar houseboys or pink collar waitresses and then felt guilty about it, their marriages going to shit because they copulated with someone other than their fat suburban spouses, mix into the soup an antiseptic dose of "classy" work written by private university-schooled smoothie minorities posing as *people of color* when their asses are whiter and their blood bluer and their teeth for damn sure straighter than anyone in *my* neighborhood—add in all that shit and I personally think we have enough perfect fucking fiction.

What we need is some *imperfect* fiction, some fiction that *does not* try to bring order to the chaos of life, but which instead tries to not only represent the chaos with chaos, but to cry *anarchy,* bring *anarchy, foster and nourish and revel* in the insanity that truly is life without a fucking trust fund, without a retirement, without divorce decrees crushing poor sons of bitches who couldn't afford lawyers, instead giving up the lives of the *crushed,* the *destroyed,* the truly hopeless and therefore the most truly alive, attuned, nerves jumping and sparkling like exploding power transformers being pissed upon in black Oakland night. John Steinbeck might not have been the best prose stylist around, but at least he had something to say that mattered. Same with Jack London and Sinclair Lewis. And Theodore Dreiser wrote the crappiest sentences known to man, but *Sister Carrie* says more, hits home more truly and rocks more than any of Pynchon's beautiful and expert and erudite jacking off. Fuck perfextion. Bend over, bitch. Let one of those perfect motherfuckers around me or anyone I know and we'll slap the faggot and take his lunch money.

You want perfect? Read someone else's fucking book. This book, if I'm doing it right, is anything but *purrfect*. I don't want you to finish it and lean back in your expensive *chaise lounge* and sigh, reassured that all the stupid shit you've done in your life really all adds up to a fine and dandy ending, your fat ass retired and happy and laying out on a beach in Hawaii drinking cocktails and watching chicks you'd like to bone hula hula in front of you while you try to hide the hardon you wish were better than a half-limp slug of dried cottage cheese. I don't want you to finish this novel and, if you're the rich fuck I suspect you are (because unfortunately my people can't *read*, and if they can they read something that matters to them like *Sports Illustrated* or *Hustler*), you think that the shit-for-life you've imposed on my people by your very existence is something that is *not your fault* and that everything *works out in the end*, your sins forgiven and your virtues rewarded in the great steakhouse in the sky, extra cheese and sour cream for the potatoes please, belch *apres*. Quite the opposite good sir, ma'am. I want you to finish my book and be a little apprehensive, just a little, a bit concerned ol' boy, good lady, that maybe, just maybe, maybe we're gunning for you. Maybe we're just waiting for our chance to take you the fuck out.

What do we think about when we think about the terminal diseases we've contracted working in your shops and factories, on your construction sites? What do you think we think about in the Busch-drunk late hours when we're paying you for our parking spots at your run-down factories with outhouses instead of toilets? What you think we're thinking about when we're signing our child-support checks to your daughters who married us because they wanted *men* but divorced us because they decided they wanted pussies like you? What we thinking about when we mow your lawns, unplug your toilets, drive past your houses with garages bigger than our apartments and trailers, when we see your daughters with braces while our daughters' teeth are rotting out of their heads and turning them into sixteen year old hags? What you imagine we're thinking when we listen to the news and hear that your hillside houses have mudslid down and you've lost your priceless furniture in the roll? You think we're feeling sorry for you? You think we're hoping that you and yours are all healthy and swell?

Don't forget, Mr. and Mrs. Comfy: I'm writing this in my garage, detached, single-car, in Warrensburg buttfuck Missouri. I started writing this in the winter, wrapped in blankets and my fingers blue, dick shriveled and never coming back and snow on the oil-stained concrete floor not melting because even though I have a space heater it doesn't do much because the holes in the walls and between the gray weather-worn wood slats whistle with subzero wind. Sometimes when the snow blows sideways flakes actually swirl in the night light like dust. I have a refrigerator, but it doesn't even have racks in it, so I have to stack my food on top of my 40s and my twelvers of Nat Light. I ended up here because I was a good man and hadn't learned the lesson I should have learned from my experience with FatDaddy Slattern. I live here because of the likes of *you*. Guess what? I don't *like* you.

I started writing this in the winter and now it's summer, and in those six months I've decided to drink instead of eat because it's either one or the other on what's left of my shit for check after I pay my ex. The booze I drink gets cheaper and cheaper. I fear the Night Train, and if you don't know what Night Train and Thunderbird are, I'm really fucking happy for you. Really. For me it's summer and I'm sweating on the keyboard. My computer is infested with roaches and spiders, and I sleep with the light on because if I don't I wake up swollen and itching and fearing death by insect. The other losers in town all know my story, and they sympathize but they won't front me a drink anymore. The women here spot me for what I am: broken, and when not broken, pissed. Get laid? Sure. Only the worst of losers would have me as I am now. My job sucks so bad I can't even talk about it, and even if I told you, you wouldn't believe it, so fuck you. Suffice it this: you've never had a job so bad, and driving and living in a dump truck was candy-times in comparison. Because of the things I've done, I live here under a name I can't tell you. And I have the kind of job that goes with that kind of territory.

What I wouldn't give to be able to have been born 200 years ago, born in a time when the property wasn't all *owned*, a time when I could just start walking in any direction and when I found a place suitable plant my ass and call the earth *home*, no taxes, no social security number, no identity, no history. There's not a cubic centimeter in the land I can go to and just sit there, just recline and watch the clouds whorl past without *paying for the privilege* of being, without worrying about either getting shot or jailed.

So I'm writing this book and by the time you finish this you'll still not have known how I ended up here, because I can't tell you. Sorry. At any rate, what I really want to write about, and what's really the important thing about this chapter, is work. After the FatDaddy experience work became a thing different for me than it should have been. I didn't want to ever work at something that wasn't something I wanted in my bones to do, and that's not what work is about. Work is called work because it's not play, like *playing* a trumpet. Work is called work because it sucks.

Not getting paid for work wasn't a problem for me. Hell, most of life is work—doing the dishes, stitching up work boots with dental floss, cooking pasta when you'd rather be ordering a pizza but can't afford it. Not getting paid to work wasn't a problem, but not getting paid for working at something I didn't *like doing* was. I decided at age ten that I'd never again work at something I didn't like doing truly. I don't do *dishes*, for instance. I have one Chinese plastic plate that I rinse off. I don't do laundry—it's cheaper to wear the fuck out of a tee shirt and then buy another at the Salvation Army than it is to do a load at the laundromat. If I was going to be prole white trash working grunt, I'd find something I liked doing, something I could talk about after work with the men at Dick's and not only not feel ashamed, but feel proud, not for the dignity of the work or the rate of the pay, but because the work I was doing was something I *loved*, something that *defined* me, something *I was*.

Because of the FatDaddy experience, I worked hard at the trumpet when I was a kid. I practiced eight, ten, twelve hours a day, played until my lip bled and my fingers cramped. Some of the kids from the neighborhood had made it out by playing horn, guys like Jon Faddis, like Carlo Carrera. I got a room at the Lemmington Hotel before they remodeled it and made it a place for pasty-faced San Francisco trustfunders. Before the remodel it was a dank downtown dump hotel, and I lived with the tramps and the whores and the destitute, with those who chose simply not to participate, not to engage. I played skanky gigs on my trumpet in my old Mexican band, Los Asesinos, and every night I got some applause and some booze and some jack to shoot on rent and gas. I was flush, and life was good.

Before my last gig as a decent trumpeter, before I had to become a scab and drive a non-union garbage scow, my girlie friend, Agnes, with whom I'd never been in the sack because she was saving herself for marriage—she was in the process of re-virginizing herself out of guilt because she'd humped about ten thousand black dudes and the entire Castlemont High football team—and who I loved because I hoped someday she would not only fuck me but make me some babies, said, "You got to get a real job. What kind of fool are you? It's freezing in here. Why? Because you live in a dump. A dump without heat." She had one of those black accents white girls sometimes get when they like fucking black dudes. "You think there's a future being a white boy playing in a Mexican band?"

I'd like to tell you I'm not sure why I was even with her in the first place, but I'd be lying. Back *then* I thought I loved her. Back then I thought she was the love of my fucking life, and I walked around with a hardon all day every day just thinking about her. Now, though, and a lot of time has passed, I know why I was with that bitch. I needed to have a woman around, someone to make me feel like I was a *man*, a man who was desirable and who would one day make me some family. That's the way I used to be. I've been with some serious bitches over the years, and for some reason I still can't figure most of them have been even more fucked up than me—junkies, vegetarians, feminists with all the stuffings—hairy legs and armpits, bumperstickers, ugly clothes, pierced eyebrows and nipples, no makeup—booze soaked sad-eyed slump-shouldered wrecks, chicks who were man-beaters, shopping addicts, self-helpers, hookers, most of them at some point boned by their daddies and uncles and priests. I tried hard and tried but somehow I never landed the kind of woman I actually wanted, a good one like a nympho or a stripper, or, better, both.

I finished greasing the third-valve slide of my trumpet with key-oil and began on the valve pistons, unscrewing them, wiping them down with an old teeshirt, oiling them and testing the slick with flurries of my fingers.

"Just look at this dump," Agnes said. "That's what I said, dump. This hotel is a dump. No bathroom, no heat, no electrical outlets, a lightbulb hanging from a wire from the ceiling. Dump dump shithole dump. Don't you get tired of putting the dresser against the door at night? Don't you have any respect for *me*?"

I nodded.

"Why don't you ever let me come with you to your gigs? You never let me come with you. It's the bitches."

"I'm going to write a symphony," I said. "An orchestral work using African percussion and Eastern winds and Oriental chord structures, a New World symphony to put Dvorak to shame. Music has become too polar, either savagely simple or refined into meaninglessness, and if I can just combine the two poles, I'll be able to create something beautiful."

"I don't know what the hell you chattering about," Agnes said. That's the way she talked, "*you* chattering about," putting on a fake ghetto-nigger accent. Her mother was a goddamn English professor at the community college. She could have talked white, or at least redneck like her father, if she'd wanted to. Another bitch rebelling against her parents, and Agnes had rebelled by going as low as she could go, all the way down to *me*.

"You sure talk the talk. I'm going with you tonight," Agnes said. "Where you going tonight?"

"A quinceanera."

"What?"

"A formal party for a Mexican girl when she turns fifteen," I said. "The girl becomes a woman. Cauldrons of food, dancing, booze, music, goat's head soup."

"You the big time. Big time almighty, playing a birthday party."

I wiped the excess oil from my trumpet and buffed the bell with a tee-shirt I used as a chamois and set the trumpet into the crushed purple velvet of the case.

"I'd rather be playing birthday parties than sitting behind a desk all day or driving a garbage truck."

"If *we* ever going to get married," Agnes said, "you needs to gets a real job."

"The other night," I said, "you were asleep I snuck out and took my trumpet with me and I drove out to the country. I drove out to the coast and took my trumpet with me and I drove with the lights off for awhile. When I flipped them on there was a white horse ahead on the road."

"You was juicing again. That's what you was doing, sitting around getting all liquored-up while I be sleeping. You always wait for me to go sleep before you do shit. I go to sleep, and then you just *do* shit, and shit."

"And I pulled over and took out my trumpet and I played. Horses grazed on the hill. I played and the horses kept grazing and even though they didn't act like they could hear me I knew they *could* hear me. They grazed and I played and it was serene and magical and beautiful."

"You didn't even tell me where you was. I was sleeping and you was out having a good time."

I don't know why, but I wanted to make her fell really rotten, like she'd missed out on something, so I started making shit up. I said, "Then a marvellous thing happened. I put down my horn, set it in the grass, and the horses started circling around me, walking, slow at first, about a dozen horses ringed around me and walking in a circle. Just like that. Then they walked faster and they walked faster and soon they were trotting and then running and then they were a blaze, a gray and white and black and pinto wash of streaks and spots, their manes feathered back in wind. And I ran. I *ran* with them, Agnes, and I caught ahold of one by the neck, an old gray horse with a sagging back, and I swung up onto his back and I rode him, the two of us together running in a circle with the other horses. And in the middle of the circle there was my trumpet, silver and black with sky and pin-dotted with stars, reflecting." It was a really cool lie. I smiled.

"Spare me the tears," Agnes said.

"And then I came back here," I said. "To you."

"I'm coming to your gig tonight."

"You shouldn't."

"Leaving me in the middle of the night. A fifteen year-old and all her young pretty whore friends?"

I nodded. "And all of them want to fuck me."

"I'm coming."

Agnes lifted her skirt. Her panties were old and white and baggy and the elastic bands around her legs were frayed. I approached. She dropped her skirt back down and pressed it against her thighs with her hands.

"Fat chance," she said. "That's all you want me for is sex."

It was one of her favorite tricks, pretending that she was going to give it up and let me finally fuck her at last and then shutting me down cold. I'd come home and she'd have let herself in and she'd be sprawled out on the ratty couch wearing stockings and garters and lacy panties and a black bra, looking like the whore I wanted her to be for me. And I'd climb on top of her and shove my cock against her through my pants, grinding. She'd let me finger her and mash her clit and roll it around between my fingers, but when I'd start unzipping, she'd clap those legs together and tell me no. One time I'd had it and I took my pants off anyway and started trying to work it in. "You fucker," she said. "You fucker! Get that *penis* away from me," and the way she said it, *penis*, was as if my cock was some kind of disease, some kind of plague, an old truck tire in the yard gathering water and scum and crawdads and dead mice maggot-eaten and foamed. "I'll scream," she screamed. "I'll call the cops. You're trying to rape me, you fucker!" The dick shriveled up right quick. I was pretty screwed up about the whole fucking business already, since I'd never yet been laid. I was screwed up, but Agnes was even worse. She was "re-virginizing" herself, she told me, and I had the blueball coconuts to prove she was doing a good job. Agnes felt guilty about her ten thousand fucks and the Castlemont High football team, and the way she figured it, if she went long enough without a dick reaming her cooze, she'd grow her cherry back. She was pulling out all the stops, too, re-virginizing. Not only had she decided to tie-wire her quim shut, but one night she used me as her Father Confessor, seeking absolution through detailing everything she'd ever done with every man she'd ever fucked, telling me *everything*. It took two solid days, no sleep, to get through her epic catalog. When the confession was finally over, she felt a whole lot fucking better about herself. She was happier than I'd ever seen her. She was fucking beaming.

I pretty much felt like shit, though. It was like some kind of torture listening to her go through the list, telling me about the blowjobs, the places she'd fucked them—in parks, on beaches, in a treehouse, on a pool table with the bartender watching, in a ditch alongside I-80, the backseats and front seats of every make of car in the world except Ferrari and those foreign cars that aren't Japanese or VWs, even once in the men's room of our Mohawk station while I was working the pumps—how many times she'd fucked them in a day, the sizes of their dicks, how many gallons of cum she'd swallowed, how many gallons leaked out of her cunt and down her leg, the texture of the cum, the taste of the cum, the color of the cum, the sound of the cumblast, the smell of the cum, how it dripped off her tits and how she wiped it with her hand and put her fingers in her mouth and sucked, how she liked it in the ass and how many times she'd fucked five guys at a time, how five was her *very favorite!* number of guys to fuck at a time because no matter what there were always three of them hard, one for each major hole.

About twenty guys in and I cracked the whiskey and started drinking. Fifty guys along I ran out of ice and chugged from the bottle. Somewhere around a hundred and twenty I felt water well in my eyes and I was through two 1.75ers of booze, the gin bottle now empty and my tequila next on the list. Midway through the second day of confession I broke down and started sobbing, and it seemed to egg her on more, and she went back through a bunch she'd already told me about and filled in some details she'd missed. She told me it was necessary for her to confess *all* so that she could be entirely pure for *me*, so she could be my *virgin*. By the time Agnes the Virgin finished my head was swirling and I couldn't look at her without imagining all those dicks and Agnes working them over. I'd cranked four bottles of booze, and I was nowhere drunk enough. I couldn't see and had a hard time standing, but I was sober as a Mormon.

Agnes said, "Take me to your gig and show me you love me."

The quincenera was being held at the Community Center, a dumpy sad place that held bingo night Wednesdays and checkers Saturday nights, oldsters in their wheelchairs propped on walkers shooting their social security checks because what the hell, what else were they going to do with all that money and all those years of time? Me and Agnes were the only white people, and only the members of the band would talk to us, would look at us when we spoke, and me and Agnes sat alone at the band table during breaks, me drinking plastic cupfuls of keg beer and Agnes chugging gallons of Courvoisier she'd brought along because no matter what the Mexicans could have served it wouldn't have been good enough for her.

On the buffet table was a bubbling cauldron of goat's head soup, the eyeballs boiled away and yellow foam gurgling from the sockets, hairmat horns unraveling, whole onions floating like blossomed flowers in the broth.

During breaks cumbias and rancheras played over the P.A. system, and the old white-hairs taught the little girls the dance steps, the girls standing on the old men's shoes and the old men whirling.

"The Mexicans got it right," I said.

"What?" said Agnes.

"The Mexicans," I said. I turned my head back to the dancers.

"What," Agnes said. "What you talking about."

I told Agnes that even though she'd rather be a nigger, most of the time if I had my druthers I'd of wished I was a Mexican, someone from a wonderful and ancient culture, someone who knew who his goddamn parents were and who his grandparents were and who knew his cousins by name. American white people can rarely trace their family tree back past their grandparents, and if for some reason they can, they probably got it wrong, because only the women know for sure who the fathers are, and the bitches they don't tell. We don't have dances like the Mexicans do, not even us Micks. Sure, there's always some traditional Irish dance troupe that knows how to do a jig the right way instead of the drunken pogo-stick bounce we do at Dick's when a Raider breaks someone's leg or neck, but it's not like the Mexicans who all and every one of them knows how to dance a salsa or a cumbia. Our traditional music is plastic mass-produced sentimental relic of the times when our people had some nads, something quaint we whip out for parades to try to prove to the rest of the whites that we have something resembling a history or a culture. But in America that shit gets bled out of us pretty quick. We're too busy being mean and shitty not only to everyone else but to each other. The Mexicans, though, their traditional music is *still* the stuff they dance to, *still* the stuff they listen to. Drive through the farmlands and listen to your goddamn radio. Their music isn't something they drag out of an archive or museum once a year, it's alive now and part of who they are. Then watch white people dance: it's ridiculous and it's ugly, just a bunch of history-less dorks, no tether no anchor no ballast no honor, shaking their fat bellies and wagging their asses and flopping their titties around, about as graceful as a herd of water buffaloes. Go to a Mexican nightclub and sit back and watch a culture celebrate itself, celebrate *life* and procreation and black-tie death and the births of blood.

We took the stage, a rectangular plywood platform gussied up with linoleum tile about six inches off the tiled floor. Nacho counted us off, and we played. I'm not going to launch into a musical reverie about how well we played, how we soared with the music gods and how all the people in the crowd didn't even dance, so entranced, so mesmerized were they with the miraculous beauty of the music we played for them. I could tell you all kinds of shit like that and go on for three or four pages, getting lyrical on your ass and showing off how well I write about music, since before I started writing books I was a musician, and a pretty good one, too, sometimes, and because I was a musician and even though I couldn't *play* with the union big-bands or the nightclub Negroes, nonetheless I *knew* what music was about and as a result of the combination of my experience with music and my devotion to being able to write about my people and my neighborhood I've somehow hit on a few formulas and patterns I use when I write about music, certain sound patterns and ways of matching the rhythm of words with the cadence of musical sound. I actually *think* about the pitch of the word as you hear it in your head when you're read-ing, and if you go back through what you've read, or if you read my other book and consciously listen to the tones of the words, you'll recognize passages from Mozart's *Requiem*, from Miles Davis' *Kind of Blue*, from "Suzie Q" by Creedence. This time I'll spare you the musical rapture and cut straight to what happened.

What happened is this. We were playing some hokey ranchera and I looked out at the crowd and they were dancing but there were Mexi-cans in the crowd who weren't dancing who were instead knifing people. Blades flashed everywhere I looked. Mexicans don't shoot people, but every one I knew carried a stiletto or a switch or a barber's straight. And they're quick whipping those blades, too. You don't want to piss a Mexican off in a lonely place where there aren't other people, because he'll dice you up before you can blink. Steel flashed and I looked over and Agnes was dead and the crowd was pushing toward us on stage, such that it was. If it'd been a real job with a real stage, elevated, I wouldn't have gotten my front teeth knocked out. I'd have just stood above them and watched the spectacle, because there's nothing like a serious blade fight for special effects. Instead I had my trumpet up to my lips since we hadn't yet stopped playing and some Mexican fell back and against me and jammed my mouthpiece down my throat, knocking my front teeth out en route. You know how hard it is to play trumpet without any fucking teeth? Try it sometime.

When I got back to the Lemmington I scooted on over to Duke's apartment and knocked on his door.

"You look like shit," he said. "Let me get you a cocktail."

Duke was forty years older than me, but he was my best friend in the world, and he was everyone else in the neighborhood's best friend too. I don't usually describe the way people actually *look*, and Duke didn't look all that different from the rest of the old dudes—short, beer belly, balding and the hair he had gray, tee-shirts he should have thrown away a century ago but that he still wore and that rose up across his gut and showed flesh, pants that hung low on his ass and showed the crack when he sat or bent over, but Duke had eyes that weren't like ours. His eyes should have drooped and gone dull long ago, but instead they blazed with not flame nor fire but voltage, electricity. His eyes were that pale blue that gives you the creeps on anyone else, but that on Duke bred trust. You knew that Duke would do anything for any good man, dog, woman or child. When one of us ended up tanked and in jail on a DWI it was Duke we called and he'd be there no matter what time after closing to bail us out.

One New Year's Eve I was with my buddy Ben (I can't tell you the rest of his name because now he's respectable and a lawyer with loads of kids and a house worth a couple million, L.A.) and he was frying and so he made me drive his Chevy Vega, stick. I'd never before driven a stick and I was about two bottles into the evening, but at least I wasn't frying on acid. So I tried to drive us home. It was more than usual foggy and I rolled down an overpass and cut right at the corner but the car didn't cut and instead skated across the asphalt in slow motion like cars always do when you're wrecking them while drunk and the car plowed into a house, plunk, not a slam but a gentle ride over the curb and across the lawn and into the house, the nose of the car inserted. We tried awhile to back out of the house, shifting from first gear to reverse and back and forth like that, but the car wouldn't budge and the rear tire just dug a rut in the lawn, and it used to be a nice fucking lawn that lawn. Ben even pushed his weight down on the back of the car to help it get some traction, put his shirt under the wheel too, but nothing we tried could get that Vega unlodged from the house. Funny thing—there were people home, we found out later, and the dude who lived there was a Catholic priest, but his lights never came on, and I'd plowed into his bedroom to boot. I don't know what set Ben off, but the next time I looked in the rearview I didn't see him, and I got out of the car and looked around and then I spotted Ben and he was running down the street calling out the names of presidents—Garfield, Coolidge, Hoover, Taft, some fuckers I never heard of—his arms at his sides and flapping as if he was trying to lift off like a pelican. I decided fuckit, and I ran home like a criminal. If Ben wasn't going to stay with me, I wasn't going to take the full rap for what I'd done. I was a sniveling shit.

I called old Duke, seventy years old and could outdrink any of us, called Duke and told him I needed help. It was about three in the morning, and Duke said he'd be right over. He showed up at the Mohawk with a pickup truck, a big one I'd never before seen and therefore probably *borrowed*, primer gray and with a winch on the front grille. We cruised slow to the scene of my crime and the cops were already there with a tow truck and so we just slid on past like rubberneckers. We went to Duke's apartment and called Ben's place but his mother answered and we hung up. I crashed on Duke's couch, and then at about five Duke got Ben's collect call. Duke bailed him out. What Ben'd done? Evidently Ben got spotted by some cops while he was running and calling out the names of presidents and the cops gave chase. They coon-treed Ben up a telephone pole and hauled his ass in.

Duke was the man who in a pinch could be counted on more than any of the rest of us losers and schmucks and brooding whelp bankrupt reamed out assholes. Funny thing was Duke had more to be sad about than any of the rest of us, and he *was* probably sadder than the rest of us, but he somehow dealt with it better. The test of a man is not how successful he is, but how well he deals with being fucked. I once asked Duke, when I was feeling pretty low, why he didn't just kill himself. Duke laughed hearty and big. I looked at him with question. "Why," he said, as if responding to the simplest question in the world, "I want to know what happens next," he said.

He had good Scotch, Glenfiddich, and after a few he made me open my mouth and show teeth.

"Still bleeding," he said. "You'd've thought the Scotch would've done the trick. That's some fine Scotch, too, not that rotgut Clan MacGregor you swill. You should, by the way, have some self-respect, young T-Bird Murphy."

"My trumpet's fucked up," I said. I opened the case and showed him. The bell was wrinkled like tinfoil and bent over to the side, obscene.

Duke rummaged around in his powder closet. His apartment was lined with books—history and philosophy, mostly, war books and folders stuffed with topographical maps, and his apartment was legally classified as an arsenal. He had every kind of gun you can imagine, shotguns and pistols and rifles and autos, Mac-10s and Uzis and AK-47s, a beautiful Streetsweeper with a 24 shotgun-shell drum. Man, you could take out any mob around with that puppy. You could chop down a forest. Guns were his hobby, but his vocation, his calling, was powder. Duke loved gunpowders, and he mixed his own breeds, then used his powder in the bullets and shotgun shells he loaded himself, even pouring his own lead into molds and letting it cool and filing down the bullets so they'd travel right and mushroom properly when they popped their targets. His kitchen table was a factory, loading machines and crimps and vials and tubes and lead and spent brass awaiting new cargo. Everywhere books and on the wall a chart detailing every powder mixture and its explosive qualities, what velocity the bullet would carry, how well the bullet worked in this gun and that gun, extensive and detailed analyses of a bullet's accuracy at 25 yards in pistol x, 50 yards in pistol y, the size of the hole at point blank in pistol z.

While Duke was rummaging through his closet he told me the story of Jimmy Mulefoot. "I knew a man down in Falfurrias, Texas," Duke said. "When I was working night tower. Jimmy Mulefoot, part Indian and the best derrick man south of Amarillo, where his brother Lincoln Mulefoot worked. Old Jimmy Mulefoot one night decides it's high time for him to do some drinking since he's been sober for exactly one year or so and he brings himself a bottle of the blessed sustenance to work and he stands up there hooting and hollering and pacing back and forth on the mon-key-board. Mind, he's three joints up where he can latch and unlatch the elevators—ninety feet above the platform—and this is back in the old days when we just did things as they needed doing. Work had replaced war and a man did not consult his attorney before he performed his job any more than the soldier sues for having been shot by the adversary. Back in the days when a worker accepted the responsibilities and hazards of labor. The rig needed moving and we pulled the pipe out of the hole and old Jimmy Mulefoot he wouldn't come down, wanted to stay up there for the ride. So we started rolling the rig along on some logs, old telephone poles actually."

Duke looked over at me with scrutiny, and I drank some more, and then Duke went back to digging through the closet.

"The rig tipped over," Duke said, "and old Jimmy Mulefoot rode that monkey-board all the way down. Broke every bone in his body but he lived two hours. He didn't say a thing, just lay there and bled. Night-tower shift ended and the morning-tower crew started pulling up in their trucks and you could see black clouds of bugs getting thick against the orange belt of sunrise. It's so flat in that country you can see the curve of the earth. Then Jimmy Mulefoot looked at the sky and watched it all go away."

Duke found what he was looking for and closed the closet door.

"That's what I'm talking about," Duke said.

He opened another bottle and set three leather pouches on the table.

"You have three choices," Duke said. "IMR 700-X, Red Dot, and Solo 1000."

I didn't say anything.

"Red Dot ought to do the job," Duke said. "Fast burning, quick flash."

He opened one of the pouches and pinched some gunpowder between his thumb and forefinger.

Duke said, "The bark's worse than the bite."

He packed gunpowder into the bleeding holes in my gums and he pulled a Zippo from his pocket and lit a Lucky. Duke smoked and he took deep drags. He flicked the ashes and examined the hot red cherry, then jabbed the hot end of the cigarette into my gunpowder-packed gums and the powder flashed white and sizzled. He splashed Glenfiddich in my mouth and you could hear it hiss on the smolder.

"Smells bad," Duke said. "But you'll be fine."

Duke examined my mouth. "The proof of the pudding," Duke said, "is in the shooting."

I nodded. I think I passed out.

When I next saw Duke, my trumpet was fixed. I'm not exactly sure what happened *while* he was fixing it, so excited he was to show me his handiwork, to show me my trumpet that was now better than it had been since Pop played it in the Oakland Symphony, but the way I've come to think of the scene is like this.

Duke wore his trenchcoat and his fedora and beneath his arm he carried my trumpet wrapped in a threadbare wool blanket. He crossed the tracks and started toward Skyline Boulevard, shops and BART stations and pubs and markets closed for the evening. He expected to hear his footsteps echo in the empty streets but he heard nothing but his own breath chugging into the thick darkness. When he passed through Oakland's Chinatown the smell of rotted flesh creamed through the air like a rancid soup, and the dry smoke of char-blacked red snapper expanded in his lungs like the acrid pallor of carrion and Duke gagged and hurried alongside open-air markets clouded with flies and oozing with blood. Duke walked beneath canvas canopies shimmering with fluorescent neon kanji and turned left uphill and stopped in front of a market-front picture-window and hanging in neat ranks and files were plucked ducks, slick with gelled fat, hanging by their feet.

Duke lifted a hand from his trenchcoat pocket and aimed his index finger at one of the ducks, his thumb pulled back in hammer-ready position.

"Bang," Duke said.

Duke walked and when he rose above the Oakland flats and stopped in front of a small stucco house and he turned and looked back, out toward the bay. He was above the fog line now, and Oakland's streets were gone. The tops of the few office towers rose into the night like block-shaped turrets, the Tribune tower ugly and lit. In the distance the spans and girders of the Golden Gate and Bay Bridge cut through the bed of fog like the masts and riggings of immense ships of death. Beneath the fog smothering the expanse of the industrial East Bay, Oakland and Richmond and El Cerrito, the fires of factories billowed red and orange as if the workers had set the oil-sate earth ablaze.

Duke swung open the garage doors and flipped the light switch. He smiled at the clutter which was his clutter and the work of fifty years of accumulation, a testimony to the love he still suspected his wife of harboring for him, hidden beneath her high-collared dresses and expressionless slackjawed Buddha-face. His catfishing skiff, the Garrard stereo system and a stack of old record-albums, John Lee Hooker and Sinatra and Benny Goodman and Tony Bennett and Ray Charles and Louis Armstrong, the covers black and brown with mold, his drill-press and table-saw, cases of oil and jugs of anti-freeze and his tool bench and work clothes hanging from overhead water-pipes, the clock-radio still set to the news station, caulking guns on the concrete floor where he left them twenty years before.

"She loves me," Duke said. "The bitch!"

He rummaged through his Snap-On tool box and found his soldering iron and silver-solder and he plugged-in the iron and stood waiting for heat.

He unwrapped my trumpet and laid it out on his workbench and examined. Dented bell, sprung pipes, crimped tubing, valves jammed. He put the horn to his lips and tried to blow but no air went through and his cheeks swelled until they hurt. He watched the soldering iron until he saw it steam in the cold air and then began work, re-attaching the sprung tubing with delicate traces of silver, drawing the solder along as if tracing a portrait on rice paper, wiping excess solder and flux on a wet green sponge.

Duke opened the wooden cabinet beneath the tool bench and pulled out a small acetylene torch and a tin box of metal-working tools and opened the box and set on the bench an array of rods and hammers and clamps and taps and dies, mallets and files and fine-grain black sandpaper.

The door into the house opened. Myrtle stood in her nightclothes, her hands clasped together as if in prayer.

"What are you doing, Mr. Hammerback?"

"You look great," Duke said. "The sexiest old broad north of the Mason-Dixon."

"We agreed that you wouldn't drop by uninvited until you'd quit drinking and been through Jungian therapy."

"I quit drinking every night, baby."

"What are you doing here, Mr. Hammerback?"

"First aid," Duke said. "Fixing a trumpet, Mrs. Hammerback."

"At four in the morning?"

"Emergency rooms don't close just cause the sun goes down."

Myrtle's face was young and simple and her eyes wide and alert like a genius or a simpleton.

"Odd hours," she said, "are a signal of discontinuity of the spirit. You are still not at peace with your inner self."

Duke looked at his hands.

"Fixing a trumpet is a symbol of your white male need for control over exterior events," Myrtle said. "You invented God in your own image, and then you killed him off, and you think you can take his place."

Duke went through the record-albums and found his favorite John Lee Hooker album and put on "Tupelo," a dirty blues tune that reminded him of Falfurrias, Texas. He looked at Myrtle. She was as beautiful as she had been fifty years before. A horn honked on the street outside. Rain sprinkled in soft waves and the air had the fresh dusty smell of childhood. Duke smiled big and opened his arms toward Myrtle.

"Let's dance," Duke said. "Baby."

"We're old," Myrtle said. "We ought not delude ourselves into idealizing a frothy youth we never had."

Duke approached her and took her in his arms and began dancing her around the perimeter of his catfishing skiff. Myrtle hung stiff in his arms.

"I'm a happy man," Duke said. "Your knight in shining fucking armor."

The song played and it was Johnny Lee Hooker alone with his guitar and scratchy recording-tape and the sounds of the bar, ice rattling in glass tumblers, people tapping their bootsoles on pier-and-beam wooden floor.

"You hear that, Myrtle? You hear that? Do you?"

Myrtle didn't say anything.

Duke laughed.

"That's the sound of the city," Duke said. A horn honked on the recording. "That horn! *Not* edited out, *no* artist sheepshit fru-fru doing another take of the song—No! The sound of the city, the rumble of the subways under our feet, the smell of vomit and urine on the sidewalks, the undeodorized pits of a million arms, the wind cutting into our flesh, the same wind that cuts through buildings and offshore rigs and volcanoes across the Pacific! Johnny Lee Hooker didn't edit out that honking horn, that street noise, that blast from the city. He didn't edit out that horn! Don't you see?"

Duke looked at Myrtle's eyes. "Don't you see?"

Myrtle shook her head no, she did not fucking see. Did not fucking see at all.

"Editing out that horn would be changing what's natural, changing what's true," Duke said. "It'd be like asking me to not be Duke."

Duke gave Myrtle a spin.

"Whee-haw!" Duke laughed. "Whee-haw!"

He danced her back to the door.

"We can't do this," Myrtle said. "Not until you've stopped drinking."

"Honk!" Duke said. "Honk honk. Honk!"

Myrtle cut Duke a look.

Duke dropped his arms to his sides. He stood limp. He felt his cheeks fall alongside his jawbones.

"We're seventy years old," Duke said. "We'll be worm's meat soon."

"Our souls live forever," Myrtle said.

"Not mine."

"Take Jesus into your heart," Myrtle said, "and ye shall be saved."

"Jesus can suck my dick," Duke said. "I'd like to stick my Remington up the ass of Jesus and see just how immortal that ass of his is."

"I can't talk to you," Myrtle said.

"For a social worker," Duke said. "For a social worker you don't do very well by your kin."

"I've heard this before."

"Yep," Duke said. "You've heard it before."

"Yes," Myrtle said. "I have."

"I love you," Duke said.

"Yes," Myrtle said. "I believe you think you do."

Myrtle shook her head. "Duke," she said, "what is it you're looking for in life?"

Duke laughed.

"What," Myrtle said. "What's so funny? What's so funny about my question. I'm serious, Duke. I've found what I want in life. I've been saved by Jesus. What are *you* looking for in life?"

Duke was still laughing. Then he stopped laughing. He got serious and sober. He looked at her, straight.

Duke lit his Zippo and twisted the valves of the acetylene torch and dashed the flame of his lighter across the torch-nozzle and fire burst blue into the air. The hiss of flaming gas filled his ears like air in a seashell.

"Duke Hammerback," Myrtle said. "I asked you a serious question. This is the kind of question I, as your wife, deserve an answer to. What are you looking for in life?"

Duke said, "I'm in search of the perfect bullet."

Duke'd cauterized my gums and he'd mostly fixed my trumpet, but without teeth I wasn't going to be much of a trumpet player anymore, which was just as well. I was never going to be anything more than a schmuck playing bars, and I'd seen some old schmucks at bars and they were so pathetic you either wanted to smack them or bury your face in your hands and cry like a bitch. Being an old musician is one thing. Being a lousy old musician is another.

I did tons of jobs after that. Went back to gunite for a while and worked on the California Aqueduct and the Delta Mendota Canal out in the Central Valley, got to work a long ditch job at McClellan's Air Force Base, too, and didn't have to pay for a campground because I had family in Sacramento and I stayed with them. But I saw a couple more guys die, and I'd already seen too many men die doing gunite, and so I decided adios, compadres. Gunite is a good job, but too many people die doing it. Riprapped, worked as a hod-carrier, soldered electronic components for a hippie who made negative ion generators in his spare bedroom, lumped at the docks. I worked as a janitor, worked the line at Anchor Hocking, canned veggies at the Huntz plant, served some time at Golden Grain. I worked security at an amusement park, protecting kids from perverts and cuffing the little shits when they stole something. Did freelance work rehabbing old houses for seedy landlords who didn't really want the houses fixed right, just wanted them to look nifty for suckers. I didn't get fired often, but I never really liked any of those gigs. I lost my hotel room because I couldn't seem to make rent regularly, which was fine because I just pitched my tent at the campgrounds in the area, Redwood Park, Lake Chabot, sometimes even Half Moon Bay on the coast. There are lots of worse places to live than in a Northern California campground.

Then I finally got a good job, and when I landed it, I knew things were going to start going my way.

At least the smell died down at night.

Seagulls clacked along fat and happy, and rats played in puddles. Across the bay San Francisco glittered beneath a smear of fog and the water rolled slow like tar, garbage and dead fowl adrift and caught in sludged foam you could tell was green even though at night it looked black. Thousands of hot methane gasjets hissed sulphurous and steady, millions of tons of refrigerators and diapers and water heaters, mattresses, boxsprings, deodorant cans and twisted swing sets and empty bottles of malt liquor compressing into fuel enough to power Oakland for the rest of time, and from the garbage dump mountains the shit-fume exhaled up into the world again, spouting up like geysers through dime-sized earth-assholes. Cold nights the methane geysers steamed, and at each plume a seagull stood straddled, walking a tight circle, wings outstretched like vultures over roadkill and the steam hissing at their wings and curling around their shoulders and necks and faces and their beaks stretched to the black and gray sky as if sighing permanent sighs.

I didn't like living there any more than the next guy, but since Pop was getting married, I didn't have any other choice. I wasn't the only one who lived there, either. I had plenty of company. Campfires flickered against hills of garbage, tinfoil and broken glass spangling like orange stars. Shadows paced. Once I heard the sound of people screwing slow and miserable. I was only at the dump temporary. I was only going to live there until I had enough money for a deposit and first and last months' rent. Then I'd have a place to park my garbage truck legal.

I'd run out of money for campground living, and I didn't have a check forthcoming, and so I'd sleep in my car, which would have been fine with me. Problem was I kept getting hassled. If I slept in a fancy neighborhood where people lived in houses, dogs barked all night and the cops noticed my beat up old car and shined the flashlight though my window and woke me, ran me through the drunk tests, searched my ashtray and then gave me tickets and told me to get the hell out of there. If I stayed in a regular neighborhood, someone'd bust out one of my windows or a kid would stab one of my tires for shits and grins, and one time some asshole pissed through my cracked-open window and doused me and took off when I sat up and he ran off down the street laughing and cackling, his pecker still out and swinging and streaming and piss glinting like tinsel under the yellow streetlight. And you don't sleep in your car where there's warehouses. You just don't do it. Downtown? Nope. Try a park or an empty lot or some tucked away corner of dark—cops love those places. So when I finally got a job driving a dump truck for the father of one of my high school buddies, I figured, Cool—I'll just sleep in the lot at work. Trouble was there wasn't a lot at work. Mr. Vieira was an independent contractor. He rented his trucks out to Oakland Waste Company, and the truck was the driver's responsibility. You either took the rig home at night, like most of the old dudes did, or you left it at the dumps and picked it up in the morning before your route. I was an independent contractor, and I had to find a place to park the damn thing myself.

Independent contractor, shit. That's the nice way of saying the rotten truth, which was I was a scab, and the only thing lower than a scab is a scab who's not ashamed of being a scab. Scabs take your paycheck, your food and your rent and the money you might have spent on your last beer, and they deserve to die. Scabs are lower than lawyers. They're lower than the women who sic lawyers on their men. Scabs are scummier than friends you think are your friends and who hit on your woman when she's drunk and you're not looking. And I was a scab, and everyone in the neighborhood knew it, and it sucked hard. Mr. Vieira ran a scab outfit, I worked scab for him, and my dump rolling down the road was an insult to everyone in the neighborhood.

Just try parking a garbage truck somewhere other than a yard. It's hard enough even if it isn't a scab truck that everyone hates. You want to see a bloated white-shirt lawyer shitbag get pissed? Park your garbage truck on his block. I love those guys, those money fucks, the way their whores have those distorted faces that look like they used to be cutie little rich bitch cheerleader faces that got swelled with Crisco lard and you know damn well the dudes have been getting handjobs on San Pablo since the day after their bachelor parties, the fatso wives getting nookie about once a century and that one time knocking out another future fattie idiot homemaker. I love them. I really do. You think I'm kidding.

Can't park the scow on one of those greenback streets, and with commercial plates, hell, you can't even park it in front of a friend's house or in his driveway. You can't even park a rig on his lawn. The cops give you tickets, and even your cop friends, the guys you grew up with and smoked pot with and sold with—even those guys won't let you park, cause they're afraid to get cited by their captains, cause captains always come from the fancy neighborhoods where people own. You got a goddamn motor home and piss yourself in your adult diapers, you have an oxygen tank rigged to your asshole so you can get air to your brain directly because you drive a fancy Winnebago, well, yep, you can park where you want, wherever the hell.

You drive a dump?

Fuck you.

You drive a *scab* dump?

Well, fuck you more.

So I left my stationwagon just outside the dumps next to the slaughterhouse, and nights I slept in the truck at the dumps.

When I got the job driving scow for Vieira, my first thought was that

I could just park my rig at the Mohawk station where Pop worked. Pop was in the lube bays smooching with his fiancée, Mary. She was kind of plumpy, but she had fat titties and wore little skirts and low-cut shirts and heels that made her lopsided ass look porkable. When she laughed, pigeons flew off telephone wires in clouds and cats screeched. But she had one of those blowjob mouths, and Pop bragged about it to everyone who came into the Mohawk station. "You check the mouth on my little bitch?" he'd say, and he'd wink and grab his nuts and everyone would nod and smile.

Mary was fooling around on Pop, and everyone knew it, even Pop. When I caught her in my car screwing the bums who were living in it, even though I didn't have the heart to tell him at first, I eventually did.

"Pop," I said. "I'm sorry."

"Nothing to be sorry about."

"Did you hear what I said?"

"Do I look fucking deaf?"

"Well?" I said.

"If they fuck around and they come home," Pop said, "it's different than if they fuck around and don't."

Some of the guys in the neighborhood who'd boinked her told Pop. Mike, who worked mornings at the Mohawk, once even caught her playing naughty with one of the waitresses who worked at Dick's, and he told Pop about it, and Pop said, "She's always back by morning. Where's your bitch right now?"

And she was always home by morning—at least we could say that for her. If she was screwing around on Pop, he figured it was the best he could do, and he was probably right. Mary was loyal to Pop—if someone ever messed with him at the restaurant where she worked, she'd run around the bar and smash a bottle on the dude's head. She loved Pop, and Pop knew it and he was relieved. She was fooling around on him, but that meant he'd be able to get guilt-free nookie on the side, too. Pop had given up on fidelity long ago, having lost two cheating whore wives already.

Mary had three kids, all from different fathers. I'd not yet met the oldest one, a girl named Rhonda, but Mary's two little kids were playing in the old truck tire casings, crawling through tunnels and splashing each other with the slime-green greased water. They giggled and played war with the old flaps and tubes, swinging them and smacking each other's faces. Me and my now dead brothers, Clyde and Kent, we used to play in those tires—many of them probably the same ones—and we laughed and screamed and pulled ourselves through them, through the mantled rain-water inside the casings, and we piled them high into towers down which we climbed and in the bottoms of which we made forts, hideouts, shelters where we were protected from Oakland, California, from the Mexicans and the blacks and the Filipino gangs that wanted to skewer us with their switchblades and bludgeon us with brick and club and bone. We built magnificent castles of 10.00X20s, tires from the big rigs, castles that would take more than a quaker to bring down. Summers we patched the blown out inner-tubes of the trucks and made rafts out of them and launched them at the ends of the Oakland docks and floated out into the San Francisco bay, floated into the muck and slime and rainbow-slicks of diesel and gasoline and we bobbed and floated until the coast guard skinheads arrested us and made Pop come fetch us at the Treasure Island detention center. Winters, Pop loaded us into the back of a service truck and we headed to the Sierra Nevadas, and when we got to snow, in Placerville or Auburn or sometimes all the way up to Deer Valley or Donner Pass, where the Donner Party ate each other in proper California fashion—when we got to snow, Pop unloaded us and started up the compressor and aired up inner-tubes and we bobsledded down the mountain slopes, riding backward down the hills, watching the mountaintops and trees recede and laughing with fear knowing we might end up bonked against a tree or a granite boulder and we didn't give one fuck.

And now, now Pop's new kids, Mary's kids—our replacements—mine and Kent's and Clyde's—were playing in those same tires, slapping each other with those same inner-tubes and flaps, dusted with the same soot—and watching them made me think of how great a father Pop had been, letting us play with tires instead of sending us off to some kind of tennis racquet or soccer ball or summer camp pussyville.

"Just because the last two didn't work out doesn't mean that this one won't," Pop said.

"That last one was a pig," I said. "No class. What kind of woman won't even do the dishes? What kind of woman is that?"

"We don't need to go into that right now," Pop said. "I'm ready to start a new family, and this one's got three kids." He smiled with a kind of glee I hadn't seen on him since I was in elementary school. It was a smile that didn't have any pain, that didn't hurt his face. And then his smile went away, and he said, "It's going to be tight in the Airstream."

"If I can just park the scow here," I said. "I'm not asking to come back and live in the trailer. And maybe sleep in my car on the lot?"

Pop said, "No." He said, "No you won't. It's time to shape this ship up, and it wouldn't look right, my own son, a grown man, sleeping in his car right outside. What kind of goddamn example would that set for the kids?"

Pop looked at me.

I didn't grudge Pop. My scow stank pretty bad, even when I'd dumped my load. No amount of chemicals or steam cleaning or sandblasting could have gotten the stink out of the steel. Who'd waste their time cleaning a dump truck anyway? It'd be like scrubbing your hands during the day when you clean toilets for a living.

"No sleeping on the lot," Pop said. "Mary's got kids, and they don't need to know anything more about the way things work than they have to. I've learned some things. I taught you and your brothers too much."

"I'll be gone before anyone gets up in the morning," I said. "Route starts at four."

"No," Pop said. "No sleeping on the lot."

"It was always dandy when I lived with you and *you* had a date," I said. "T-Bird, sleep in your car tonight, trailer's going to be crowded."

"Who pays the note on that trailer," Pop said.

He looked at me hard.

"I'm really happy for you, Pop," I said. "She's a really good woman, that Mary."

"Don't you give me any of that she's a good woman that Mary shit," Pop said. "You're still not parking that garbage truck on the lot. It stinks like shit."

"It's a garbage truck," I said. "It stinks. That's why god invented it."

"He invented it to stink like shit somewhere goddamn else," Pop said.

You'd think the dumps would be the rottenest place on the planet, but get this: the whole bay is ringed with dumps, or what used to be dumps anyway. Berkeley, Oakland, San Leandro, Hayward, Fremont, San Jose, then up the other side of the bay through all those snotty towns all the way to San Francisco—what's their bayshore? Dumps. Fancy marinas and parks and mini-cities of condos and hilly golf courses and lagoon systems set up like imitation Venices, Mexican gondoliers poling along through the muck and couples smooching as they pass arroyo-side banks of restaurants that sell shitbred mussels and clams and oysters dredged from the water that cuts through what used to be dumps. Dumps are some prime real estate.

I had one of the best views in the Bay Area from my dumps at the end of Davis Street on the Oakland/San Leandro border. Man, I could see everything at night, all the way to Berkeley to the north, its football stadium and towers, down to dirty San Jose and its rows of warning lights marking the low-water mud, the San Mateo Bridge lit by some sadistic architect with fluorescent lights strung together to hypnotize drivers into late night blear and wreckage, across to San Francisco, which used to be a place where people lived and worked but was becoming a place where rich people just bought things and drank coffee instead of whiskey.

San Francisco, shit. One time I walked for nearly an hour downtown looking for a bar, and the only places that served hooch were hotels where beers cost an hour's pay and where you couldn't smoke a cigarette, where doormen gave you the eye if your clothes weren't as fancy as their gold-button dry-clean uniforms. All the crappy hotels I'd worked on restoring in the Tenderloin District when I was in construction, dives with hoboes sleeping in the basements in beds of used condoms and Army surplus blankets and rusty needles, now those shitholes, those shitholes were trendy condos filled with businessmen who had shiny shoes and used umbrellas when it rained. Even the bums had gotten fancy. I saw a dude there tap dancing for quarters and he had a stereo better than any I'd ever owned. I saw one drinking Jack Daniels, juice I could never afford. A black dude wearing a jockstrap and some kind of tribal headdress did an epileptic nigger-jig at the Powell Street cablecar turnabout, his ass wagging and jiggling and cymbals tied to his knees a-banging together, and hundreds of people, I mean *hundreds*, were throwing wadded-up dollars at him.

I accidentally went into what I thought was a bar one time and instead it was a *poetry reading*, and everyone was dressed in black and had short hair and drank water or *wine*, and the fucks turned and looked at me like *I* was the freak. A skinny chick with black-rimmed glasses stood on a platform reading from her *poetry*, and it was some shit about her period. I remember some of it. It went like this:

I am woman.
I am all strength.
I like to fuck.
I bleed! I bleed!

And then she hiked up her black sack dress almost to her twat and there it was, dried up crusty blood on her cottage cheese thighs. It might have been ketchup or food coloring, but it looked enough like the real shebang to me, and next thing you know she's weeping, standing up there crying about her period, and these dorks clapped when she was done, all hunched over on stage and wiping her eyes, clapped like she was the living shit itself. In the San Francisco I knew, someone would have told the bitch to get a tampon and go back to Berkeley and hug a fucking tree. Then some huge dude, huge and burly and wearing a Harley jacket and beer belly tight and solid, this big dude got up there and read a love poem dedicated to his *boy*friend. Well, that was about all I could take of that shit. Fags are fine as long as they don't fag it up in your face. I got right on out of there.

I could see it all from the dumps. I could see the whole Bay Area because I always parked my rig on the highest hill of the day.

I wasn't the only one who lived at the dumps. There were all kinds of people there—hoboes that had been run out of Berkeley and San Francisco for the election season, Mexican apepenadores making their living collecting up the best of the garbage to sell at Oakland's flea markets, lunatics who'd found a place that understood them, criminals who'd nowhere else to hide. At night their fires oranged the sides of the hills, reflecting off bent up chrome and crumpled cellophane. The kids played and threw things at each other. Sometimes the smell of burnt meat cut through the sour and sulfur.

Even though there were plenty of people living at the dumps, Jones was the only stable resident. He lived in a little camping trailer parked in the best spot, away from the garbage and down by the clean-fill—no shit or food or rotting cats and dogs, just dirt and demo-rubble from streets and buildings and cracked concrete pipelines and twisted up rebar—right on the edge of the bay and on a rise so he had a view of both San Francisco and the Oakland and Berkeley hills. Man, he had everything you could imagine, ran it all with a gas powered generator that chugged like a chainsaw through the night. He'd strung lights from metal poles around the perimeter of his space, and he'd rigged up an electric stove and a meat freezer. He had television sets galore, all turned on and tuned to different stations but none of them with the volume up—just silent movies and newscasts and sports games flickering blue and gray in the night—and he had stereos, dozens of them, and they always clicked on when the sun went down and the scows stopped dumping their loads and the radios blasted the classical music station. When a mass would come on he'd turn up the volume so loud the garbage mountains shook like Jell-O.

The first day I worked spilling loads, Jones came to my truck and jumped on the running board. He was a little old dude. He wore a bow-tie and white shirt beneath his orange vest.

"Jones," he said, and he reached his hand through the window to shake. His hand was scaled and flaked and red with scars. He smiled and some of his teeth were missing, but not in an ugly way. "New on the job, these are the rules. This is my dump, and here I make the decisions. You don't follow my instructions, you don't spill here. Hills rise where I make them rise, and valleys cut where I make them cut. If there's a butte or a ridge, a cave or a crater, it's because that's the way I want it. You make your spill where I tell you to make your spill. Understand so far, mate?"

"You from England or something?" I said.

"Australia," he said. "And I've been dumpmaster all over the world. England, Wales, Scotland, India, New Guinea, Argentina, Alaska, the Farallons, half the civilized islands in the South Pacific."

Nights Jones welded. He welded anything made of metal—old kitchen sinks, car parts, shorn girders, refrigerators, the legs of cheap kitchen tables, bent up and green brass lamps. He was making some kind of weird sculpture, a whacked out tower that didn't look like anything, really, but a bunch of junk welded together and curving into the sky. He wasn't building it to show off or to make some smarmy save-the-earth statement for all the world to see. He wasn't raising it in fear of the apocalypse. Eventually, it would have to come down, be buried beneath tons of fill. No one even knew it was there except me and the other commercial drivers. Each day it would look a little different, a stove jutting out to the side and making the tower look as if it was going to topple over and crush his trailer. One night he welded a honeycomb of toasters together into a creepy chrome face that shot beams of light over the compound the next morning and sparkled like city lights during the next night's moon. Once he collected all the banged up musical instruments—French horns and saxes and trombones and a corroded tuba and arranged them into an orchestra without players, and with his music booming through his speakers you could almost see the players behind those horns, old men back from their graves and children struggling with scales and generations of Oakland's ghosts playing their lonely and spectral encore.

He'd be up there every night anchored to his heap with a safety belt tied-off to some twisted lightpost or Chrysler bumper, his torch aflame and sparks showering down through the maze of metal, and he made a moaning sound that you could hear even over the blasting of Beethoven or Stravinsky or Bach's *Passion of St. John.*

"What's this thing you're building?" I said.

"What do you think it is?" he said.

He smiled. His teeth were crooked and green and brown and one of them was black.

"I don't know what it is," I said. "That's why I asked you."

Jones said, "It's *mine.*"

Jones, he'd invite me over to his compound for dinner once in a while, and we'd eat like kings. I never asked him where he got the chow, and he never told, but he'd have food spread out across a pair of tables and the food steamed in the cold air and there was always enough to feed ten porkers. The dump kids stood in the shadows and their hungry eyes slimed and shone and Jones waved them to the table and told them to take as much as they wanted and they did. They loaded food into their pockets and carried more in their arms than kids could carry, food spilling on the ground as they ran and seagulls and rats and cats swarmed over the droppings. And when we finished eating, he used a rusty snowshovel and scooped the food off the tables and tossed it down the hill toward the bay and you heard the shrieks and scurries and clack and slobber of fowl and rodent happy.

One time after feast, the both of us tight and full and I'd brought Busch beers and we'd knocked back a few sixers, he stood up and said, "Come for a stroll with me, mate."

He poked along on his skinny legs and used an aluminum cane even though he didn't need one. He smoked a pipe and the tobacco smelled like cherry and tree bark. We walked along as if cruising through a treeless park, away from his clean-fill area and toward the shit.

"You hear that?" he said.

"What."

"The breathing," he said.

Waves crunched and foamed against the garbage shore. Gulls trotted along and their babies squawked for food. A police siren dopplered down the Nimitz freeway. Somewhere a firecracker or a gunshot.

"The breathing," he said. "The sigh and exhale of the earth."

He reached down and held out his palm as if about to feel for the heat of a manifold or radiator, and then he said, "Listen to it breathe."

I leaned down. He was talking about the hiss of the methane gas, the little geysers of heated garbage cooking.

"That's the earth purifying itself," Jones said. "Making itself clean again. Everything in the world becomes the earth's garbage. The animals, the plants, the people, and all they make and unmake becomes the earth's garbage. And the earth," Jones said, and he looked at me serious and stern, and then he kind of smiled a bad tooth smile, "the earth don't care one bit it don't. The earth just cleans its own self right back up. That's what I'm talking about."

He took something from his pocket and then leaned back down. He clicked a Zippo and held it for a second, then touched it to a jet of gas and the gas popped into a blue flame and it hissed louder as it licked the air.

I looked back at Jones' compound. A wind blew across the ocean and through the Golden Gate and skimmed the bay. Jones' lights swung like the lanterns of the dead and his metal junk sculpture danced in the shadows.

After work I went to Dick's to complain and drink away the ache.

Louie poured me a draught and a Scotch when he saw me walk through the door, and the place was nearly empty since my route began early in the morning and I usually finished up before everyone else got off work, day's end whistles and bells sounding around Oakland's factories and wharves and warehouses. A couple hungover waitresses drank bloody Marys and Old Gull, toothless and wearing his fisherman's floppy, sipped martinis. Old Gull nodded, and I nodded back.

Louie leaned over the bar and blew cigarette smoke. "Hey hey, young T-Bird Murphy," he said. "You come on over here. I got some words I need to be talking with you."

"What."

"Your papa is worried," he said. "About you he's worried."

"Worried," I said.

"He won't say nothing to nobody, but I can tell, and so can everyone else." Louie looked over at Gull. "Gull," he said. "Hey. Bud Murphy— what's he think of T-Bird here?"

Old Gull's face pinched tight, and he sucked in his lips. He closed his eyes and looked down at his martini.

"See?" Louie said.

"Well."

"Your papa he's always bragging about your jobs," Louie said. "But we all know and so the fuck do you." Louie cracked a beer and handed it to me. He said, "When you're not working is most of the time. Your papa he ain't fooling nobody no one. Not no one round here."

"I got a job," I said.

"Scab," he said.

"I'm steady."

"You need to settle down and get a career. Where's your kids? When I was your age I had three kids."

He smiled and he bucked his hips and he winked. "Time for T-Bird to get to work!"

"Need a woman to have kids," I said.

"Women," Louie said. "They're everywhere. You just hang on to this job of yours long enough to show you not some flake, they'll be crawling all over you. You see."

I looked over at the waitresses. They looked at me through the blood-shot. They nodded that Louie was right.

After my route one night I went to Archibald's Playhouse where old black dudes played jazz and Mr. Beasley spent evenings listening and drinking gin. The guys at Dick's didn't know it, but I'd sneak over the tracks to the nigger neighborhood and hang out at Archibald's as often as I could. I wasn't black, so I couldn't ever be a *true* regular there, but for a white boy, I was regular as a man could get. Before I lost my teeth at the quinceanera, every other week or so I'd sit in with the old black dudes who played there night after night since the beginning of time and would probably still be playing there after the last shiftwhistle of doom. The train moaned past every hour, its horn rumbling through the jazz. The howls of dogs ached in the police siren night. Archibald had painted the splintering wood bright purple, so bright that even at night it glowed and shone. It was the only building in the neighborhood without graffiti or burglar bars, the only lot around that didn't sparkle with broken glass.

I parked my scow in the lot and walked right on in there, and I brought my trumpet case inside with me in the event someone stole my scow and took my trumpet along for the ride.

Oscar James waved at me from the bar. Oscar was the best altoman I'd ever heard. He could make his alto do things that no one else could or had even thought of. He never talked about the men he'd played alongside, and if anyone ever mentioned the old days Oscar'd cut them a look that shut their traps cold. What people said when he wasn't around, though, was that he'd played alongside Arnette Coleman, Cannonball Adderly, alongside Miles and Trane and Art Blakey and Max Roach and even Clifford Brown. He'd done something, though, something horrible and unspeakable, something that blackballed him forever and for good. People conjectured up all kinds of stories, everything from turning in the guys using dope to wrecking record contracts of guys he was jealous of to actually sticking the needles into the arms of some of the men who allegedly O.D.ed themselves. No one at Archibald's had a problem with Oscar, though, because whatever'd happened to him, whatever he'd done, was long in the past and he'd paid. He didn't have any toes and he only had three fingers on each hand. One of his eyeballs was gone and he wore a black patch like a pirate to cover the hole.

At Archibald's I was one of the only regulars who had all his parts, teeth excepted. Most of the men were missing something, an arm, a leg, fingers, an ear, one of their hands. But you never heard such men play. Everyone who came to Archibald's could play a horn or bass or piano or drums, and there they'd be, up on the plywood platform stage, rickety old men and young men with instruments customized to accommodate their deformities—a one-footed drummer for instance with a double pedal rigged with wires and pulleys so he could knock the bass drum and work his high-hat with one foot by rocking that foot back and forth heel to toe—playing like men possessed with angels and devils and playing like men about to die but whose music warded off the escorts into the next life, whose music went so far beyond anything the gods could muster, the gods themselves cowering and wilted and shriveled, subdued by the cries of earth and men and the jazz that is both.

Walker the bartender saw me and set a Bud and a Scotch on the bar.

"You ripe," Oscar said.

"Not that much," I said.

"Ripe. What you been doing? Digging in dumpsters?"

"Garbage truck," I said. "Drive one. Pays the bills and more glamorous than running a cash register. The chicks, man. I do it for the chicks."

"Yeah," Oscar said. He pointed at my horn case. "You gonna play tonight?"

I smiled, flashed my toothless gums.

"Whose lady you been messing with?"

"Wish I could play," I said.

Oscar said, "We always let you."

"Always let me," I said. "But never get me a gig. I'm the sit-in man."

"That's cause you sound Mexican. You be playing them straight chords and shit. Sound like a machine. Some kind of mariachi accordion harmonica machine. That horn of yours all razzle dazzle custom going to waste on your white ass."

"What you expect? Miles? Clifford Brown? Maybe Clark Terry? It don't sound bad when I play. Least I don't crack my notes, dried up worn out lip like some these oldsters round here."

"Yeah," Oscar said. "Like some us oldsters round here."

He lifted his whiskey and we tapped glasses together and he put his arm over my shoulder, turned us toward the band.

I swigged Scotch and tasted the fume of garbage, the sour, the childhood scent of going to the dumps with Pop and the joy of backing up the service truck and kicking and throwing junk into some pit or onto a sagging heap of old bicycles and tree branches and splintered dressers and toys, toys as far as you could see, toys I knew were broken but wished weren't. Scotch is the best thing for getting rid of the taste of garbage. Rye whiskey is pretty good, too. Vodka doesn't work for shit.

The guy on stage sitting in was new. I'd never seen him before and he was light-colored and gray-bearded and playing a beat up old silver trumpet, so wrinkled with dings and dents and varnish-stripped and corroded that it didn't even reflect light. Red and green rubber bands held the bell-tube to the body.

The band played "Love For Sale" and the soloist took his turn and when he played he hardly played at all, a note and then silence, but it wasn't silence because he was still blowing through his horn and moving his fingers, and even though he wasn't playing notes you heard what he was playing, the clicking of valves against pads. Someone turned up the mike and then you heard his airsong, the whispers of breath through horn, the phrases and pauses and whole notes and half notes and runs through scales and leaps through octaves of air, pushing song rather than vibrating it, solo bleeding into the room.

He tried for a high note and you heard the pinch as he stretched, and he cracked it.

And even though it sounded good, even though it sounded *right* that he'd cracked that note, I leaned over to Oscar and said, smug as shit, "See."

"Yeah," Oscar said. "See."

"Mistake."

"You think so," Oscar said. "All those men playing the gigs, they cracking notes too. You know so yourself."

"I don't crack notes," I said.

"That's might white of you."

I showed him my pink palms. "You black dudes have all the gigs locked up. If I had a steady gig, I wouldn't be driving a garbage truck."

"You ain't getting no gig ain't got no teeths," Oscar said. He laughed. "T-Bird, you got the blues for sure," he said, and he pinched his nostrils closed between his fingertips. "Baby boy, you got the blues. You got the 'Ripe Boy Blues.' Problem is you don't know how to play them."

I laughed, and we drank up and got another round and we drank that one down too.

"Where's Mr. Beasley tonight? Already liquored up and gone home?"

"Mr. Beasley," Oscar said. He waved for another round and he looked at me and when the drinks came he handed me mine. "Mr. Beasley, he dead."

We drank them down.

"No one told me," I said.

"You got to come round more," Oscar said. "He wasn't your only friend round here."

"How?"

"He was tired," Oscar said. "That's how most all of us die. We gets all tired out."

I couldn't stop thinking about that trumpeter and his not-notes that were notes and how *good* he sounded, how much better he was than I'd ever be. On the way back to the dumps I decided to drive through a fancy neighborhood, Piedmont, plenty of hills so juice would leak from the back of my scow and onto the street where in the morning when the sun came up and the sons of bitches got ready to go to their cushy jobs stealing money from people who worked for a living the juice would ripen into a reminder that there are some things that just won't go away no matter how far you cart them. When I got back to the dumps, I found a good hill to park on and I took my trumpet out of its case and I looked at it and imagined myself playing, imagined listening to the sound of my horn get soaked up without any effort on its part to linger, and the more I imagined playing, the more I wondered what was wrong with my horn and with me and why neither ever seemed to sound quite right.

On the north side of the Bay Bridge freeway interchange, where I-80—the freeway that goes all the way to New York City—meets the Pacific Ocean, mud flats stretch along the edge of the bay from Oakland and through Albany and Richmond and Pinole and all the way to Vallejo, where the Sacramento River fans out and dumps its silt. The flats used to be nesting grounds for birds, they used to be oyster beds, they used to be red with brine shrimp. When I was a kid, Pop took me and my brothers to the flats and we ran along them, mud sucking at our shoes and pants legs, oysters and clams and mussels squirting water through the mud and into the air like little geysers, protests that made us happy and made us want to stomp the mud more.

On the flats people gathered the washed-up wreckage. They collected the bottles and the drifting planks from bulldozed houses, the floating toys and syringes and life-savers and they made sculptures—a train, complete with engine and all the kinds of cars and the caboose, an Aztec sun that was as big as a house, a sundial that actually told the time of day, driftwood families standing in the mud, a mini-San Francisco skyline that if you looked at it right obscured the real one sitting beautiful and unattainable and chortling in the gold-leaf distance across the bay.

In the neighborhood, just off 98th Avenue, Mr. Bronsky had been building an iron ark since before I was born. It was huge—took up five or six lots—browned with rust and every night after he got off work at Anchor Hocking he'd be welding and grinding, rattling with an air-hammer socket, banging nuts onto bolts and riveting and about once every five years he sandblasted the entire ship, hanging from ropes and scaffolds with the sandblast hose between his legs and gently sweeping the spray back and forth and back and forth again. He was a strange one, Mr. Bronsky—never came into Dick's and never talked to anyone at work, but we all liked him plenty. There wasn't a one of us didn't wish he'd get to be on that loony ship when the big one blew or quaked in Hawaii and sent a tidal wave or tsunami our way, a giant wall of water roaring across the Pacific and standing taller than the TransAmerica tower in S.F., when that wall blasted San Francisco and Oakland and rolled all the way to the Sierra Nevadas and the flood we'd all been waiting for finally came and submerged all the shit, washed it clean and pure and permanent. Mr. Bronsky would have time to finish his ship, though, because the flood wasn't coming any time soon and we all knew it and we bided our time and waited and we waited some more.

Jones might have been the immediate master of the dump, but even he had to own up. He had bosses, and they were assholes, white-shirts with pocket-protectors and the whole nine yards—beepers, calculators, company cars. They'd be out there on the dumps every few weeks with their blueprints, checking up on the progress of the dumps.

"That's not where the hill goes," one told Jones. He spread out the blues on the hood of his fancy Chrysler, and he squinted and he pointed with his pink finger at the prints and then pointed at Jones' hill. "That hill should be fifty yards or so to the south."

"That's my business," Jones said. "When I'm done, every hill will be where it should be."

"It better be," the architect said.

Jones smiled. "You think I don't know what I'm doing? I been doing this longer than you've been alive, young man."

"The hills will be where they should be?"

"That is my job," Jones said.

The architect said, "Right," and he pointed at Jones' junk sculpture. "Then what the hell is that monstrosity?"

"That," Jones said. "That is integral to your blueprints, young man. It is what is beneath the lines on the paper. It is what holds your plan together, what brings not only structural integrity to the whole but that which codifies the individual units, which sanctions the enterprise."

"Of course," said the architect.

"Making a dump is not something to be done haphazardly," Jones said. "Combustibles—and you don't know what those are, do you? Compounds what will *eventually* combust, not just immediately explosive and flammable, must be buried deep enough to not ignite the entire mound and create an infinitely burning heap. Tires, for instance, when they reach a critical mass of weight and therefore gravitational pressure, will spontaneously combust and cannot be extinguished with chemical or compound. Households contain a different variety, and must be treated accordingly. The hills shift, are mutable during the creation of the eventual landscape, and it is my profession, *profession*, young *sir*, my chosen and studied vocation to properly situate, mold and manipulate the excess of humanity into the bounty of man's future."

"We'll be back regularly," the architect said. His two colleagues turned to walk back to the company Chrysler. It was white, the Chrysler. The whitewalls were dusty. "You are expendable. East Bay Municipal Utility District will hear of this."

Jones smiled. "Oh yes," he said. "I am expendable to East Bay MUD. But it is not only I who is expendable. Man has come and man will go, but his garbage, his garbage will endure."

Jones tore off his orange safety vest and threw it to the ground. He stretched his arms out wide and scanned the dumps with his eyes.

The architect rolled his eyes, and I didn't blame him. Jones was about to say some of his weird shit and get all philosophized about garbage.

And Jones knew we weren't listening, knew the architect couldn't take much more and only wanted to get back into his car and blast right on out of there, and Jones he played it up, standing there like he was going to go off on a tirade and leaning toward the white-shirt with promise, with threat of words, and I backed off behind Jones and lit a cigarette and the architect walked backwards toward his car as if he had something to do, somewhere to go, as if he were listening to Jones, hanging on every psycho word, truly heeding.

Jones didn't say anything. He just leaned and leaned, promising to say something but not saying anything, chasing the shitbag away with not-word, scooting him right on out of there with threat.

When they'd left Jones looked at me and did not smile.

"What?" I said.

Jones shook his head in disgust.

Music was playing on a boom box. Mexican tunes, Tito Puente. On top of one of the mounds danced a little girl. She wore a lacy dress and she danced, and she danced like both a little girl and like a woman, her face lush with sex and body lithe with pureness. Her hips swiveled figure-eights to bongos banging off-beats in merengue and her fathers and forefathers would have been both ashamed and proud and heavy with anger and pride and shame and they would have been happy. She danced and the clouds and fog of the bay sky moved in some kind of strange and slow off-beat knowing and approval. The trumpets brassed the beat of her slender hips, and Jones and me, we watched.

Rich fuckers. It sometimes seemed kind of funny to me, hauling their trash to the dumps, just a mile down the road, sometimes seemed funny and sad that it felt like their trash wasn't really going away at all, that it was just being shifted around, and that soon the trash would creep back to their homes, would slither beneath the ground and overflow from the landfill hills and crud their lives. And while the trash boomeranged back to them, rich people would live in condos on top of the landfill heaps and get nice views of the city, and they'd play golf on landfill courses and they'd go jogging in their faggy running suits in the mornings on trails that wended their way along the hills and gullies that Jones was raising and carving.

When I first started driving dump for Vieira, the most cool thing was getting to see just what kinds of things people actually *had* in their trash. I'd linger over a dumpster or a can and go through it, finding silverware, faded wedding pictures, boxes of letters and journals people had kept for years and years, sex accessories and bails of porno magazines, china and crystal and things you'd think no one would ever throw away. One time I found an entire box full of military medals and awards, and even the poor sonbitch's air force wings, tossed out no doubt by ingrate kids or some wrinkled and bitter old hag wifey glad to finally be rid of her hubby. But after a while witnessing the remnants of other people's pain and anguish and despair and hate got to me, and I stopped sifting through their trash. The only things I liked about driving the scow were the mindlessness of it—the thinking and zoning time I got by doing a job any retard could do—and when I got to sub someone else's route and did a rich neighborhood.

The rich neighborhoods in the East Bay, in Oakland and Berkeley and San Leandro, are all in the hills. That way they can see the niggers and the white trash like me coming when we get uppity and pick us off with their rifles. They live in the hills and sit up there with their binoculars fearing the day when we all get together and instead of killing each other charge up the hills and burn them down and give them what they deserve. So far we're stupid, though, and when we have riots we steal from and kill each other. Some day, though—some goddamn day there's going to be a really *good* riot, a class war instead of a race war, and we're going to take them out, the fuckers. We're going to burn their homes and burn their banks and burn their fancy cars and even through they'll just get insurance to pay for it at least they'll know that just because they have cops and alarm systems and motion-detector spotlights and Dobermans and bullshit laws, even though they actually are protected from just about everything including death—they just sit by the freeways waiting for one of us to die so they can buy our spare parts and Mickey Mantle them into their fat carcasses—even though there's not much we can actually do to them, at least they'll know that they're not invulnerable, that they're mortal. Like us.

Well, driving dump in their neighborhoods is a joy. You always get an extra early start when you're hauling for the rich so you can wake them up. Our jobs start at six—we have to be there to serve them when they get to work at nine—and so when you haul in their neighborhoods you crash the cans and clunk the iron scoop over and over on the rig and you accidentally honk the horn as often as possible. You drop the scoop hard, let the fucker free-fall against the truck. You rev the engine. You skid to stops whenever you can. But waking them up isn't the best part. What's best is leaving them some ooze. When you do your route, you make sure to always have the nose of the scow facing uphill. That way the sludge and slime and swill runs out the back of the truck and down the street, or, if you've angled the rig just right, into their driveways and yards. You leave them some of their own. The smell of the swill is worse than the smell of the actual garbage for some reason. And it sticks. It don't go away. It's our gift to them of their gift to us.

One night I decided to go out on the town instead of hanging with Jones. I took the hike toward the slaughterhouse just off Dolittle to fetch my stationwagon and ramble around town a bit, catch a shower at a college locker room and maybe go find a bar and get some nookie.

The slaughterhouse was a great place to leave a car, or anything else, because it smelled so bad no one would go near it unless they worked there chopping up pigs and cows. The smell was shit, clean and pure. Shit and rotten eggs. There were some houses close, sure, but they were houses for people who didn't have the guts to just do the right thing and live in their cars, houses for people who thought that just because they lived in a house instead of an apartment they were some big goddamn middle class deal—uptown—homeowners, Jack, and landed like blue-blood Lake Merritt *very* big deals. Poor sons of bitches mowed their foxtail lawns and larded latex over the peeling lead paint every spring. They'd be out there Sundays waxing the oxidized paint of their rusted jalopies, Armor-Alling the cracked vinyl of their dashboards, sending their ratty children to the market for celebratory brewskies after duct-taping a cracked window that buzzed and rattled and kept everyone awake at night when the train rolled past.

If you live in your car, it's because you're hoping you'll end up better off someday. You're knowing you'll be better off some day, since after car living, you get the welfare and a place with all the good things, digs that don't rock when you walk down the hallway because the floor ain't set on wheels, the plumbing is connected to pipes and not a garden hose, the sewer isn't a bucket you carry but a pipe down which you flush.

But dig: if you own a shack next to the slaughterhouse, if you're paying the note on it and you've got the payment schedule scotch-taped to your refrigerator and you're counting down until you finally own the dump— it's over. Everything else surrounding the slaughterhouse was abandoned. Construction companies, the old shooting range, the truckstop and Fernandez Salami and Chin Ho's Laundry and Break Fast Bakerie. No one could stand the stink after the slaughterhouse came in.

When I turned the corner and saw my stationwagon I felt good, felt like everything was right in my cosmos.

My car—I bought it when I was fourteen years old. A '67 Dodge Polara stationwagon, navy surplus. Some old dude pulled into the lot of the Mohawk station and the wagon was flaming from under the hood, fire licking through the grille like snake tongues, black smoke curling around the wheel-wells.

"Fifty bucks," the oldster told Pop.

Pop laughed. "It'll take more than that to fix this one," Pop said. "It's a goner."

The oldster said, "To take it. Fifty."

Pop looked at me. "Two months of morning shift, it's yours. I sleep in, you open."

Took me three years to get it running and bondoed into shape. Tranny, cam, carb, seats, bumpers, rings, valves, alternator and generator, battery, radiator wroughted-out, master cylinder, shoes. I spent weekends in the junkyards that rim the bay cruising for parts, chrome mouldings and armrests, taillights and u-joints. A steering wheel. Lug nuts. When I brought interior parts back home to the Mohawk station—armrests and floor pedals and seats and parts for the dashboard, I took them pronto to the solvent bin and used a wire brush to carve off the matted hair and black-cake blood. Sometimes I found chips of skull, little flakes like broken seashells. Fixing up that car of mine was like redeeming the world, making it right and good and complete. There is something very sad about a car that isn't being fixed up, that's just sitting on someone's lawn or parked on some station lot and rusting and sagging and rubber hoses and bushings drying out and chassis turning to dust. Old crumbling cars are sadder than toothless adult-diaper oldsters because medicine and operations and love can't fix someone that's croaking. People can't be fixed back up, and most of them shouldn't. Cars can, and most of them should.

My stationwagon looked like hell—red and gray pancakes of primer, four different hubcaps, the whitewalls all different sizes. But it was a car no one fucked with. When I hit the blinker and started into another lane on the Nimitz Freeway, I never looked to see if I was cutting someone off.

And I liked seeing fancy dudes in their Camaros and Firebirds and 280Zs and Monte Carlos making way and making way and making fucking way.

That car was tough. One time after a gig in San Jose when I was playing merengue and salsa with Los Asesinos a low rider tried to shimmy his 1939 Ford coupe around my car in the parking lot, got the cars somehow wedged together so that there was no way to move either without scratching or denting them up. He got out of his customed-up diamond-tucked sled and started screaming at me in Mexican, and a crowd gathered. People cracked beers and sat on the hoods of cars to watch. I wasn't too worried about getting sliced up—hell, I was with the band, and that counts big.

"No mi problema," I said. "You're the one who wedged the cars. I'm not moving mine."

"You move that shitheap," he said. "Gringo."

"Nope," I said. "Muchacho."

He made toward me, and the band members circled round. Nacho, the bandleader, told me to just move my car. "You have witnesses," he said. "The accident will be his fault."

So I got in my car, dropped it into drive, and instead of trying to ease my car away from the coupe, I punched the pedal. My rear bumper grabbed the fender of the coupe and tore it off. The fender lay on the ground like half a doughnut.

I took a look at the damage to my car: sprung bumper, about six inches out of whack.

The low rider dude was kneeling next to his severed fender.

I pulled my wallet. "Let's exchange insurance info," I said.

He shook his head. His cheeks were wet and shined taillight red.

"You don't have insurance?" I said.

"You owe me money," he said. He was shaking. He picked up the shorn fender and slung it over his shoulder like it was a fainted woman. "Lots of fucking money."

"We need to call the police," I said. "We need a police report about this. It's illegal to drive without insurance, isn't it?"

"Fuck you," he explained.

He opened his trunk and stowed the fender.

"Adios," Nacho said.

The trunk wouldn't shut. The low rider drove off, the trunk bouncing and clanging against the fender.

The next morning at the Mohawk I told Pop the story of the low rider and his fender. I showed Pop my sprung bumper.

"We'll fix that right up," he said. "Nudge the nose against Doral's building. Keep the car running. Set the emergency brake, leave the car in gear, and keep your foot on the brake. Hard."

When I had the car against the cinderblock wall, Pop lit a cigar and started up one of the tow trucks. The truck had a wide flat bumper made for pushing broken down vehicles off the road. He pulled in about 20 yards behind my car. I saw him sitting in the cab, smoking his Roi-Tan, smiling. I heard him rev the motor.

Pop yelled, "Hold on," and then I saw him coming and I braced myself.

The truck smashed against my car so hard I thought I was going to mess up my face on the windshield. Then Pop backed up again and revved the motor and made a second charge at my car.

We got out to look at the work. We were making progress.

Seeing my car in the nightlights of the slaughterhouse parking lot made me feel damn good. I wasn't going to be living in the cab of a dump truck for long, and I knew it, and soon, amigo, I'd be back in my car and soon after that I'd have a place to park it in front of and a refrigerator that wasn't built into the wall with food in it that I didn't have to eat that very day.

The windows of my car were fogged. The car was rocking.

It was rocking and when I got close enough I could hear pigsqueals and grunts and I saw a greased foot pressed against the back window.

One of the doors squeaked open and then slammed and a shirtless black dude walked away from my car and toward the slaughterhouse.

I'd brought my flashlight from the scow in case I needed to do some work under the hood to get the wagon started, and I always carried my Buck, and I crouched down low and scrambled to the side of the car and squatted next to the rear tire and I took a deep breath to get ready. I think I smiled. Then I stood and pulled the doorhandle and clicked on the flashlight and readied my blade not for cut but for plunge.

"Aw fuck," I said. "Aw," I said. "Fuck."

What I saw? I saw asses—three or four of them—naked black asses pointed my way and pumping and a-rocking and under them was a fat chick rolling around in the back of my stationwagon in a pile of fast-food wrappers and weird junk—broken trophies and golf balls and picture frames and antique liquor bottles, pints mostly.

"Hey man," one said. "What the fuck."

"Fucking fuck, fuck," said another.

"Aw fuck," I said.

"Get the fuck," one of them said.

I lowered my flashlight and turned to walk away and I thought about slamming the door shut but I didn't.

I heard one of them getting out of the car and I turned back and shined the flashlight at him. He was pulling up his pants—blue doctor's scrubs.

"Turn that light off," he said. "Hurts the eyes."

I didn't, and I shined the light at his eyes for spite. He walked toward me.

"Stop," I said. "There, stop."

He stopped. "You got a cigarette?" he said.

"Probably a pack in my glove compartment," I said. "Why don't you ask your lady to hand you one."

He shook his head. "Your glove compartment," he said. "Well."

"My glove compartment," I said.

"Far as I can tell, that's not your glove compartment. Not that glove compartment."

"That's my car you and your friends are breeding in," I said.

"Way I see it," he said. He laughed. It was a slow laugh, like he had pity for me. "Way I see it is this. Ain't no one been near that car in a month but us. Cops tried to tow it away twice already, and we saved it by moving it round the block. Registration expired three months ago. And in the state of California, squatter's rights are observed according to the housing code, section 53b, paragraphs 3-18. You can check it yourself."

"Squatter's rights," I said.

"Squatter's rights," he said. "And if you really want to think about it, that car would have been towed. Sixty bucks for the tow, a couple hundred for the impound fee, twenty a day for storage. That car just got a thousand dollar invest. You owe us a grand you want that car. If there's gratefulness in this town."

One of the other dudes stepped out of my car. He didn't bother to put on pants. His skin shone like motor oil. He leaned forward and blew his nose onto the asphalt one nostril at a time. The woman giggled, and she giggled more, and then she was laughing. The guy in the car started laughing too. They were having a good old time.

I stood outside with my flashlight and my knife and I laughed once like a cough, and then I shone the flashlight at the car and I saw the faces of the woman and the man. He was an old man, hair white and close to his head, and he was laughing and so was the woman and then I started laughing for real, and the naked man by the car, he started laughing too. The housing code expert let out a whoop and laughed deep from his belly, and we were all laughing and you could hear the echoes of our laughs banging against the slaughterhouse and the abandoned warehouses and the streets of Oakland and we laughed and coughed and the old man and the woman in the car lit cigarettes and laughed and none of us could stop laughing and maybe never would.

I went back to the dumps and slept in my rig. I couldn't shake the image of those rumps bobbing around in my car, those dark asses and the look in the woman's eyes when she saw me—a look not of surprise or shame or even anger, no—a look rather of intelligence and lust, a look that said she'd figured something out that no one else ever before had, that said, You, you the fool, boy. You, boy, the fool. And curled up on the seat of my rig and listening to the shrieks of gulls and the scrambling of rats and dumps-kids and the all night shufflings of Jones, the Dumpmaster, at work on his screwy iron junk sculpture, the sound of his torches popping and hissing and showering sparks into the methane night—listening to the earth burping up compressed chemicals through the puffed-out lips of dirt-mouths that sometimes caught fire and danced blue and purple when Jones' sparks touched them off I thought, Well, Pop's getting married soon, and soon I won't have to live at the dumps because I'll have enough checks built up to cover a deposit and first-and-last-month's rent and utilities deposits, and I'll keep saving money and some goddamn day I'll have enough money to get new teeth installed and I'll have time enough to practice my trumpet properly and get good enough to show my face in Archibald's and hold my own with the jazzmen and I'll be able to make a living gigging at clubs and I'll never get up again before noon as long as I can smoke a cigarette and pour my own drinks.

If you work hard enough, if you just stay honest and good and true to your job you'll eventually win out. That's just the way the world works. Isn't it?

Pop laughed. "Now *that's* a nigger rig," he said. "Hey Joe!"
Joe Rondinone was filling his van and eating an egg sandwich he'd

gotten from the catering truck. He said, "That's me," and Pop told him the story of my stationwagon. The catering truck driver didn't have any more people to sell to, but he hung around to listen to Pop's story and he laughed all the way through it. Pop laughed so much he coughed, but Rondinone didn't laugh. Rondinone just shook his head.

"You don't think it's funny?" Pop said.

Some rich dude in a new Bonneville pulled up to the ethyl pump. He told Pop to fill it up and check the oil. Pop stabbed a screwdriver into the oil can and pried the top open and poured a quart into the plastic funnel. The rich dude told Pop to check the transmission fluid, and Pop checked it. Then he told Pop to check the radiator, check the brake fluid, the wiper fluid, check the air filter, the anti-freeze. The pump stopped short of ten bucks' worth of gas. Check the air pressure in the tires and make damn sure it's 32 pounds per square inch.

Pop was sweating, and he wiped his brow with the back of his hand and smeared grease across his forehead.

"Check if there's anything else needs checking," the rich dude said. He was fat and his hair was gray and full. He wore a goddamn tie. He wore sunglasses.

"Nine eighty-six," Pop said.

Fatso gave Pop a ten-spot. "Keep the change," he said.

Pop smiled. "Thank you, sir. Thank you so much." Pop even bowed a little. "Thank you so much. Please come again. Sir."

Rondinone and me snickered to each other.

When fat boy had driven off, Pop looked at us and smiled big. We smiled back.

"How far's he going to get?" I asked.

"Tires'll be flat before he hits the bridge," Pop said. "When it rains, and he runs his washers, the windshield will be oiled properly—half a quart in the valve cover, half a quart in the washer-fluid reservoir. Radiator cap's loose—it'll overheat once it gets warmed up."

Pop shook his head, sadly.

"And it's a real shame," Pop said. "A real shame about those brakes. Fluid's full, but I just don't know how far he'll make it down the road before all the fluid runs out through those loose fittings on the master cylinder. Sure hope he doesn't have to make any sudden stops."

Pop smiled, and so did we.

I was pretty damned proud of Pop. He was getting back to his normal self. He hadn't been the same since he torched a house full of Mexicans and they killed my brother Kent in retaliation. That was a long time ago. Years ago. It was about time he got his spunk back.

Pop said, "Back to the matter at hand. Rondinone, you don't think it's funny those niggers in T-Bird's car? You don't think it's funny?"

"Shit," Rondinone said. "No. Not funny. I seen that before. They got my son-in-law's car just like that. They got my son-in-law Joey's car right before he was going to fix it up. It was only two of them living in his car, but there was pecker tracks all over it. A nice old Ford. He never did get that nigger smell out. Had to sell that little Ford. It was a terrible thing selling that Ford. Poor kid never recovered from it. Never been right since."

Pop said, "If they're in your car, you can kill them. That's the law. Just don't let them get out and start running. Then you got to drag them back inside the car."

"If I call the cops, the cops'll ticket me for the expired reg and probably cut me an entire pad of fixit tickets. If I don't call the cops, I have to fight for my car, and it's not worth it."

Pop's face got serious. He cut me one of those looks.

He said, "A car," he said, "is always worth fighting for." He pointed his finger at me. "Might be one of the *only* things worth fighting for."

"Sorry," I said.

"I'll make some calls," Pop said. "After work, tonight, we can help you take care of the business. Hell, there's plenty sit around for years just waiting for the chance to catch the sons of bitches and give them some payback. Joey Mason's boy got knifed by a nigger and the nigger got away. Frankie McMalley's girl," Pop said. He lit a Roi-Tan. "You remember what happened to her. Nigger."

"I'll take care of it myself," I said.

"Good," Pop said. "Be a man. Besides, I got shit to do. I'm busy. The wedding."

"I thought it wasn't for three weeks."

"Three weeks," he said. "But there's arrangements. Mary has me doing all kinds of shit."

Rondinone paid his bill. Pop took the cash into the shop office.

"T-Bird," Rondinone said. "Come here for a minute."

I walked to his van. He leaned out the window and put on his sunglasses. "You be careful with those niggers," he said. "You be careful now. They're smarter than they let on."

I nodded. "No shit," I said. "*They* live in a car. *I* live in a garbage truck."

"That's what I'm talking about," Rondinone said. He looked over at my parked scow. He shook his head. "There's things not right with this world."

"Sometimes that's what I think," I said.

Pop had cleaned up the shop's office. Snookie the dog lay on a new towel Pop had taken from the trailer. Pop had framed the newspaper clipping from the *Oakland Tribune* that featured a big picture of him and Snookie by the tomatoes that grew wild in the back of the shop, Snookie sitting dignified at Pop's side, Pop kneeling in his Mohawk coveralls, palms outstretched, huge ripe tomatoes in his outstretched palms. The header of the article read, "The Only Water they Get is Snookie's!" In the picture Pop was smiling. The peanut vendor was filled with fresh nuts for Snookie—customers would put nickels into the slot and turn it for him, and then Snookie would open the metal flap with his tongue and lick them out. A picture of Mary was nailed to the wall over the register. She stood behind the bar at the Mediterranean Lounge, where she worked, cigarette in one hand, cocktail in the other, smiling, and she looked pretty good. The floor was swept, air-valve cores from inner-tubes and shavings from tubeless tire grindings and brake-shoe springs and leftover screws from rebuilt carburetors and Snookie-hair swept into a neat pile in the corner. He'd taken down the Snap-On Tools girlie calendars and replaced them with a calendar that had pictures of redwood forests and California beaches and the Golden Gate bridge and Yosemite's Half-Dome and seals and whales and all kinds of pretty shit no one ever sees in real life.

"Look," Pop said. "I have to send out all kinds of shit in the mail. Invitations to her relatives and friends, these little pictures she wants in every envelope."

He spread them out like playing cards across the counter top. The pictures were of him and Mary standing in front of the big tire service truck, the one Pop used for serious jobs. She wore her waitress outfit— black mini-skirt and white button-up shirt—and Pop was in his coveralls and leather tire-beating apron. They had their arms around each other, and between their heads you could see the "Bud" that was written in red cursive letters on the truck's door.

"I don't like the apron," Pop said. "I think it would have been better if I wasn't wearing the apron. It's not like I'm *always* busting tires."

"She's in her work duds too."

"Hers are clean," Pop said. "There's oil and grease and tire soot on my apron. I look like a slob."

"You look like you *work* for a living."

Pop bristled up. "Damn straight," he said. "Some of us have to."

"That's right," I said. "If they don't like a man works for a living, they don't need to come to your wedding."

"What I say," Pop said.

"Damn straight," I said.

"You know," Pop said. "She's one swell bitch. Really swell. I could get used to having her around."

"She's swell," I said.

"One swell bitch," Pop said.

Pop asked me to meet him at Dick's after work, and I got there before him. I'd finished my rounds and cleaned up with the hose at the dump and I had some money in my pocket. Not enough for a deposit and first-and-last-month's rent, but I was pretty flush.

Everybody was there, and they were complaining about their ex-wives. Joey Polizzi had to live in a tool shed because when his wife divorced him she was boning her divorce lawyer and could afford to rack up nine grand in legal fees for Joey and he finally had to quit fighting. Joey was an old biker, a Hell's Angel, one of the dudes my mother used to ride with after she dumped Pop. Polizzi's wife got the nice house, the kids, the cars, the fishing boat that had been his business, even his high-school yearbooks and his penny collection he'd put together as a kid. Joey got all the debts.

The tool shed Polizzi lived in was behind Dave Campos' shack, which was all *he* had left after his divorce. His wife got both the good houses, the roofing business, the kids, even all the old cars from his backyard, cars he was going to fix up someday and now would never get the chance to.

When Shapiro's wife tossed him, the next day he went to his apartment and it was cleaned out—nothing left, not even his work boots. He'd never seen her since, not even during the divorce. She lived in Texas somewhere, and she'd married a lawyer, like they all do. His wages got attached, and he had to work side jobs mowing lawns and pouring driveways and being a Mr. Fixit just to pay for the trailer he parked on the lot of the slaughterhouse where he worked.

Carlo Mendez, who didn't come to Dick's much anymore, came home one night and found his wife humping Bob Foutz, and he just walked out of the house. The next day he went to Oakland City Hall and got a wrecking permit. He came back to his house around noon with a dozer—he ran an earthmoving company—and he chugged right on into that house of his, plowing. His house wrinkled and splintered, and we were all there watching because he'd told us what he was going to do at Dick's the night before, and his wife and her fuck came running out of the house, her titties a-flapping and his dick shriveled. Carlo dozed the house, razed it clean to the foundation, and he spent the whole night rolling back and forth across the ruins crushing his couches and tables and family pictures into pulp, and we had a barbecue when he was done and that was a really good time. Carlo's joy-day made the papers, and Louie had the clipping behind the bar, framed, the bulldozed house, Carlo standing in front of the wreckage and smiling big.

"Bitch got a boob job on my credit card two weeks before she left me," Joey Polizzi said.

Shapiro's head was already hanging low, and he swung it.

"I never even got to squeeze those titties," Polizzi said.

"Buy him a drink on me, Louie," Dave Campos said.

"It's been three years, and I've only paid one of them off," said Polizzi. "When she dies, I want those puppies back. I'm going to use them for bookends."

"You don't have any books," Campos said.

"Doorstops."

"A pound of plastic," Shapiro said. He laughed, but his laugh was ugly and swollen.

"It'll be all right, Shylock," Polizzi said.

"No," said Shapiro. "No it won't."

"Why shouldn't we trade you in?" one of the old waitresses said. "Why shouldn't we trade in our fat drunks on better models, ones that make money and get us something better than a six-pack of Schlitz on Valentine's Day?"

Somebody said, "What you want? Heineken?"

"Why the hell you have our children, then?" said Polizzi.

"Good hardy stock," the old waitress said. "Wouldn't want to breed with any of those faggy rich boys. We want their *money*, just like you do, and if *you* could marry them, you would too."

That was her usual joke, the one she always made when they guys were cranking it up about their ex-women. And the way she said it was always just right. We knew she was serious, but we knew she loved us, and that's why she was at Dick's and not some snot bar on Lake Merritt.

Shapiro slipped off his barstool. Another one of the old waitresses came over and helped him back up, planted his forearms on the bar. "Get him a stiff one, Louie," she said. "He needs it." Then she laughed. She thought that "stiff one" joke was pretty damn funny. It was kind of funny, actually. The old waitress was the only one laughing, though.

We all knew what was going to happen now. Shapiro was going to start crying. He used to be a school teacher before his wife threatened to leave him unless he got a better paying job, so he took work at the docks as a lumper loading and unloading boxes on and off rigs. He'd been to some college back in New York, and all he ever wanted to do was use his education to teach kids things about the world outside of Oakland, teach them things other than how to fix cars and lay concrete and tar-mop roofs. He was going to cry and blubber and howl and someone would have to drive him home.

Polizzi put his arm over Shapiro's shoulders. "The offer still stands, Shylock," Polizzi said. "Me and the boys can take care of the business pronto. Just give me an address, and I'll make some calls, and I can have some friends waiting outside that lawyer fuck's house in the morning, and when he comes out in his robe in the morning to get his paper, after he finishes pissing all over himself we'll cap him and that bitch ex-wife of yours. Just give me an address."

Jorgensen took the stool next to Shapiro. He said, "I can take care of it with no one knowing. From three hundred yards I can cap his knees, cap his elbows, take out his dick. We can make things better. Say the word, Shylock, and it's done. Say the word. *Please*, say the word. I'm itchy."

Jorgensen's eyes were big and twitching like they always did when he was thinking about being happy.

Shapiro was crying even louder now, moaning and choking and slobbering on himself and shaking. "But I love her," he said. "I still love her. I'll always love her."

Polizzi and Campos sneered and then Polizzi said, in a high faggy voice, "*I love her. But I love her*," and then Campos joined in saying "*I love her. Oh, I love her*," and they were saying it in unison, and Shapiro cried more and louder and it was getting pretty ugly, Polizzi and Campos dancing in circles on their tiptoes like queens saying, "*But I love her. I love her so much. Oh, oh, I love her.*"

It worked, like it always did, and finally Shapiro stopped his blubbering and we all bought him drinks and he drank them all and everything was back to normal and we were all having a good time again.

That's when Pop finally showed up.

Everyone cheered.

"The wedding boy!"

"Nuts in a vice!"

"Lover boy!"

"Listening to the little head instead of the big one," the old waitress said. She tipped her drink at Pop and slugged it.

Pop beamed. "A round for all my friends," he said, and Louie poured one for everybody and took a shot for himself.

But instead of taking a stool, Pop tipped his head and motioned me to a booth. He sat down. He looked serious.

"Son," he said. "I'm getting married, and I always wanted your brother

Kent to be my best man at my wedding. But he's dead. And so is Clyde. You're the only son I have left, even if you're not really my son. I still think of you like a son."

"You're Pop," I said.

"I've been rough on you," Pop said. "I had to be extra rough on you, since you were going to be more on your own than your brothers. You understand that."

I nodded that I understood. And I did.

"I can't have you for my best man," Pop said.

He looked at me like I was supposed to say something.

He said, "If I had you standing up there next to me, I'd just be thinking of your brothers. It wouldn't be right. For either of us."

Old Gull walked in, and he sat down next to Shapiro and Shapiro started up again. You could hear him going, "But I love her. I miss my kids. I love her so much," and Gull stood up and gummed something at Shapiro and Shapiro gave Gull a funny look. Gull said whatever he'd said again, and Shapiro laughed, and Gull nodded and let a toothless grin. His gums were black.

"I understand, Pop," I said.

Pop got out his wallet and pulled a ten-spot and he handed it to me. "You stay and have a good time," he said. He smiled. "I have a date."

After my rounds I parked my rig at the dumps. I'd cleaned up and was hosing the suds off when I heard Jones behind me laughing.

"Mate," he said. "Mate, you look damn funny there with that hose over your head."

"I don't have a trailer like you," I said. "I ain't no uptown dude from England who gets to be a boss."

"I'm not a boss, mate, and I'm from Australia, if you remember. I have bosses. I just don't pay attention to them. They don't know the first thing about garbage. All they know is blueprints. Put a hill here, a valley there, an easy rise over yonder. They don't know the first thing about how to distribute the bounty."

"Your job's better than mine. My rig doesn't have a shower," I said. I started toweling off. A breeze pulled across the bay. My nuts were raisins. "Or a stove. Bed."

"I'm a lot older than you," Jones said. "There was a time. That doesn't mean it's not funny to see someone else during their time."

"Well," I said. "I'd be sleeping in my car, but the niggers laid claim to it. Caught them screwing in my car last night. A pile of them on the queen and fucking away. Boomboomboom."

"As well they should be," Jones said. "If you're not using it, why shouldn't they?"

"It's not theirs," I said.

"It's not yours," Jones said.

"It's sure the hell mine," I said. "I paid for it. I built it. I've lived in it. I can tell you where damn near every part on that car came from."

"Do you think this garbage," Jones said, sweeping his arm outstretched across the rubbled and rotting terrain, "is mine?"

I finished toweling off and pulled on my shorts and pants. I lit a cigarette.

"Because it's not," Jones said. "Everything is temporary. Permanence," he said. He laughed. "Permanence is the realm of only the very powerful and the very stupid. We, my friend, in all likelihood, are neither."

"I'm pretty stupid," I said. "I live in a dump truck. My friends went to college, and I became a bum. My enemies deal drugs and have lots of loot and I live honest and can't afford work boots. My brain is a swamp. My car is a fleabag hotel."

Jones shook his head. He spat. "You see that?" he said. He pointed to his junk tower. He'd welded a pair of refrigerators, doors open, to what was now the top. "You see that?"

I nodded.

"That will not last."

"Nope."

"It's what I do."

"Yep."

"It's what I *do*."

"Do something else," I said. "Something that *will* last."

Jones laughed.

I changed my clothes, but I couldn't get the stink out of my skin. The sun set behind me, but you could hardly tell through the fog. The gray sky turned a darker tarp of gray. I looked up for some reason. It'd been a long time since I'd looked up. In Oakland, you worry about what's in front of you, to your sides, behind. There weren't any stars. It seemed like there never were. I wanted my fucking car back, is what I wanted.

I unlocked the door with my key and I pulled the handle and the door started to come open but wouldn't open more than a few inches because it was chained shut with a bicycle lock. Pigeons roosted on telephone wires picking fleas and shitting on the sidewalks. A catfight screeched and a train sounded its whistle. Bells went off at a crossing. Somewhere someone shut off some lights and it got darker, and then some lights came on somewhere else and it got lighter again. My back hurt, a low pain in the small I'd had for a few years that wouldn't go away except when I was at work.

I went around to the passenger side of my stationwagon and tried the door, and it was chained too. And the rear door.

I shined my flashlight through the rear window and took a look. Unoccupied, but full. An old Hoover upright vacuum cleaner with the headlight broken. Six-pack of toilet paper, opened and one roll missing. Empty tampon boxes. Dirty clothes in one corner of the bed, a neat stack of clean clothes—male and female—in the other corner. A photo album, opened, but I couldn't make out any pictures. Spider webs hung from the headliner. Beneath a few tools—a screwdriver, a staplegun, three ball-peen hammers—lay a high school yearbook from the fancy side of town. A wrinkled condom was stuck to one of the rear side windows. In an open box and packed neatly in crisp white tissue a wedding veil, beautiful lace and pearls trimming the headband. Dirty socks stunk.

A piece of paper was taped to the windshield, and I walked to the front of the car to take a look. In the front seat was a styrofoam head with red hair and one eye gouged. The piece of paper was a note. For me.

—Joker's Lounge tonight. Sorry about the locks, but this is a bad neighborhood.

I shone my light into the car again and scanned the rubble. On the driver's side floorboard was a box I hadn't before noticed, and in it neatly folded was what looked like a wedding dress, white and lacy, that thin packing paper used for fancy stuff neatly folded over the edges. Next to the box was a withered corsage. The shift siren sounded at the slaughterhouse, and you could hear the building sigh.

A squad car drove slowly down the street, and when he saw me with my flashlight poking around in a car, he U-ied around and pulled up alongside me.

"You're under arrest," he said. "Up against the wall, motherfucker."

I grabbed my crotch. "Eat this," I said.

"How you been," he said. "I heard you were doing construction work, some nasty shit."

"Fired," I said. "Clubbed the foreman's kid with a shovel after he pulled a knife on me. Now I drive a dump truck for Vieira. You still with Roxanne?"

"Naw," Joey said. "Bitch left me for Campos, skinny little shit. But that's OK—you'd be surprised how much pussy the badge gets you. Chicks just love the badge. The baton, the cuffs, the pistola."

"Driving a dump truck ain't no nookie bait," I said.

Joey nodded. "What's a matter with your car?"

"Nothing," I said. "Just checking on it. Lent it to some friends while I don't need it."

Joey pulled his flashlight from its holster and clicked it on and swept the light around through the window.

"Some friends you got there," he said. "Looks like niggers to me."

"Black folks on hard times," I said.

"They give you any shit," Joey said. He patted his iron. "You just call dispatch and tell them T-Bird needs a hand. I'll clear them out quicker than they can peel a banana."

Joey got back in his car and pulled out his timesheet and wrote something.

"How do I get to Joker's Lounge from here?" I said.

"Joker's Lounge?" Joey said. "Why you want to go there? That's Africa."

"Jazz happening tonight," I said. "Thought I might sit in."

"You and that trumpet," Joey said. "If you'd have spent as much time working during high school as you did playing that trumpet, you'd own a house by now," he said. "Like me."

"You the man," I said.

"Walk down the tracks is the fastest way," Joey said. "Down to the old cannery. Cut between the cannery and the scrapyard and head toward the bay. Down by the docks. Joker's Lounge—you'll smell it before you see it.

"How come I never seen it before?"

"No sign. Just a yellow bulb outside the door. You watch your ass there. You'll be the only gringo."

"Like that's new to me, José."

Joey laughed. "Adios cabron," he said. "Vaya con dio."

I sat on an empty 55 gallon oil drum and lit a cigarette. Fog snaked through alleys and between the rusted water heaters and refrigerators and twisted car doors and washing machines of the scrapyard behind the cyclone fence. Tugboats groaned and trains hammered the rails, the sounds muffled in the mist. A candy factory pumped scorched sugar into the air, and somewhere a dead dog or cat or maybe something bigger skunked. Cigarettes help with the stink of the world.

When I opened the door I couldn't see anything but barlights. One flickered in convulsions. Pot smoke and cheesy Booker T. and the MG's organed and when the people came into focus none moved, not even the bartender, and no one even looked at me. A row of red leather booths along one wall, the bar made of rivet-stitched tin, stools a miscellany—an old steam radiator, two shipping pallets nailed together with two-by-fours, a few oil drums, a real bar stool, a foot locker turned on its end.

My tenants sat at the end of the bar—the old dude with the gray hair sipped a gin or vodka, the three young ones drank beers, and the woman had a cocktail in each hand, one clear and one brown.

I pulled a twenty from my wallet and flagged the barkeep. "Drinks for them," I said. "Scotch for me."

"Scotch," the barkeep said. His face shone with grease. He wore a white shirt and tie. He was bald.

I looked at the bottles lining the wall. No fruity mixers. No Bailey's. No tequila. No kahlúa, no Scotch, no call drinks except Jack Daniel's and Beefeater's. Hennessey. Courvasier.

"Beer," I said. "Bud. And whiskey. For the house."

He didn't even nod at me, and he didn't take my money. I shoved the

bill to the edge of the bar and lit a cigarette. He popped the beers and
poured the drinks and handed them to the gang and me. They tipped their
drinks at me and I tipped back and I knocked mine down. The barkeep
brought me another round.

The oldster tipped his head, motioning for me to come on over.

"Glad you could make it," he said.

I drank.

"Name's Harrison," he said. "After the president."

"T-Bird," I said. "After the car."

He nodded. "I got a friend named Brisket," he said. "Know a woman
named Mydol."

The jukebox ran out of money. No one put in quarters. You could
hear bodies exhaling. You noticed the sour and the wheeze of the world.

"We all got jobs," he said. "We ain't no bums."

"That's something I understand," I said.

We drank, and we drank a long time and we told some stories. At first
the stories were about other people, things we'd seen and places we'd been,
shit jobs we'd quit and other shit jobs we'd been fired from. It's spooky
how much we white people have in common with the niggers, when you
get right down to it.

"Those two," he said, and he pointed. "They got jobs at the slaughterhouse. No commute for them. The other one," and he looked aside with
his eyes. One eye was rimmed with blood. "That other one, he's touched.
He has hard times keeping jobs. He's all right though. Works at the school
right now as a helper. One of my sons."

Harrison's son was the one I'd seen walking away from my car the
night before. He was huge. His legs were like pylons. His head was shaped
like a cinder block. He never smiled.

The woman finished her drinks. She was all gussied up, wearing a
purple hat with tassels and her dress was shiny green and tight even though

she was really fat. And even though she was really fat she still looked sexy in a fat kind of way.

"I work at the library. I put the books back where they belong. I know lots of shit, man. I read lots of books. Everybody trying to figure out if they different than cockroaches, trying to make up some reason to go to work in the morning, to have babies, get married. You know what, though?"

I nodded.

"What is this, what," he said. "I'm a philosopher of the stomach."

"That's right," I said.

"Might of read that somewhere," Harrison said. "But when I read it, it was something I said myself. I want to digest."

"I want to drink," I said. I tossed one back and the barkeep brought me another. He was starting to sweat pools but he didn't look like he minded.

"The lady," he said. He smiled. He had a gold tooth with a design scrimshawed into it, some kind of spiral thing. It shone green and red with the neon and it flickered. "The lady, she's our wife."

I nodded.

"We married her."

"All of you?"

"Except my son," he said. "That wouldn't be right, a man and his son married to the same woman. She's a fine lady, she is. She's what we work for. Yolanda. That's her name. Yolanda."

Yolanda heard him talking about her and she leaned over and talked in my ear. "Don't let him give you no too-much about me. They my husbands, but they my babies, too. I just make sure everything's good with them and they remember to go to work in the morning."

"You're a good woman," I said.

She laughed. It was a high-pitched laugh. Not a cackle or anything bimbo, but a nice laugh like a lady.

I put down another twenty and the barkeep brought more drinks and everyone drank and the woman looked even prettier.

Yolanda whispered in my ear. "I'm bringing my mens a present tonight," she said.

"What kind of present?"

"You so nice," she said. "You come on by our place and maybe I'll share my present with you too."

I tossed back another drink. I was feeling pretty right.

I had to piss bad, and I stood to go to the can. I was pretty wobbly. Some dude slapped me in the back when I was waiting outside the door. On the door was a big black and white poster of Willie Mays. Willie was smiling and holding his glove in front of his chest in a basket-catch pose. I got slapped again.

"What?" I said.

"That's a blacks only toilet," he said.

"Where's the whites toilet?"

He was skinny and his chest was sunken and his lips were cracked and leaked motor oil.

"Ain't no whites toilet here. White toilet on the other side of town."

Harrison's son walked up. He picked up the skinny dude gently and set him aside against the wall. "T-Bird is our friend," he said.

The skinny dude nodded real quick, like he was shaking but he wasn't, just nodding too quick.

"We like T-Bird," Harrison's son said.

"I like T-Bird too," the skinny dude said.

Harrison's son almost-smiled and he said, "We like T-Bird."

After the skinny dude walked back to his booth, I looked at Harrison's son. "Thanks," I said.

He looked at me with question. He tipped his cinderblock head sideways.

"Thanks for helping me out there," I said.

"We like T-Bird," he said. He shrugged. He went back to the bar.

When I left, I shook hands with the guys. Yolanda hugged me, and I felt a little funny. Harrison bought me some beers to go.

I walked toward the docks. A bitch-dog pulled itself alongside me, teats drooping and its haunches bony and brittle, legs thin as tire-irons. I stopped and she stopped too, her legs curled beneath her rump, and she whined and licked between her legs. I patted her head and my hand started itching.

"Go home," I said. "Go home, gal."

She looked at me. Her eyes were clouded with scum.

"Go home," I said. "Go goddammit home. Go the hell home. Take care of your goddamn puppies."

I lifted my arm as if to whack her, and she slunk into herself and I felt the water in my eyes and I said, "Go the goddammit hell home," and I started walking and when she walked along behind I walked faster and faster and still she followed me and I picked up my pace and by the time I lost her I was panting and I needed a cigarette and I cracked one of the beers Harrison bought me and smoked a few.

Giant cranes walked back and forth over the barges and ships picking up containers and stacking them in iron cities, making streets and alleys and condos bigger than any project or apartment complex you've ever seen. Get a set of cutting torches and some window frames and those containers would beat any Airstream or double-wide around, and they'd all beat the hell out of a stationwagon or a dump truck's cab. All those places to live in stuffed with boxes full of things for ritzy people in the suburbs to buy and wear out and throw away. Televisions and new refrigerators and walkers for their snotty brats and new dressers for their fancy bedrooms with attached bathrooms and curtains that matched their gold-threaded comforters.

Across the bay San Francisco glinted on the water and lit the fog into a halo. Cars tinseled across the Bay Bridge, and millions of champagne glasses bobbed in the water. Somewhere my dead brothers fed worms. My mother was humping my newest stepfather in a field, and Pop snored and had workmares, remembering in his slumber a tag he'd forgotten to put in the till, a tire he'd patched improperly, a boss he'd offended that would sic his sons on him in the night. I could see the dumps from where I stood, dark hills rising against the glow of the bay, and I could see the glow of Jones at work on his crazy junk sculpture, and seeing that glow, knowing that Jones was at work shoving his metal into the air and ramming it up the asses of the gods, I felt good. I felt as if everything made sense and that in this world there are some things they can't take away from us and those things are the things we *make*, the things we create just for the hell of it without any hope of ever making a buck or fucking someone out of their check. Someday I was going to buy me a mountain, a granite motherfucker, and I was going to spend the rest of my life with a jackhammer in my hands blasting away the excess until what was left of that mountain was a reflection of my own soul, a big-ass monument to work and honor and fear and courage and the blood of the bone.

I lit a cigarette and stood looking at my car for a while, then walked up and knocked on the window. A door opened.

It was Harrison's son. "We like T-Bird," he said.

The rest of them were asleep, coiled up together. Yolanda sat up. Her teats were black and swollen and her nipples were hard like tire-valves in the cold. I didn't know what to say.

"We have a guest," she said. "Let me pour you a drink."

She cracked open an Olympia. She handed it to me. She said in a low voice, "I have a sister, now, and my mens have a new wife. To help me out."

I drank beer.

"She nice," she said.

I nodded.

She leaned into the car and pulled a blanket back to show me.

It was a white woman. She had a plumpy face. Her hair fell across her cheek.

Yolanda pulled the white woman's hair aside.

It was Mary, Pop's fiancée.

I pulled up in the Mohawk lot around noon. My load was full from the morning rounds and leaking pretty bad so I parked near the curb so the ooze would smear into the street. Snookie was chasing his tail between the pumps, going round and round and snapping at his tail with his teeth bared as if he'd kill that tail if he ever caught the fucker. Pop sat in the office doing the books. He'd nailed pictures of Kent and Clyde, my dead brothers, above the register, and pictures of his soon to be step-kids leaned against the wall. One of them was a chick my age, and she didn't look too bad except she was pimply. Pop had framed one of the pictures of his father, Granddad Murphy, standing on a rooftop in Oakland, the squat skyline of San Francisco in the background, a roofing rake in his hand, a sober look on his face and his little club feet astraddle a bucket of tar. The sky was cloudless.

"Drinking?" Pop said.

"Never," I said.

"Well I'm not lighting a cigar until you get out of the room," he said. He smiled some.

"Pop," I said.

"Is this a social visit?" he said. "I got work to do."

Snookie yelped. I looked through the window. His tail bled. He started chasing it again.

Mary's clunker pulled up and she got out. She looked good, had her makeup done good and her hair brushed. She wore her waitress outfit, and she'd bought a new skirt. She walked across the lot to Pop.

I walked to my scow and opened the door and stood on the running board.

"Baby," Pop said.

She handed Pop a paper sack. "Sandwiches," she said. "I need my man strong. Roast beef, ham, cheese, pastrami. We need to keep your energy up."

Pop beamed. His face had a hardon.

She put her arms around his neck and smashed her titties against his coveralls. She kissed him, tongue.

"Hey," Pop said.

"Hey hey," I said.

"Ain't she the best bitch around?" Pop said. "Ain't she just the living shit?"

"One swell bitch," I said.

Pop smiled. He pinched her ass through her skirt, or maybe from under it. I couldn't tell.

Mary giggled.

A couple of cars smashed into each other in the intersection. The drivers, a man in a Ford and a woman in a Dodge, got out and slammed their doors shut and started swearing at each other.

Pop started laughing, and Mary laughed too.

Day before Pop's wedding, day's end, the sun setting brown beyond the dumps through the coaled filth of stagnant carboned East Bay factory diesel air. The airshit hung low, and the dumps were so high now that I was above the crud. I could watch it move, the air, watch it move like greased burlap, slow and slushing and with waves that if you listened close you could probably hear cream against the shores.

And I could see the neighborhood, 98th Avenue stretching from the dumps where I sat in the cab of my dump truck all the way to the Oakland hills, to the Mormon Temple squat and gold-spired and guarded with an army of angels whose names I couldn't pronounce, to the forest line that sliced the concrete like the laughter of an unassailable enemy, to the glint of lakes shimmering with a sunlight that only shoreline owners ever saw. 98th Avenue ran the length, from shit to Shinola, serf to Czar, from us to them.

These are the roads my grandfather built, I thought. These roads. My roads. But these are *not* my roads. We do not own what we build, only what we buy. And blood is not legal currency. It don't buy more than a decent bottle once a month. I could see that neighborhood of mine pretty clear, and I was building a dump that would become a playground for people who hated me and thought I was an insect if they thought about me at all and who would play a well-funded tax-deductible cosmological Mexican tune and do a hat dance to that tune on the sod-turfed lawns and chase me and all my kith and kin around like roaches while we dodged their shiny heels, finally squashing our guts with an obscene whoop of triumph.

Jones made me dump half my load on one hill, and half on another. He was working on two conelike peaks. "I have to vacate by morning," he said. "I have been fired, terminated." And he went back to work.

He'd torn down his compound, speakers and televisions and tables ground into the dirt by the iron belts of the bulldozer, floodlights turned into glitter. He'd moved his trailer to the dump's entrance, and it was hitched up to an old Chevy Impala.

The dump was starting to not look like a dump anymore. The hills weren't rounded, the graceful sweeps of the canyons and valleys were gone. What was once something that looked planned and nice was starting to look haphazard, jagged. The hills were scarred, the valleys were rubble, and the once calm methane gas-jets were blasting so hard the air was thick with dust. I wanted to smoke, but there was no way I was going to light one up, not in that hissing fume. The dumps looked like shit.

Jones was moving earth. He was going to show those blueprint suits they'd fucked with the wrong man. He was going to mess up everything like any man would, waste it thorough and complete and proper so that it'd take them a year to re-survey and plant their little red flags marking out the elevations for the foundations of their country clubs and fancy restaurants and swank condos. He worked it hard, and the dozer sweated brown hydraulic fluid from its hoses and tubes, and oil and grease bled black from fittings and bearings, Jones atop his machine methodically pulling levers and working the pedals, moving mounds and cutting trench, cutting caves and gullies and razing rounded hills into buttes.

"Jones," I said, and he didn't pay attention. I yelled, "Jones!" and he kept a-dozing, working the pedals and levers, his white shirt becoming brown with dust, his red bow-tie coming untied, face streaming with mud-gullies of sweat.

He'd circled his sculpture with mountains of fill, and all you could see of it was the tip poking above the hills—last night's work—a rusted sheet of corrugated tin that had been stripped off some old shed swaying slow in the breeze. Welded to the tin sheet were a few dozen handsaws. They looked like teeth.

"Jones!"

He turned and looked at me, and it seemed like he looked at me forever. He was smiling, the few teeth he had brown with caked dirt. I couldn't smile back at him, I just couldn't do it, and then he turned and looked at the mounds circling his sculpture and he gunned the engine all the way up and threw the dozer into gear and it lurched forward, black smoke chugging from the exhaust pipe like a warflag in the air and the scoop hit the mound and the garbage shifted forward. He backed it up and charged again, and the mound shifted forward more, rebar and dirt and garbage crunching so loud the earth shook. He backed up again. It was going to take him a while to finish the job, and he had to have it finished by morning.

I climbed out of my cab, and I stood there and I looked at Jones, sweating and at work, and then I walked over to the row of parked dozers. I fired one up and I put it in gear and threw one lever forward and pulled the other back and it ground a circle as it spun around and then I pushed both levers forward and made a run for the hills that circled Jones' sculpture.

Jones saw me coming. He revved his engine.

He made his run.

It only took us a couple hours to bury Jones' sculpture, to obliterate it from the world. We sat next to the Cats and Jones split a six pack with me. We didn't say much, just sat there and stared out at the ruined dumps and San Francisco beyond, its lights clear in the fogless night. A breeze wisped the sounds of tug and barge, seamen telling each other splendid lies in voices that were older than any voices that have ever been spoken.

The little girl we'd seen dancing on the dumps stood atop the highest mound with her arms at her sides. There wasn't any music, but she started moving, slow, deliberate, tranced. She danced with the grace of a nation and a people that had either not yet appeared or had been long since expired, and her dark silhouette against the shimmer of the San Francisco skyline and the lights of the Bay Bridge moved like a ghost, like a blessing.

And me and Jones, we watched her and we finished our beers and we did not speak. And then she was gone.

Jones, he'd looked peaceful, content, as if burying his own sculpture was the logical consequence of the labor of life. But then he looked at me and his face changed and he gave me some kind of look like he was sizing me up. Then he stretched his arms out wide, like he was gathering up the dumps, the bay, the whole earth, and he said, "I'll tell you something."

He turned to the side, his arms outstretched, then turned all the way around like that, like Moses parting great seas of trash, and he said, "I've worked all over the world, and seen every kind of garbage. Every breed of man makes its own kind of garbage. Different chemicals, different foods, different soils and concretes for clean fill, different botanical mixtures, different deads. But the garbage," he said, "the garbage, mate, when it's all packed tight and together, the garbage—it all smells the same."

Jones was gone, towed his trailer right on out of there. Everything was quiet, and the dump fires were dark coal, the lights of San Francisco and Oakland and Berkeley sparse, buildings lit only a floor at a time while the janitors did their work. Cars on the Nimitz sounded like gusts of wind, and you could hear the scuttle of night beasts and the flutter of roosted birds ruffling their feathers to keep themselves warm. The chain link fence creaked in the breeze, and the dump smelled bad because Jones had shifted things around, exposed the compressed rot.

I climbed out of the cab of my scow and walked to the center of the dump, what used to be a crater but was now a mound, and I stood at the base of the mound and leaned down to listen, and I heard the methane hiss.

I took my Zippo from my pocket and clicked it open and spun the flint-wheel with my thumb and looked at the flame for an instant and then swept the flame across the ground. Two jets popped to life, blue fire. I circled the mound, torching, and then walked away from the mound, my lighter close to the ground, listening for the hiss and lighting jet after jet, first dozens and then hundreds of gasjets wagging in the black sulphur night.

I must have been at it for a couple of hours, and the sun still hadn't begun to rise, and the dumps were lit like some strange voodoo-man's den of candles, thousands and thousands of tiny blue and orange and red and purple and green tongues licking the air just above the ground, curling through rock and mud and steel and smoking styrofoam and plastic and paper and the smell like arc-weld ozone, dry and harsh and electric.

And when I'd lit enough, I climbed to the top of the mound beneath which Jones' sculpture stood and I looked out over the bay at the lights of the city, and I looked back down at the flaming dumps, each gas jet like a home, a campfire, a porchlight left on in welcome, and I sat down and I closed my eyes and I knew that I would never sleep again, not ever.

I wanted always to know what happened next.

It was the day of Pop's wedding. Pop hadn't shown up yet, but the wedding crowd was beginning to assemble on the big lawn in front of the General Electric plant.

Pop set up the wedding for a Saturday night at sunset, after everybody got off work so they could sleep away their hangovers on Sunday and not miss any ball games and make it back to work Monday just fine.

The GE lawn was a magic place. When we were kids, my brothers Clyde and Kent and me played football on the lawn, and other kids played there too. The school lawns were just dirt and weed clearings no good for anything but blowing up firecrackers. You get tackled on a school lawn you're likely to get your face broken and a mouth full of rocks. The GE lawn, though, the GE lawn was always green, even in the summer, and it was moist and cool from being watered every night. We came home to the trailer wet and muddy and laughing and listened to the A's on the radio while Pop barbecued burgers on the pit.

Pop wanted the wedding ceremony held outside, in the sunshine, and the GE lawn was the biggest open space around that wasn't a field filled with and concrete and re-bar rubble and rusted washing machines and burned out cars—insurance jobs rigged by Joey Polizzi and his brothers. Besides, Pop was connected—he knew the night manager of the GE plant personally, and got special permission to use the lawn for his wedding.

From where I sat at the dumps, the cracked vinyl seat pinching my ass and the smeared window obscuring my view, the gulls clouding above the haze, from where I sat I saw Pop's wedding assembling just a quarter-mile down the hill, across a lagoon, everyone dressed up in their respectful best, cars and trucks and vans shined and polished in respect. Those shined cars—each of them a day's work—and seeing those shined rigs—something you didn't get a raise for doing—seeing what the town and neighborhood was doing for Pop—it made me understand just how truly big Pop was not only to them, and not only because both of his sons had been killed, and not only because he'd taken me on even though I wasn't even his own kid—seeing what the folk were doing out of respect for him and admiration and approval of him, it made me more proud than any other son has ever been of his pop. I was the son of Bud Murphy. I wasn't his best man, but I was the best man he had left in this world.

The street was lined with cars and work trucks from nearly every business in the neighborhood. The Camozzi brothers were there, and all the drivers, a long row of white Camozzi Carpet vans lined up on one side of the street. Joe and Frank Camozzi opened the back of one of the vans and pulled a carpet out and carried it on their shoulders to the center of the field, and then they unrolled it and it was red as blood and long and beautiful against the green grass. The Yandell Trucking guys were there, and some of them had even brought their shiny big-rigs to add to the spectacle. One of them was blasting his airhorn and I heard it loud and sharp all the way to the dumps. The Markstein Beverage guys brought a beer truck that was loaded with cases of Bud that were about to be reported stolen. You could see the Concrete Wall Sawing guys and their pasty brown trucks, demolition men with arms as round and solid as telephone poles from running jackhammers all day long, bearded and walking around slow and limping from getting slammed by falling cinder blocks and slabs of concrete. Neighborhood kids played football on the lawn and a short fat kid dragged three other kids all the way to the endzone and scored a touchdown and everyone cheered. One of the Markstein guys opened the back of the truck and started handing out the beers.

I drove my scow right on up to the wedding. When I pulled up and the guys saw it was me they all held their noses and laughed, and I took a bow.

The band pulled up in two old Cadillacs. One was a hearse with plenty of room for drums and the electric Hammond organ. The band was a bunch of players I didn't know, black dudes and white dudes both, probably fancy guys who played San Francisco. They looked like pros, had that walk that says, Hey, I don't sit around wishing I was playing—I play.

And there were people I didn't know, that no one knew, relatives no doubt of Mary, and they didn't look like the rest of us. They were either skinny whelps with pockmarked faces and long hair, junkies and cranksters, or they were fat chumps who wore plaid shirts and khaki slacks like Baptist preachers from Mississippi or Texas or even worse, and the fat dudes and their blimpy wives with birdish haircuts looked like they spent all their time shaving and plucking nose hairs and waxing their blackheads off so that their faces looked doughy and pink like the feet of pigeons. They were all fucked up and they knew it. They hovered together like a bunch of hogs protecting themselves from butchers. They were even afraid of the scarecrow half of their own family.

Granddad Murphy trotted over to me on his club feet. His hair was wild and gray and his teeth shone like he'd buffed them.

"Playing?" he said.

"Jazz," I said.

He shook his head in sadness, then shrugged. "With the niggers?"

"They do it better than us white boys," I said.

"They let you play with them?" he said. "You must be pretty good. They never let me even sit in. Not even once, those coloreds."

"Using the family trumpet," I said. "The one you and Pop played. When he lets me."

"Just don't be using it when you drink," he said. "The sugar gums up the works. And the alcohol don't clean it out, either," he said. "Don't clean out the sugar."

His new wife rolled over to us. She was fat and blind. But he said she was a great lay. The best fuck of his life, he told me, was one time when they pushed the single beds together and humped so hard they split the beds apart and ended up on the floor bucking like mules and nearly broke their backs. "That's the way to fuck," he said. And his shit-eating grin told me it was true.

Granddad Murphy pinched his newest wife's ass and she giggled and the soapy rheum in her eyes glowed as if she could see something. He leaned close to me. "Weddings," he said. "They're the best place in the world to get laid." He winked.

He was right. The women who aren't getting married get gooey and drunk and I'd seen it hundreds of times before playing wedding gigs on my trumpet. When that bride throws her garter, there isn't a one of the babes isn't wishing she was going off on some romantic week-long fuck-fest camping in every National Forest in California in some swank rented motor home off the Courtesy Chevrolet lot.

And if you're in the band, if you've got a horn up to your lips and you're breathing your soul through the silver pipes of a trumpet or vibrating your lips on the gin-soaked reed of your sax, the curve of the tenor up against your crotch all night long and all the gals just a-watching you writhe against it, the bass guitar slung just below your nuts or your fingers tripping and stroking the ivories of the Hammond—if you're in the band you're guaranteed the bitches are going to be all over you by the end of the reception, especially right before the bride and groom take off for their night of bang-bang. They envy the bride, and they know what she's going to spend the night doing, and they'll be damned if they ain't going to get banged and give the dude a better show than the bride will give her groom. After the show's over, when the divorced dudes are whaling, harpoons poised over the cows, the band dudes are running lines and blowing smoke with the babes, who always pretend that their ride home has already left.

Man, you could be playing in the corniest cumbia and ranchera band, the lamest salsa or merengue ensemble, and as long as you're up there on stage, you get first dibbs on the goodies. You could be up there doing nothing more than playing the cowbell with a drumstick or stroking the wooden fish and all you got to do is stare into the eyes of one of the bridesmaids a few times and the first time you get a break, the first time you don't have a part to play in a tune, she's tugging you out to the dance floor and mashing her titties against your chest and doing the grind thing to check out your package. I'm not kidding. Check it out for yourself.

So Pop's wedding—What I'm thinking? Get laid. Get laid. It's time for your balls to drop, young man. This time I'm not going to chicken out, and I'm not going to get so drunk that I don't know if I got any nookie or not. Pop's getting married, and I have a better job than he does, and he shouldn't be the only one around here who can nab some pussy.

Murphy men always outlive their women.

Not that the gals don't try their best. Hell, they do everything they can think of to outlive us. They poison us with boxed and canned chemicals, they screw our best friends before and sometimes after our nuptials hoping we'll get in duels over their honor and die with bullets between our eyes, they make us take the nastiest, most dangerous jobs since building the fucking pyramids. They screech about the long hours we work and the connections we have to maintain after work at Dick's, and they nag us into strokes and heart attacks. But no matter what they do, no matter how hard they try—and you'd be surprised how hard some of them have tried, knives, guns, emptying the liquor cabinet into the toilet hoping we'll beat them for it and end up jailed with the niggers and get sodomized to death—or worse—we outlive them.

By far. We outlive them by generations. I mean, a Murphy man usually buries four or five bitches before he's through. And as far as I can tell, this's been going on since the old Irish famine days, when a Murphy man would eat half an earth-apple a day and his family would stuff their faces fat with mutton, and they'd all die young and he'd have to hitch-up to another wench. Granddad Murphy had already outlived four.

A chick with a really good body and a pimpled up face, looked like one of the crankster clan, walked up to me. Her dress was thin and tight and white and she wasn't wearing a bra and her nipples punched out like lug nuts. She had a beer in each hand, and she finished one off and tossed it away and cracked the other and took a big guzzle.

"Are you T-Bird?" she said.

"That's me."

"You're going to be my big brother," she said, and she smiled and her pimples went away. "I'm Rhonda."

I thought, Shit. Oh shit.

"I just graduated," she said. She smiled again, and she kept looking at me. "From high school. Right after my *eighteenth* birthday."

"Aren't you a little old to be Mary's daughter? She's not much older than me."

"I'm her step-daughter," Rhonda said. "What's *that* make you and me?"

Mary's little kids ran over to us. The boy had yellowed skin and kinky orange hair and wore a Raiders tee shirt. The girl was fat and round and probably only ten but her hair was in pony tails and her skin was deep brown and she looked like an ancient Indian squaw ready to sprout the grays.

"How about grabbing me a couple beers," I said.

"I was just going to ask if you wanted me to get you one," she said. She smiled one of those smiles your sister-to-be isn't supposed to smile at you, or anyone else. And I watched her walk toward the Markstein truck, and she turned around to see if I was watching and smiled again when she caught me.

I couldn't see a panty line beneath that tight white dress, but it looked like she had on some of those whore panties I'd seen in *Hustler*, the ones with the string that runs up the ass and up over the hips.

I got a hardon, of course. It seemed like my hardon never went down. Even in the scow, that smell everywhere and nothing to look at but heaps of trash, I always had a hardon. And I was twenty-one years old and I'd never gotten any nookie I could remember. It wasn't like I hadn't had any chances, I was just the world's biggest chickenshit. I'd had plenty of chances. Hell, I'd had women actually *tackle* me at bars and nightclubs during the breaks at gigs I was playing on my trumpet, tearing at my jeans and yanking at my dick. But I'd get spooked, and I'd shove them away and scram on out of there, go back to the bandstand and make like I was checking the equipment or oiling up the valves of my horn. I'd be shaking and scared. I was the biggest coward on earth, and sometimes I even wondered if I was fag.

But I knew I wasn't, because it was chicks, not queers, that I thought about when I'd get a thinking hardon. If it wasn't bad enough that I had a hardon when there weren't any chicks around, imagine how bad it got when a babe was anywhere near. My dick was like a goddamn divining rod over the worldwide ocean of cunt. And the women, they knew. Hell, how could they not know unless I was wearing a trench-coat or hunched over at a barstool, as had become my custom. Some babe—hell, even a below average piece with some special good part—a sexy pair of eyes or long legs or the right mouth or good tits—would walk into the bar and *boing!* I wouldn't be able to walk for the rest of the night and I'd have to jack off forever and ever in my scow just so I could get some sleep.

It didn't take Rhonda long to come back with the beers. She brought four, since she'd finished hers off. Two for each of us. We cracked a couple open and knocked them together and when she drank from hers she didn't look at the can but looked at my eyes, and she stood close to me and I felt really wicked and nasty. Like some slime from Arkansas or Eastern Oregon or Warrensburg, Missouri.

I slammed my beer and cracked another can.

And Rhonda slammed hers and did the same.

"Sorry for the smell," I said.

"What smell?" Rhonda said. She tipped her head back and sniffed, and I thought I was going to die looking at her neck like that.

"I drive that scow over there," I said. "The dump."

"I *know*," she said. "My mom told me you had a steady job," she said. "Non-Union." She looked at me nasty. "*Scab*," she whispered, and the word never before in the history of man sounded so good.

"I won't be a dumptruck driver forever," I said. "I play trumpet. I might go to college. I have a laborer's union card. I have options."

"Well," she said, "you don't smell to me. Not one bit. I wish I *could* smell you. I got really drunk one time, and I fell down a flight of stairs and knocked my head. It was pretty bad. Hospital and everything. I can't smell or taste anything."

"Whiskey's like water?" I said.

She nodded. "Do *I* smell?" she said. "I can never tell. I worry about it sometimes."

She leaned close to me, pressed against me so I could smell her and my face was nuzzled in her armpit and sandwiched against her tit and that was it. I never felt anything so good. I was a goner for sure.

A train was coming, and the ground started shaking, and the kids ran to the tracks to see how close they could get and feel the wind sucking at their faces. You could tell it was a long train by the sound of the whistle, the pitch getting higher and higher, and you could feel it rumbling and punching down on the wooden ties and slick iron rails and everyone there on that GE lawn turned to watch it, and you could tell that everyone brewing up on that lawn wished he was on that train and rolling away and away.

A couple of years before I might have gotten laid, but I couldn't be sure, so it didn't really count.

I was working a gunite job shooting concrete on mesh to make the mountains for a ride at the Great America amusement park near the Lockheed plant in the South Bay. The ride was called The Demon, and the mountains were supposed to be black, so we had to dump hundred-pound sacks of powdered concrete dye into each batch we shoveled up. The powder fogged into the air from the churning paddles of the gunite rig's hopper, and it was always hot near the rig and you sweat a lot shoveling sixty ton of sand and breaking four hundred sacks of concrete a day. By lunchtime my face and neck and hands were black and shiny as wet roofing tar. Even my lips and teeth and tongue were black. The lower rims of my eyes should have been blood red, but they looked like black worms. The only thing that got that crud off my skin at night was powdered dishwasher detergent, the grainy kind that grates your skin until you're red as a stoplight.

The amusement park wasn't open yet. They were waiting on us to finish up The Demon, the year's main attraction. We were already a few days late, and so the bosses at Oakland Gunite Company had two crews working twelve-hour shifts round the clock, a thirty minute lunch break after the seventh hour.

Great America hired a bunch of high school kids to be the Great America Marching Band, and they practiced corny Sousa marches and showtunes all day long. If the gunite rig or compressor ever stopped, all you could hear were songs like "76 Trombones" and "It's a Grand Old Flag," and it made you want to fix the rigs yourself and get back to work.

And they were snots, too. I asked one of them once, a punk trumpet player with a perfect face, what kind of horn he was playing, and he said, "An *expensive* kind of horn."

One day during lunch break the band was taking a break too. My friend and shovel-mate Fish, a black man bigger than any man who's ever lived and stronger than two, walked alongside me. At the workers' cafeteria we ate buffet salads so we wouldn't get cramps when we went back to work. When we left the seats had to be scoured, and one time some kid started to give Fish some shit about the mess we made from the black dye and Fish just looked at him hard and said, "I don't want to have to go back to Quentin," and nobody ever messed with us again. On the way back to The Demon we passed by the band members, I saw the perfect-faced punk sitting on the step of an imitation old-town store, and I stopped. He even had blue eyes. I hated him.

"That's a trumpet, right?" I said.

He sneered at me. He said, "An *expensive* trumpet. Get it right."

I said, "Can I try it?"

He looked at me like I was nuts. I could see him looking at my black hands.

"Please?" I said. I pulled a clean white cloth from the inside of my hardhat. "I won't touch it with my hands. I'll use this."

Band members crowded around. Lots of them were girls. They were all good looking, pretty boys and girls whose dads were rich and moms were the kind of good lookers that rich men always get because good lookers are trained from birth to go for money like dogs are trained to shit on command. They were the kinds of kids who could afford to take crappy minimum wage jobs in the summer for "life experience" instead of because they needed the cash themselves or had to fork over their checks to their parents. The kind of fucks who work because they *like* it, and they *like* it because they're not really working. Shopping mall bitches who work for a day at a vet clinic because they think they like animals until one pukes or shits or pisses or bleeds on them, and then they only like animals that aren't sick or bashed into pelts. Caddyboys who get new cars when they turn sixteen and spend their weekends washing and waxing and Armor-Alling the leather so much that they can't even take an onramp curve for the slime-slipping across their seats. These were the kinds of kids that used to drop down out of their fancy hills when we were in high school and trash our old beat up cars. Once or twice a year they came to our school in their Porsches and BMWs and Jaguars and destroyed the junkyard heaps we'd repaired into barely running condition—smashed our windshields and slashed our tires and spray-painted their school logo over the bondo and primer of our twenty-year-old Ramblers, Falcons, Galaxies, and Polaras. In retaliation, we stalked them at their local hangouts, late, and with baseball bats and tire-irons evened the score—not on their cars, but on their bones. Nothing ever happened to the rich kids for destroying our cars. We told the cops, the cops asked for our proof, we told the cops we were eyewitnesses, and the cops said the eyes ain't proof. We, on the other hand, went to juvy for assault and battery. At crosstown football games, halftimes when our fat little cheerleaders sweated away with their ragged and frayed pom-poms, they drove around the track in Corvettes and Porsches and landed helicopters on the field with their dads the city councilmen or state reps or doctors jumping out and waving at their bleachers.

"Let him try, Bucky," they said. "Let's hear him play us a song."

Their teeth were white and straight and you could actually see them sparkle in the sunlight.

A dark-haired girl who looked sexy and naughty even in her wool red-white-and-blue marching uniform sat down next to Bucky and whispered in his ear.

"OK," Bucky said. He set the trumpet in my handkerchief.

I made like I had never held a horn in my life. I grabbed it like I was holding a basketball. I said, "Like this?"

"Show him how to hold it," the sexy chick said. "Give him a chance."

So Bucky stood next to me, showed me where to put my fingers, and I put the mouthpiece to my lips and honked a blast that sounded like a diesel's airhorn.

Bucky smirked, and everyone else laughed it up pretty good.

Fish stood back and shook his head and smiled a little smile but it wasn't a smile of being happy. It was pained and sad and he crossed his arms over his chest like a prison guard.

Bucky's mouthpiece was a 7-C, standard school issue, the mouthpiece you use when you're five or six years old and thereafter if you suck, like Bucky did. It's like playing a trombone. You never miss a note, but you can't hit anything higher than a D. I wasn't going to be able to rattle off a primal scream like I could have with my Shilke 6A4A lead piece, my scorcher.

I thought about John Hunt, one of the oldsters at Archibald's playhouse, who had only half an upper lip and had to play to the side. His range was only an octave and a half, and most hornsters can do at least three. What John did was use the notes he had by leaping between them. He never played two notes next to each other, but jumped around, knocking notes back and forth that no one had ever considered coupling.

"Nice try," Bucky said, and he reached for the trumpet.

"One more," I said. And I put the horn to my lips and I blew. I blew a long tone, a mid-range G, soft and light and delicate like lace, and then everyone was quiet because it wasn't just a note, it was one of John Hunt's notes, one of those notes that makes you stop and listen because it's pregnant and you know something's coming that's going to make you feel relieved. I held the note as long as I could, and then I dropped off it and muttered with a flutter of valves, and then picked up a lower note and held it, popping the valves breathy once in a while to hint at the notes even farther below. And then I did a couple of John Hunt jumps, ba-dee, boo-whee, boo-dee, going up and up, jumping ladder steps through the range, and then when I'd reached as high as I could go on the 7-C, I flittered backleaps down through the bars, thirds and fourths and punching tight and loose and bee-bopping down and fading and then coming to rest at the bottom of the horn, fade and fade and then hiss and more hiss.

I said, "Thanks."

I didn't look to see their expressions, didn't look at Bucky. I just handed his horn back to him and I said, "Thanks," and I walked off.

He ain't getting that blowjob the sexy bitch promised, is what I thought.

I'd thought I'd feel really good about it, showing the rich fuckers how they didn't know shit and could do even less. But I didn't. I felt really rotten. It didn't make sense. I felt like an asshole. I feel like that sometimes.

Fish and me didn't talk about it.

After work, when we were standing around in the sunset stripped down to nothing but our pants and workboots and blowing each other off with an airhose from the compressor, I saw the dark-haired girl and one of her friends standing beyond the construction zone and watching us, watching *me*.

The next morning I stood on a street corner somewhere in downtown San Jose crazed and sore, sweating and shaking and feeling like I was going to hurl out an organ. I was still drunk, but I was also stoned on something else and I didn't know what it was but it made everything sharp and clear and bright, the edges of the buildings suddenly something I noticed, the cracks and webs in the plaster, the spiders ducking in and out of tiny holes, a trail of ants marching like businessmen through a crack in a windowledge. A shopping cart coming down the sidewalk being pushed by a toothless hag wearing a sweatshirt for a headdress made a noise that was louder than any train that ever cut through a city and I could hear the ball bearings in the metal wheels, the squeaking of the wheelbraces twitching back and forth. Every building's paint seemed a slightly different shade even though they were all painted either brown or white and usually just looked like a smudge of filth. Three cats fought somewhere behind the row of not-yet-open storefronts and I heard a big rig fire up its diesel on the other side of the world.

My back burned with streaks of pain and I could feel sweat bead and trickle slow in salty ball bearings and then pool along the waist of my pants. I reached my arm around and wiped my back, and when I brought my arm back around I looked at my hand and it was slick with blood. I pulled up my shirt and turned so I could see my reflection in a storefront window and my back was carved up, long bleeding scratches crisscrossing and curling and sometimes broken like the dividing lines on an interstate. I heard the blood leak.

A cop drove slow past and the cop gave me the get moving or I'll pound you look and I dropped my shirt and started walking and trying to remember what had happened. What I knew for sure was this: I'd followed the girls to an apartment complex somewhere off Capitol Expressway in San Jose, and I'd gone into their flat. It was small and stark and sweat stains streaked the walls and cut gullies through a hundred years of foulness. They both played clarinet, and music scores lay about like old newspapers and an old upright piano pressed against one of the walls of the main room. Some of the white keys were missing and the keyboard looked like an ugly smile.

"Connie really likes you," the blond one said when the sexy dark-haired girl went to the bathroom.

I smiled through my black teeth.

"But you'll need a shower. You can use ours," she said.

"You got any dishwasher detergent?"

She laughed. "The dishes are clean."

"It's the only thing takes this crud off," I said.

She went into the kitchen and Connie came out of the bathroom and sat down next to me and started kissing me and running her hands under my sweatshirt. I saw the other girl peek around from the kitchen, and when she saw us she ducked back and made like she was doing dishes. Then she coughed a couple of times and when I opened my eyes she was standing there in her panties and bra and she had that space between her thighs that makes me think nasty. She had a decanter in one hand and three glasses in the other.

"We should have drinks," she said. And she sat down on the dusty couch next to us and poured into the glasses and Connie stripped down to her panties and bra too. I drank my drink, it tasted like vodka and pepper, and the blond poured me another, and Connie downed hers and the blond poured for her. One of them took my sweatshirt off. There was a hand on my thigh working. I got really happy, and I took off my glasses so I couldn't see.

More drinks and then Connie's passed out and sprawled on the floor like a chalk crime-scene outline. The piano and sheet music disappear and I'm kissing someone and I hear the blond screaming at me, "You're such a fucker. How can you do this to Connie? She's my best friend, you fucker. Oh, you're such a fucker."

Then I'm on a street corner in downtown San Jose.

I still had my wallet, and change weighed down my pocket, and nothing was missing but my soul. I didn't know where the apartment complex was, where my car was, where I was. I found a payphone and called my crazy friend Blewer, the writer. I told him I needed help, and he couldn't refuse since I'd bailed him out of jail twice, once on a DWI and the other time when he got jailed for telling the president of the college he worked for that he was going to set himself on fire and walk through his living room. Then I bought a beer at a 7-11, a 24-ouncer, and sat on the curb next to the other shellshocked niggers.

When Blewer showed up, I showed him the scratches and told him what I remembered and that I might have gotten laid but I wasn't sure, and he laughed and laughed. He told me to read some books and I'd feel better. I've read a lot of fucking books. They've never made me feel any better.

From down the street police sirens sounded. A train of garbage scows headed toward Pop's wedding and skidded to a stop like some obscene herd of tailed-up elephants, and you could hear the trash shifting back and forth in the slosh. It was the Vieira men, the other guys that worked scab with me, established men who rented houses that had driveways and yards they could park their scows in at night, men who came home at night to good meals and good wives. Sheets of sluice spilled, and if the orange-rind sulfured smell of the dumps hadn't already been in my nose I'm sure I would have smelled the juice. The cops got closer, nearly a dozen cars, lights flashing and sirens full tilt and they pulled to a double-parked stop and in the middle of the train was Pop's Ford Fairlane, and he'd had it painted white and shiny and he'd gotten new chrome moldings and slapped on some mags a set of 60-series Goodyears and we all knew where he got *those* and that unless he'd rigged the books there'd be hell to pay from the boss when he went back to work on Monday.

The band's drummer was changing the skin of the bass drum. There was a logo on the new skin. It read, "Bud's Hot Five."

When Pop stepped out of the Fairlane, everyone was silent for a second. We couldn't believe what we saw.

Pop looked like something from a black and white movie, all decked out in a tuxedo and top-hat, his barrel chest making the jacket hang as if he had his shotgun holstered at his side beneath. He wore shiny white shoes that looked like they'd never take a scuff, and you just knew that his cane was really a sheath for a sword. He looked like the classiest gentleman that ever stepped foot in Oakland.

Someone let a war whoop, a call we'd all heard and that most of us had brayed, our neighborhood battle cry, the one you heard on both sides of the creek when there was about to be a shootout or a serious block-fight, the sandpaper-throat gut-chuck vein-pop call of joy and hate and don't-you-fuck-with-me-or-mine that was followed by everything true and honest and without censor or restraint.

Everyone made their way to the Markstein truck and grabbed hand-fuls of beers and started chugging, chanting, "Bud, Bud, Bud! Bud, Bud, Bud!" and they laughed a lot at the pun. Two fatties—both of them with skinny rednecks—lifted their tube tops and cupped their boobs for Pop, and everyone cheered and some people laughed. The boobies weren't that bad, actually. They would have been really great boobies, first class, if they'd been attached to other women. Boobs are like that sometimes.

"My aunties," Rhonda said. "Lura and Tura, my mother's sisters," she said. "Twins."

"Quadruplets," I said.

"They have really big tits," Rhonda said.

"They're both on the big side."

"Still," Rhonda said.

She looked sad. She was looking at her own tits.

"You don't have anything to worry about," I said.

She looked at me with eyes that made me want to drag her off to a place without factories or warehouses, without garbage dumps and seagulls carrying the guts of anything once living and now dead into the sky to make the sky stink as bad as the earth below, a place that smelled of pine trees and licorice and eucalyptus or the Pacific or fields of poppy, a place of all that was good and right about California, the place Spaniards found when they sailed up the coast in galleons and thought they'd discovered the Garden of Eden and knew that God and the angels had protected this paradise from the evil of man. I wanted to tell her that she was the most beautiful woman that ever walked the planet, and that if she'd marry me, now, on the spot, I'd care for her the rest of her days and caress her wrinkles when she was old and drink wine with her over a smoldering pit of coals while the sun set over the world and while we both died at the same time, our breaths wheezing their last as we embraced for the final time.

I wanted the pickup truck, the barefoot kids, the single-wide, the fishing rods and a workshed, and I imagined myself working on a car in the winter and my knuckles bleeding from banging wrenches against manifolds and my woman, my Rhonda, bringing me coffee and brandy and red rags to wipe my forehead. I saw myself with a child, a *son*, my *son*, a trumpet in his hands, his lips pressed against the mouthpiece, the finger-grips too big for his small hands, his mind focused on pressing the valves at the same time as he shot his breaths and remembered the names of the notes, and me sitting beside him next to the music stand, the transcribed sheet music of Charlie Parker's "Ornithology" spread out and the only etude my son would ever need to know, he, my son, the child who would redeem every fucked up thing about my own fucked up family, he, this son of mine, the light burning through generations of soot, of grease and oil, of concrete dust and asphalt fumes and the noise of the jackhammer, he, my son, the reward for work well done and honestly performed. My child, Rhonda. Give me my child. Your tits? I love them. I love them with or without you, but with you they may suckle my son, and you, mother of my child, you may be the redeemer of centuries of Murphy toil and anguish and drunken earth-soaking tears and faux joys of men bruiting in the flickering fires of hearths of desperate hope. Your tits, Rhonda? They're just swell with me.

"Really," I said.

I tossed back my beer. So did Rhonda. Lots of people were tossing back beers. Lura and Tura hadn't pulled their tube tops back down. Pop was walking toward the Markstein truck, and every three or four steps he chugged a beer someone pushed his way. It was going to be a good wedding.

A white Cadillac pulled up, tinted windows and brand new with gold insignias and gold-plated lug nuts. The door opened and a dude in a shiny silk suit stepped out. His gray hair reflected the sun and he was tall and skinny even though he was old, skinny like he'd never eaten a bag of Fritos or chugged a twelver in his life. He stared at us for what seemed like a flick of time but we all knew that for this dude it must have seemed an hour, his eyes going pale and shaky as he took us in, the truck drivers and jackhammer operators and cops and the titty twins dangling and no one in the crowd who didn't have perma-filth scored three layers of skin deep, no one of us without biceps bigger than his pinhead. He walked around the Caddy and opened the passenger door and a woman took his hand and he brought her to a stand. He took a pair of sunglasses from his coat pocket and slapped them over his eyes so he couldn't see us as good.

His bitch wore a white dress, low cut, slit up the side to show some leg. Her titties nearly dropped out when she stood, and she had to rearrange the dress to hold them in. The diamond on her finger as big as a hubcap.

It was my mother.

Pop acted like he didn't give a shit, stood there in his suit with a beer in each hand and his tie crooked and his Florsheims spotted with foam.

He acted like he didn't care, put on the face, but we all knew he did. Mom—she was the reason Pop ended up living in a trailer next to a gas station. He'd married her when I was already born of another man, and he'd raised me, the bastard son, along with two sons she'd popped out for him, one of which was no doubt his own, and while he'd been working four jobs trying to give her everything she wanted—a new Chevy Impala, a new house, new clothes, her own washer and dryer and a fancy television/stereo console—while Pop was driving a tow truck, pumping gas, working as nightwatchman at a junkyard, and spot-gigging in the Oakland Symphony on his trumpet, Mom was boning the Oakland chapter of the Hell's Angels.

The night he beat her up, she hopped the fence and told the bikers, and when they came round the block on their choppers, Mom sitting bitch behind one of Barger's boys, Pop was ready for them. He'd unfolded a lawn chair on the driveway and he'd cracked a beer and sat down. He was tipping the beer back when the first chain cut the air and cracked his chest into splinters. Me and my younger brothers, Kent and Clyde, watched from the living room window as the Angels tore into Pop, and each time they'd knock him over he'd set the lawn chair back upright and crawl back into it and take another swig from his beer. When they finished with him, he was sitting upright in that chair, blooded. And that's where he was when the cops showed up, Mom stepping out of the lead car, and took him off to jail for beating Mom.

When he got out of jail, she'd given away or sold off all the things he still owed money on, divorced him, and stuck him with alimony and child support. It was damn near impossible for Pop to get a job, since he was an ex-con, but Joe Fernandez, owner of Joe's Tire Service, which operated out of a Mohawk gas station, owed Pop a favor for something Pop had done that no one ever talked about, so Joe gave Pop a job. Pop lived in the office of the Mohawk, slept in a swivel-chair with his feet propped up on the counter, until he saved enough money to buy a 19 foot Airstream trailer. Joe let him park it next to the Mohawk, behind the stacks of truck tire casings.

We kids lived with Mom for a while, hopping from house to house, staying with Hell's Angels and dopers and hippie freaks and fags, living in the projects for a while, the only white kids always and getting slammed around like dogs. To this day I get a physical reaction when I'm in sight or smell of a black ghetto, and I get sweaty and my insides get quivery as if I'm a kid again and a herd of niggers is about to beat the living fuck out of me. I can't shake it, and I've tried to, but I can't. If it had been a goose-stepping army of Krauts, I'd feel that way about them. But it was niggers. And they truly loved beating the shit out of little fat white boys. Their parents had taught them *we*—little poor-boy white trash geeks—were the reason they were niggers, and wasn't no way we were going to convince them otherwise.

I can't even write about the stuff we saw or that happened to us, and I don't want to either, and I probably never will, either, because it might make you think I was asking for your sympathy and compassion. It was bad though, and kids usually don't realize when things are bad because they're kids and whatever their lives happen to be they just assume that their lives are normal, that there isn't any other reality. But it was shitty enough that even we knew it was fucked up, it was *wrong*.

Mom got tired of us after a while because we got in the way of her fucking, and she shucked my brothers into foster homes and ditched me with Pop, and eventually Pop got all three of us and we all grew up in that trailer, Pop paying child support and alimony to her the whole time.

The only times Pop mentioned her was if one of us did something wrong and got caught. Then he said, "You want to live with your mother? You think the grass is greener on the other side? You want to live with your mother, you just keep fucking up. You keep fucking up, you live with the bitch. Understand?" And we cried and shook and begged Pop to forgive us. We told him we'd never get caught again.

I hadn't seen her in a few years, not since she brought her last husband to town to flash him around. The last one was younger than me, and he worked for the railroad riding around in a caboose, easy money union job. We got drunk together, him and me and Mom, and the last glimpse I had of him was Mom smacking him around because he'd forgotten to bring her some booze.

And here she was, Mom, slutted up and stepping out of a Cadillac with some swanky dude that wasn't pimp and had bucks anyway, that looked like his loot was earned easy and long, that stood and carried himself like a man from a world none of us had ever known or ever would. He seemed *nice*, and there was a dignity about him that was disarming, that made it so even though your first instinct was to bitch-slap him and take his lunch money you knew you shouldn't because he was not deserving of a bitch-slap at all. Instead, what he deserved was to be commended, to be stepped aside for. He made you feel ashamed of hating rich people, made you suspect that not all of them were assholes that would fire you and starve you out just for shits and grins. We wanted to hate him, we knew we *should* hate him, but we couldn't. And that made us hate him more. Otherwise, we'd have to hate ourselves.

"Everyone has better tits than me," Rhonda said.

"Fake," I said.

"How do you know?"

I said, "My mother."

"Well shit," Rhonda said. She spat on the lawn. It was substantial. She wiped her mouth with her forearm. I loved her.

The congregation was so quiet you could hear the chain banging against the flagpole, the soot filth flag wagging like a greasy shop-towel.

Blewer drove up, his Rambler backfiring like gunshot. My mother and her man ducked, but none of us did.

"Fine party you got going here," Blewer said.

He took his flask from his pocket and slammed one. He passed it to me. I took a pull. Blewer's Everclear with lime juice. Rhonda took it from me. "Bottoms up," she said, and she smiled a nasty smile that would have killed any man on earth and sent him home jacking off like a chimp for days and days.

Pop's face stretched into a grin. I could tell it hurt his face. It was the kind of grin you don't like to see on a man, a creepy show of teeth that made your own smile sink down into your throat, the kind that means some bad shit is about to happen, and if not soon than sometime before long, and when it happened the grin would still be there hurting his face because it was the kind of grin that wasn't face deep but went clean down to the bone.

"We aren't *too late*, are we?" my mother said.

Pop just stood there grinning.

"T-Bird?" my mother said. "Is that you? Is that really you? You're such a hunk! Hunk hunk hunk! I hardly recognize you. Do you like my new dress? What do you think of your ol' ma now?" And she walked right on up to me, her man trailing along behind in his sunglasses like a politician's hired goon.

People started talking again, and Lura and Tura packed their titties away in their halter tops. The guys in the band flipped the power and tested their mikes, warmed up their horns with quiet scales and whole tones. The beer bottles were already running low, so one of the Markstein guys cracked a couple kegs.

"Well, I just *couldn't* miss your father's wedding. I heard about it from one of the old gang and since *I* just got married again and found the love of my life, I thought, to myself I thought well, if Bud's getting married he certainly wants me there to witness his bliss and joy because I *am* the mother of his children! My children would want me there!"

"Kent's dead," I said. "So's Clyde."

"If Bud's getting married, he must be as happy as I am! And I know he'd be just so happy for me too."

"They're dead, and I'm not his son."

"Gail is the perfect man," my mother said. "He's kind, and he's handsome—as anyone can see—and he has the means to provide a *proper* home for a *lady*. Where are Kent and Clyde, my other two darling little boys?"

"Dead," I said.

I put my arm around Rhonda's waist and turned toward the kegs and
then I couldn't walk. I couldn't move. My mother stood behind me saying,
"What? What?" and her voice got more and more quiet and the sound
of the party rose and Rich Kuam pulled his 4-wheeler onto the lawn and
cranked up his stereo and opened the doors and the ground shook with
Creedence Clearwater Revival and I'd never before felt anything like what
it felt like to have my arm around Rhonda's waist. Her waist was slim and
soft and beautiful and I could nearly wrap my arm all the way around
and touch my own ribs. My forearm touched the undersides of her tits,
and I couldn't see anything at all even though my eyes were open. I could
only feel her tits, her waist, her hair over my shoulder, the heat of her
body shimmering and the bass guitar and drums of Kuam's stereo, the
rimshots of the bandman's snare as he tuned it, the rumble of a train and
Jell-O shake of the landfill beneath my feet. Rhonda leaned her head on
my shoulder, and her mother, my soon to be new step-mother, looked at
Rhonda and winked. A flock of seagulls swooped toward the linguisca
vats, and broken-haunched dogs sat drooling in the street.

The wedding party was assembled, the band was ready, the preacher—
Father Camozzi—set down his beer, and the ceremony began, Mary with
Lura and Tura at her side, Pop with Louie the bartender as his best man
and Joe Fernandez, Pop's boss at Joe's Tire Service, as Pop's other man.
When Father Camozzi opened his Book of Common Prayer, Lura and
Tura, at the same time, turned and flashed their boobs at the crowd, and
we all cheered, and Pop and Mary looked less nervous. Tits count, even if
they're attached to pigs. Don't try denying it.

Pop tugged at his coat and tie and even though I'd only once before
seen him duded up like that he somehow seemed natural that way, seemed
as though in another life he could have been some fancy real-estate guy or

a salesman, someone who didn't come home from work and wash his hands and forearms and neck with Ajax, someone who got to talk on the phone and have expensive sandwiches and beers with people and call it work.

My mother'd somehow sidled up next to me and Rhonda, and she leaned against my arm as if I was her man.

"T-Bird," she said. "You need a bath."

"I work at the dumps," I said. "I stink."

"Dead?" she said.

Father Camozzi was getting on with it.

"Dead," she said, and she kept on saying it, dead, dead, dead, dead. Dead, dead.

"Dead end road and Mexicans," I said. "Same difference. Dead. A long time dead. But don't worry, it wasn't painless."

I didn't know why I said that, why I intentionally made it sound as bad as it was, since they really did die rotten deaths. I wanted to make my mother hurt. I wanted the bitch to feel the neighborhood again, feel what she'd evidently escaped. I wanted her to remember where she'd come from, her roots, us. I wanted her to know that just because she'd married some rich fuck didn't mean the world she'd brought children into didn't still exist, and wasn't still chewing its own legs off and chewing off the legs of any nearby animals just for spite. I wanted to demolish her. I hated her for bringing me into this spinning hairball we call earth.

So I told her all about it. I told her about it while Pop was standing there straight-backed and proper and proud and finally with a woman who would stay with him and sometimes even be nice to him, who would make him some goddamn coffee in the morning and crack a can of chili for him and have it hot in the pot after work, crackers and cheese shredded on the side, beer fresh from the fridge.

I started with Clyde, told her Clyde died after getting drunk one night with me and trying to drive back to Pop's place, wrapped his car around the barrier at the end of my dead end street. No one reported that kind of shit in my neighborhood, because that means the cops will have to talk to you and you'll have to scour your place for stuff they'll bust you for, which might be anything depending on how dark your skin is or how long you keep your hair. So Clyde sat mangled in his car until noon the next day—about eight hours—with a steering wheel carving semi-circles in his throat and belly. Died on the stretcher.

I didn't tell her that I'd always hated that little fuck, that every time he ever came to visit me I always got him drunk, that every time I ever got him drunk I hoped he'd get in his fancy Camaro and drive head-on into a semi. I didn't tell her that somehow I'd always known that I wasn't Bud's kid because of the way he treated Clyde, how he loved on Clyde, how Clyde would get a report card full of Cs and Ds and Pop would snap him a c-spot for passing and when I'd bring home straight A's he'd say, "You might get straight A's in school but you flunk out in real life." I didn't tell her that every time I saw Pop's boy I wanted him to get so drunk he'd hyperventilate and convulse and quake and choke and die swallowing his own bile and puke. I didn't tell her because I can maintain. I can be cool when I need to.

And Kent, well, I didn't tell about it in the last book because an editor said it was too gory. Editors don't come from neighborhoods like mine. When you tell the truth about the shit they say it's "over the top," so you have to tone it down and leave out the real shit. Here's what really happened.

The way Kent died? Mommy, here's how. He walked out of a 7-11 and saw a low rider, and the car was stuffed with the same Mexicans that had cut off Clyde's ear and beat the living fuck out of him for fucking their sister, and when Kent saw the car he said, "Mexicans." And they jumped out of the car, and wham! they'd knocked him to the ground and they were stomping his chest and neck with those Mexican shoes of theirs, the ones with the heels. A little shit, after Kent was down and after I had a knife to my gut, wrapped Kent's chest with a chain and then it took three of them to drag Kent to the trailer hitch welded to the ass-end of the Chevy Impala low-rider. Then they got in the car and backed up, and I don't know if they ran over him or not, because I didn't hear him scream and because one of those fucks had sliced my arm across the vein—that's the scar I have, see it?—and they drove off, drove with those little 78-series low-rider tires and ass-end of the car dragging even lower from the weight of Clyde being towed behind across the asphalt.

I tied-off my arm with my tee-shirt, and it was dark and foggy and the streetlights made nimbi like schmaltzy angel halos and I wear glasses, you know, and my glasses were misted and wet and fogged but I could see the taillights red and fuzzed and I could hear Clyde being carved and sliced by the asphalt rough. I got up and I ran, and I ran and I saw the asphalt ahead shine with the bloodslick of Clyde's life reflected in the taillight haze and candleflame from Catholic ceremony and dread in bayframe windows. I kept running, my arm leaking, and then I saw ahead a lump dark and heavy and when I came to it the lump was Clyde's leg, jeans shorn, legbone gray and sticking out of the pantleg like a plastic piece of PCV pipe, drooling with red gobs of curd. I nudged it with my foot, Mom, and it rolled over, and then I think I might have howled, but I'm not sure, because howling is not a thing one can be certain one has done, not if it is a proper howl. Have you howled? If you have, you're not sure, not absolutely certain that you have. You haven't howled if you're sure you have.

And I kept on after them. I don't know why, since Clyde was either dead or going to die, and since if I caught them they'd kill me too, as is their custom.

I found more body parts, but the more body parts I found, the less I was able to tell them apart. The more body parts I found, the more they started to look like car parts soaked red in transmission fluid, springs, wires, gobs of grease, rubber hoses.

When I found Clyde, what I saw was not something I will describe. I don't want you to vomit while you're reading my book.

We buried him with a closed coffin funeral.

Telling my mother about Kent and Clyde, I knew what was going to happen. She was going to flip out and make a scene. Years before, when she was married to some other dude—an airline pilot who made a shitpile of money and had a health care plan—my mother cooked up a great scam with a shrink. That didn't surprise me. Rich assholes all go see shrinks so they can blame their shitbaggery on someone else, anyone else, anyone other than their own fucking selves. *My daddy spanked me too much, and so I'm a fatass pedophile adulterer. My mommy never let me play with the other girls, and so I beat my husband with a frying pan and fuck his friends silly whenever I can.* Shrinks.

The Self-Help section of the bookstore is bigger than the Literature section. Have you ever looked at a Self-Help book? Crap, that's what. I know, because nearly every bitch I've ever boinked has thought it necessary to give me one, handing it over with emotion and a stupid look they suppose resembles philosophy, holding the paperback like it was a gold-gilt Gideons. They read like horoscopes, catch-all bullshit that applies to every simpering dupe who flips through the pages:

Are you lonely? Are you sad? Do you feel like your parents didn't love you enough?

You are a co-dependent whose Inner Child was not nourished enough!

Horseshit. My Inner Child wants to pop bugs with a magnifying glass. My Inner Child wants to toss cherry-bombs down the toilet at school. My Inner Child wants to spin the old family cat around over my head like a lariat. My Inner Child is a serial killer I have to keep in check. He doesn't need nourishing: he needs a life-sentence in Quentin, or one helluva spanking.

I met a girl one time, a Self-Help addict, a twelve-step devotee, little rich bitch who never had to worry about a thing in her sheltered pampered cable TV life except deciding which college her dentist parents were

going to pay for her to attend, what clothes she was going to buy for
the new season's fashions, what goddamn dress she was going to wear at
her parents' dinner party with the neighbors. This little cooze got pissed
off, fucking *wept*, because her parents didn't buy her the kind of car she
wanted. Bought her a Honda instead of a BMW.

"Rich people have problems too," she said.

"Too?" I said. "I don't have problems. You see me having any problems?"

"I'm trying to work things out from my childhood."

"Get over it," I said.

"You're just in denial," she said. "You're ignoring your problems, the
issues you should be working through. That you don't acknowledge the
problem is proof of the problem."

"Get over it," I said.

That's what I said, and that's what I say now. Get the fuck over it.

For you rich fuckers having existential crises, I've got a recommenda-
tion: Get a fucking job.

Poor people don't see shrinks.

They get a fucking job.

And that's what you should do, you fuck. Build a fucking pyramid.
You won't need a shrink to help you with your angst and dread. You'll need
a bath, a meal, and a fucking beer.

My mother called me when she and her shrink cooked up her excuse for
bitchery. "T-Bird!" she said. "T-Bird, there's a *reason* I was a bad mother and
used to beat you boys. It's because it *wasn't really me* doing those awful things!"

"Of course not," I said.

"It wasn't really me! It was the bad alters! I have M.P.D. That stands for
Multiple Personality Disorder. My bad personalities were the ones doing
the bad things, not my *core* personality. I have 95 personalities in all!"

Most of my mother's gang were bitches. When we were kids, if me
or my brothers woke her up, she'd scream like she'd been set afire, and

she chased us through the house, her robe flopping open, eyes twitching, calling us little fuckers, little assholes, little sons of motherfucking bitches. When she caught us she dragged us by the arm, or the leg, or the hair, to her room, where she kept her special whipping belt—a belt studded with metal rivets and a buckle the size of Texas. She beat us until we bled, our legs and arms and asses torn open and one time my brother Kent's arm broken. I once popped a bicycle tire while riding through a thorny field, and when I came home, one of my mother's husbands doled out the punishment: he trapped me beneath a bed and blasted away at me with a BB-gun.

She had a nice alter who popped up every other Christmas or so, bought us some candy or came out of the bedroom after having been awakened and gave us a hug or took us to the grocery store. The nice alters didn't stick around for long, though.

When my mother's alters began to surface, her shrink told her she needed to call everyone in her past she had a gripe with. So she got on the horn and told off some of her ex-husbands, her father, her step-father, her half-brothers and sisters, her former bosses. The shrink also told her she needed to get things out into the open with her three sons. She called me, and wanted to come to visit so we could have a heart-to-heart chat and so I could tell her everything I remembered from my childhood. "Not a good idea," I said. "I'd rather not." She insisted, and said she was coming to town.

She came, brought her husband (I can't remember that one's name) and about 8 bottles of wine and a couple bottles of Scotch. She was ready to talk.

So I let her have it. I told her some of the shit I remembered, and not just the woe-is-me bullshit about the times she'd beaten me and my brothers, the burns and broken bones and bloody noses and whip-marked backs and fronts and faces from the garden hose she used on us, the weeks of deafness from getting our ears boxed over and over again, the time she ripped all Kent's hair out of his head and how his head looked like he'd been scalped and how he had to wear hats and grease his skull with Vaseline for months, how the scabs leaked green pus onto his forehead and down into his ears and down his neck while he sat sniveling on the school-bus with the other kids calling him the creature from the black lagoon, the time she pounded my head with a ballpeen hammer and knocked me out cold, no: *Hey, Mom, feel right here, just next to my shin: I still have a B-B there. Feel it. Touch it Mom. You stood watching, Mom, and you screamed,* "Show the little fucker. Show that little fucker to respect his possessions."

Hey, Mom, you remember when I didn't do my homework before dinner, and so you stabbed a pencil into the back of my hand, cranked the pencil sideways and broke the tip? The lead's still there, Mom. Hey, Mommy, remember when I came home from school and told you my tooth hurt, me a first grader, and so you got a pair of pliers and yanked my tooth out and I bled for days? Hey, Mom, remember how at night I used to fall off the top bunk of the bunkbed and how one time when I fell off and cracked my head and I was bleeding while you were fucking a bunch of dudes in the living room you came into the room naked with one of the men, naked too, and you beat me for making a fuss, bloodied my thighs with that belt of yours, made me bleed for, as you said, "interrupting your grown-up time," and how you told me if I fell off the bunk again you'd make me cry forever and wish I'd never been born? Hey, Mom, remember how you used to tell me it was all for my own good, that Jesus would save me, but how Jesus wouldn't save me if the Devil was in me, and how the Devil had to be beaten out of me if I used a fork with my left hand? By the way, Mommy, I don't need a fucking shrink to deal with this shit. I need a shotgun.

Her husband nodded like a social worker, or a pussy-whipped piece of shit with no guts no balls and no sense of when it's time to dump the bitch or at least crack her one good, but Mommy's face as I talked began to contort, to writhe and twist, her lip curling, her eyes fuzzing over and then flickering like chrome in the sunlight.

Her husband went into the bathroom. While he was gone, my mother began quivering and twitching. I lit a cigarette.

I poured myself a drink.

Then her face wrenched, and she opened her mouth, and she howled, and the howl was in the voice of a man. She kicked and flailed her arms, and then she clawed at her face with her fingernails and said, "Bad. Bad. Bad."

"Hey," I said, calling to her husband. "You need to come out here and deal with this shit."

He walked out of the bathroom and pinned her down on the couch and stopped her from scratching her eyes out. I remembered I'd forgotten to take the trash to the curb that morning.

"It's George," her husband said. "One of the bad alters."

Her husband began his routine: he told my mother that he was locking George into an air-tight casket. He used both words and hand gestures to catch George, to open the casket, to stuff George into the casket. He even tightened the screws down. His hand gestures kept getting interrupted because whenever he'd let go my mother's wrists, she would scratch at her eyes, so he'd have to grab her wrists and pin her down again. Finally he managed to padlock the casket shut and blast it into outer-space. He even equipped the casket with its own rocket propulsion system, because my mother asked how the casket could keep on going forever just on its own, without any help. In outer-space, my mother's husband kept telling her, George could never get to Molly or any of the other good alters. It worked, and my mother stopped trying to scratch her eyes out. Funny thing, though. She didn't draw any blood on that face of hers. She was a fuck of a lot better scarring her sons than she was ripping into herself.

I've seen plenty of the "alters." Sometimes they call me at night when my mother has slipped away and she's on the freeway being driven around by a bad alter, or even a child alter who is afraid of driving. Other times they call me and cuss me out.

So I knew that my mother was going to flip out, lose it for everyone at the wedding to see so that they'd pay attention to her and not to Pop, upstage the wedding and draw a crowd of sympathetic onlookers to console her and tell her everything was all right.

Father Camozzi was about to wrap it up and pronounce Pop and Mary man and wife. They put the rings on each other. Pop got one of his old wedding rings shined up special for the new marriage, and he got Mary a ring from Franco Flores, who specialized in watches, rings, and stereos. Her ring had a diamond on it the size of a doorknob, and it only cost three hundred bucks. Flores told Pop she could wear it anywhere this side of East 14th Street. They kissed, and Pop grabbed Mary's ass and lifted her wedding skirt. Mary grabbed Pop's cock. We all cheered and clapped and laughed, and then the band played the recessional march and Lura and Tura lifted their tube tops and wagged their titties like water balloons and Pop and Mary walked through the crowd, Pop's hand on her ass still and Mary tugging away. We threw rice at them. Pop was really happy.

The band kicked it into gear and played a disco song, one of the old black dudes trying to make his voice sound fag. People danced. Kids threw footballs and frisbees. Kegs bubbled and slobbered on the grass. Rhonda stuck her tongue in my ear. I got a hardon.

My mother leaned against me and pressed a fake tit against my chest. It felt like an overinflated inner-tube. She said, "Bad. Bad. Bad bad," and Gail had a look on his face like he'd eaten something nasty and was about to fart and was really working trying to hold that puppy in. Lura or Tura was standing next to Blewer and banging her tits against his chest, and her husband, Leroy, eyed Blewer pretty good. Grandpop Murphy's wife stood up and danced like she used to be a stripper a million years ago when she wasn't fat and old and blind.

Pop walked up to the band. They cut the disco crap mid-riff. The amps buzzed and we were quiet. Pop took his horn from its case. It shone through its soot tarnish. His hands were inked with grease even though he'd probably scrubbed them raw with an SOS pad. He took the mike and said, "This song is dedicated to my bitch!" and the band kicked in and it was a slow blues, "As Time Goes By," sleazy and sexy and washed with all the sadness and joy and asskick hosewhipped gruel of our place, of our Oakland, of the docks and piers and factories and of the railroad tracks and the slaughterhouse fume and the Hershey acrid stink that somehow became chocolate, of the General Mills plant that made you yaak your throat into your hands when you walked past, of all the Chinese and Negroes and Japanese internment survivors and of the Okies like us who came to CA desperate for a vine to bite and a piece of dirt that would give grain, and the beat of the music and the walk of the bass and the slow and sparse chords of the Hammond organ slipped into the air like the slimy ooze of late night tenth time in the day fucking. Man, those boys set down like there was only, in the universe, the song they were playing, the great and almighty song of fuck and fuck and more fuck more.

And Pop brought his horn, the old family trumpet that had been the trumpet of his father before him and that someday when I could again play and when Pop deemed me worthy of the horn's ancestry would be mine, brought the horn to his lips cracked with ten worlds of radiator fanned wind and creased with valleys of oil and grease that would never wear away, brought that horn up and pressed his lips to the mouthpiece and with the bellows of his chest, with the force of all his anguish and love and lust and will to endure, the force of all that constituted what he *was* and the force of what he *would* be and had been, the force of a man who should not be standing surefooted and planted but who should instead have been piledriven into the asphalt earth like the ruins of a splendid society the likes of which man would be better off never having known—with force and yet restraint, the restraint of a million years of doing the shit work for brutes bigger or smarter or less compassionate and therefore more powerful, the restraint of the man at work upon whom his family depends for sustenance, for bread and water and fire and skins, the humility and seething rageboil of a man for whom a ten-state murder spree is never more than an insult away, never more than a single instance of despair from becoming a plan, a vocation, a mission, a relief and justification for a life of endless and constant pain and silence and sucking it the fuck up. To be an American, to be an American and a man, an American a man and a working man, is to be a sultan of restraint, gorgeous enslaved and eager quims wagging in front of your face and you with no hint of hardon. If there weren't laws and we weren't so shitscared of them, each of us each day would kill, and not just kill with discretion, but with sure and steady and satisfied impunity. Find me an American man who claims he does not want to kill at least once in a day each day of his life, and you've found one lying son of a bitch, one you'd better watch out for, because he just might want to kill you. Trust me. I never lie.

And even though I shivered watching Pop swell I wanted to see Pop other than he was. I had some questions I wanted to ask Pop.

I wanted to ask Pop why he quit playing his music though Pop had made excuses, blaming the bitch, the whore, the cunt, the cooze, my mother, the cause of all that was shit in not only his life but in the lives of all men, my mother the ruin of Oakland, the downfall of the unions, the reason the gooks kicked our asses in both Korea *and* Nam, the reason the blacks overran the nice neighborhoods of old, the reason car parts were going over to the metric system and hardworking American mechanics were having to retool their socket sets, my mother the slut behind the conspiracy to destroy the non-homo white male and replace him with a pantie-weary army of three-piece Florsheim-wearing faggots—that's why Pop couldn't play the goddamn trumpet anymore, for if he did, the divorce gods would descend and strip him of all he had left, his trailer, his new bitch, and his tools.

I knew all this already though, knew it by heart and by cadence, and I wanted to ask Pop if though he no longer played he still heard music in the world, if there was music in the clack of jackhammer, in the hydraulic moan of dynahoe, the whine of Bobcat and the arc-sound wrecking ball swing, if now that he spent his time breaking down truck tires and felt in his hands the sledgehammer instead of the trumpet, felt his viscera vibrate with the rhythms of air-compressor instead of with string-bass and piano and his own fingers caressing the pads of the trumpet, if now that he beat things level with earth instead of ascending with the muses and angels he had achieved some hidden sinister goal, some act of revenge against himself, his family, his people, and his mysterious nameless gods. I wanted to ask Pop if the music of his past, the music of his blood, the notes of mothers' and fathers' voices before him haunted him in his dreams. I wanted to ask Pop if he was like an old piano whose keys had not been touched in a generation, the marrow in the white and black keys dried and drained for lack of touch, for lack of flesh on bone.

When I was a boy I used to listen to Pop play trumpet at the Baptist church with the old jazzmen, white-haired men with workblacked faces wearing shipyard blues and machinist coveralls, their names stitched to their workclothes in red, horncases beaten like toolboxes. I listened to Pop and I sat on the pews and looked at the cross in the shadows of the after hours and the church smelled of cigars and gin and menthols, the pastor at the piano singing his chords as he played them, his voice many voices stacked upon each other as if Babel instead of being a cacophony of noise were instead language turned chorale and that chorale turned jazz-mass by the magical solo fugue of the pastor, his voice booming like a section of perfectly harmonized trombones. The drummers in this church and with my father not drummers but instead musicians who understood that the drum no more carries the beat than does the bass or the horns or the piano but is itself an instrument of music and each drumstick against calfskin or sheepskin contains within the stroke and impact the possibility of not merely a single percussive punctuation but the certainty of all notes playing at the same time, and each tom-tom and floor-tom and bass-drum and cymbal and high-hat contains in itself the expanse and range of the sounds of nature, the drum not something beaten, but something played, music lifting rather than being hammered out. The trumpets and trombones, ores mined from earth and forged and wrought into brass and silver extensions of veins and arteries and lungs and I would squint so bright were the starfires that shot from the horns twisting in the candleflames and pit-lights, these horns born in the fires of earth and even when pianissimo seemingly crouched and waiting to attack with the ferocity of beasts untamed and primordial with lust and passion and the sex of the earth's ongoing creation, these primal heralds the troubadours of war, goat-hooved satyrs of cities ancient and rising phoenixed into the dark and darkening skies of jazz. The upright bass and its womanly shape, bassists never sitting but standing and not just standing but entwined with the wood and gut-string and pressed into the instrument like lovers into loved, always restrained, eternal foreplay, fingering the strings now in gentle strokes and now plucking as if to punish, and the sound of the bass itself rolling slow through the church. But none of these instruments, none of the sounds made by the transformation of nature into the appendages of man struck me as did the sound of my own father's horn, and I could tell the sound of Pop's trumpet amid a line of fifteen. I could tell the sound of Pop's lips on the mouthpiece, the old silver Conn held together by Pop's father's own handicraft with soldering iron and file, its sound when Pop played cascading over the other players like a room of strings downbeating at the opening of a Mahler symphony, which I the child did not realize until the first time I heard Mahler, many years later when I was in college and trying to impress a girl and took her, therefore, to the symphony, where, when the downbeat of Mahler's *Resurrection Symphony* stroked I said, "Pop," and

I wept, the girl at my side dumbfounded and saying, "Yes, it's beautiful," and I with my face in my hands saying softly and again, "You don't understand, you can't understand." This sound which issued forth from my father's trumpet was the wind pirouetting through the tulles, the sound of a storm-gale blowing over the open pipes of a playground jungle-gym, the howl of a chimney in a hurricane. Pop seemed to me then not my father alone nor the son of man but a being wholly inhuman, wholly at one with the elements from which the trumpet was made and those elements combined to bring the trumpet vibrating into life. And I (I remembered being too young to walk on my own, unable to speak the voices within myself) sitting in the pew and understanding that I was in a holy place.

Pop, Pop—why did you give up? I wanted to know. I wanted to know if the lack of courage is something you began on your own or if it was something passed on through Okie shit blood, a trait sent down through the ages from the times when our people were beaten prostrate and humbled hopeless, our courage a vice and death-sentence, I wanted to know if the lack of courage was your personal and generational invention or if it was my destiny, a destiny I would have been better off not attempting to elude, a heritage I should have understood and therefore embraced and welcomed and coddled like a retard kid, mine.

And Pop blew, and no telling whether or not the band knew the tune but no doubt they knew the *song*, negroes they, they knew the song because they'd sung it and they were singing it and they'd never in America cease to sing that fucker. They knew Pop's song, because Pop was nigger as nigger they, and so was I, nigger me, and as long as we pissed and shat in the same plastic construction site outhouses we'd always be niggers together, our shit mingling in the bowels of every urban shithole in the world. Those black boys played a chord that so made Pop's opening breath resound that there wasn't a person on the GE lawn that didn't know in their heart, in their gonads, that this note, this note that was a song, was something from

Bud, from Pop, the father of us all and all us but me, a song we not only knew but all knew was a song that told our story, our stories individual and collective, the stories of our fucks and not-fucks, the stories of our divorces and our children, the ones we could never again see and the ones we never again wanted to see, the ones we'd raised and the ones we'd not been permitted to raise, the ones we'd rather have seen drowned in the San Leandro creek—the water that separates the Negroes from the not-negroes in Oakland—and the ones we'd kill the bitches to be able to raise the *right* way, the *Oakland* way, the way of Don't you fuck and If you think *shit* well *don't, don't,* watch the fuck out Oakland motherfuck watch your ass bitch out right. Bud's song, my father's song, the song of Pop, had begun and all of us felt pride and guilt at the same time, at the same time felt guilt and pride and fuck you and up your ass bitch I'll kill you and I'll fuck you forever, and that's the way good music works. Try me otherwise.

He blew. Every note he'd ever played came back to me, the times he stood before the tropical fish tanks in the living room of our shotgun shack on 62nd avenue in Oakland, the fish themselves dancing no shit dancing to the sound of his trumpet, bobbing and swaying to the gentle and hatred echo of the bruits that issued from the metal of the family horn—I remember this with clarity that is bestowed only upon the cursed and the blessed—the fish somehow part of a universal dance that as a child only I understood, and only I will ever understand, for I am a child and always will be always.

Pop blew and his horn shone and Pop stood in an attitude of dignity and propriety that bespake something beyond the gas station and the trailer in which he lived, which went beyond the dumps and the tracks and the warehouses and the junkyard dogs but which at the same time encompassed, and more: which *embraced* them all, which extrapolated upon the fullness and spectrum of life, which ranged between dock and soiree, between cheap beer and fancy Champagne, between worn out blowjob whore and gorgeous bimbo divorce queen, between *us* and *them*, and with Pop playing there really didn't seem to be much difference between us and them at all. With Pop playing, blowing his cracked-lip air-tone soul into and through and out of the horn of our family, it seemed and most likely was true that in this life of ours the only common denominator is song. Pop's tone was so pale, so incandescent and yet ethereal, that he seemed to be playing ever more silently the more forceful he blew, as if the interposition of his being into the world was not an intrusion, not an interjection, but was instead being absorbed, embodied. Pop moved toward silence. Which made sense, which could only be, for when man made music to praise gods now dead and some recently forgotten he was attempting to silence the noise he had made, the noise which had chased the gods into circles more silent because only in silence can the whispers of the gods be recognized, so subtle are they and still.

A man with a beard walked onto the GE lawn, his beard yellow he toothless, his mouth sucked in and lipless. His mouth moved as if he would talk but did not.

A dog somewhere bleated.

The yellow-bearded man pulled out his pud and began pissing, and above the music and the wedding assembly he said, "It will get colder."

He laughed and the flesh of his face bubbled obscene with unneeded skin and the man began chanting some weird shit none of us could understand. A song.

The task of a man of music is to cancel out the noise of man. To disappear the noise man creates with noise more beautiful.

And Pop played, and the oldsters of the band backed him as if Pop were Miles Davis or Chet Baker or Clifford Brown, Pop sailing through the chords as if those chords were the echoes of all he'd never tell any of us, the reverberations of howls and pleas made in the small hours to men and women at bars and clubs none of us, the workers, the cement masons and asphalt layers and riprappers and hod carriers and dump truck drivers of Oakland would ever know, so much different was Pop, at this moment, Pop in his suit and the family trumpet to his lips and his tone slowly turning from shimmer to lip-shot hiss, so much not like us for the first time ever was Pop. I felt like I knew everything about him, every nuance and every ache and every woman he'd ever loved, and yet at the same time I felt as if I'd never known a thing about him, never known him to speak a sentence that was honest and true. And I thought, Words don't even approximate truth. The only truths in life are love and stupor and music.

Rhonda leaned into me and pressed her face against my chest. My mother whispered and shook and said, "Bad, bad, bad, bad." Lura and Tura flanked Blewer like fleabag dogs rubbing themselves against a cyclone fence, Blewer beer in one hand flask in the other. Leroy eyed Blewer with hate.

When the song ended, no one clapped, no one cheered. Everyone drank, tipped their beers and their flasks and their screw-cap half-pints and drank, a communion holy and reverent and solemn.

Then Pop leaned toward the mike, and he said, "For my bitch!" and we yelled, and Pop bowed and walked toward Mary and Mary mashed herself against him and they kissed. If I'd have been the kind of guy who cried, I might have. But I'm not that kind of guy.

Pop and Mary peeled off on the lawn, Mary's blouse unbuttoned and Pop without his shirt, hairy barrel chest soaked in beer and glistening. Oil stains greased his forearms and back where he'd missed when he washed up before the wedding. One of Mary's tits plopped out of her black bra, and she didn't mind but Pop reached over and stuffed that puppy back in gently as if he were being careful with an expensive inner-tube he'd just patched. Grandpop Murphy and his fat blind wife did some kind of Irish jig I didn't know and had never before seen or imagined, rickety and beautiful and you could hear Grandpop Murphy's bones clacking like bad lifters.

My mother's husband walked through the throng and the Concrete

Wall Sawing guys dumped beer on him, but my mother's husband just smiled while they poured and the more they poured the more cool my mother's husband looked. You didn't know what to make of this guy, the way he seemed immune to everything, the way he seemed like the kind of dude who could, if he wanted to, take anyone out, but who was either too nice or too badass to do it, and the not knowing which he was—nice guy or killer—that's what made you creepy all over. Everyone was getting pretty loaded. Chuck Santos, one of the Markstein guys, puked florescent yellow in the back of his truck and then he stood up tall and beat his chest, a beer in each hand, and then he chugged them. He could really drink, Chuck Santos.

Soaked and smiling creepy with straight white teeth my mother's husband walked up to Pop.

Blewer pulled himself loose from the twins and said, "Business?"

I nodded. "Business," I said.

I stood up, my mother still saying, "Bad bad," and hanging onto my arm like a drunk waitress. Rhonda pulled my mother off me and broke her beer bottle against the rim of a Yandell 18-wheeler and handed me the jagged neck. She smiled at me and then she slipped her arms over my shoulders and around my neck and kissed me, tongue. I got a hardon. I pulled her close to let her know. She pushed against it. I squeezed the bottleneck in my hand. I was ready to rumble.

Leroy grabbed Blewer's arm. "What you been doing looking at my woman?"

Blewer laughed.

"You been looking at my woman," Leroy said, and Blewer looked Leroy straight. Some more of Mary's relatives started toward Blewer, seven or eight men with crooked teeth and ugly wives, and they swayed and their eyes spun with booze. Father Camozzi set his Book of Common Prayer and his Bible down on the fender of one of the Yandell trucks and rolled up his sleeves and started toward Pop and Mary and my mother and her new husband. Father Camozzi was an expert at weddings. I'd played my trumpet at Mexican weddings that broke out in gang wars and one time I saw Father Camozzi crack six guys' heads open with the billy-club he kept under his habit. By the time Father C was done with those guys, everyone stopped fighting and went back to drinking like the family they had become and would remain.

Father C reached his arm beneath the robe and pulled out the billy-club, and man we all made way and made way and made fucking way. But Mary's clan didn't. They were probably from some part of town that didn't have priests or they'd have known to back the fuck off.

Leroy slapped his woman, Lura or Tura, and he said, "Put your fucking tits away, pig," and Blewer said, "Oink," and Leroy said, "You calling my woman a pig?"

My mother walked through the crowd toward her husband and toward Pop, and the guys whistled and hooted and my mother swung it up, giving leg and showing the personality I always saw whenever there were men around, and Franco Melendrez swung his arm around my mother's waist and she leaned on in and grabbed his cock through his Ben Davises and Melendrez put his hands to her shoulders and tugged her dress down so only her fake tits held up her dress. Her husband was almost to Pop, and Mary saw him coming and threw a beer bottle at him. Leroy spat at Blewer, and Rhonda looked at me—and it seemed like everything was beginning to happen all around her and she was touched by none of it, as if in this shit of a world, this stinking hellhole that was Oakland, nothing could touch her, nothing could affect her, nothing could make her a part of it or make her any less beautiful, any less a chick for whom a man would die and work the worst job in the world forever if only he knew she'd be at home waiting for him with a beer cracked and a roasted chicken on a plate, as if while we all fought and battled and gutted each other like shit-for-ditch fish she, Rhonda, would hover over all of us like an angel, like a warrior goddess who would choose a side and whose choice would decide all our fates—Rhonda looked at me with a sparkle and glint and crooked lip I'll-fuck-you-love-you-and-never-leave-you look that let me know that whatever happened, no matter how bloody I got, no matter how many of her relatives kicked my ass and sliced me up, she'd bring me a beer while I soaked in Epsom salts and pretended I didn't need to cry.

Everyone was smacking someone now and the melee swirled, arms flailing, men breaking beer bottles against their trucks and pulling the Bucks from their belts and flashing steel, Blewer swinging Leroy around by the neck and Lura and Tura slapping Blewer upside the head, Mary holding my mother by the hair and slapping her down to the ground, then yanking my mother's hair again and again slapping my mother to the ground. Mary's relatives scrambled and some of the Overhead Door guys hauled them back into the fight, and no one knew who was fighting who and Concrete Wall Sawing Bob, the biggest jackhammer operator in the East Bay, stood in the center of the mess laughing and laughing and beating his chest like a gorilla. Grandpop Murphy sat down at the edge of the crowd and rested his head against a keg, his wife bouncing around in circles like she was doing some obscene fat blind Mexican hat dance.

My mother said, "Yes, yes, yes," and someone pulled her dress down, and my mother's husband turned to look when he heard her voice and Pop cracked him upside the head with the family trumpet and I threw up on someone.

Lura or Tura was bleeding. Blewer and Concrete Wall Sawing Bob were laughing together, clubbing anyone who came within fist. Grandpop Murphy's wife was a slut with no one to fuck. Grandpop Murphy was dead.

I cut my way through the crowd and checked Pop mid-swing as he was about to crack one of his new relatives. Mary danced and swung a beer bottle around her head like a lasso. She looked really happy, Mary.

I pulled Pop toward me and I kissed him on the forehead.

"You gone fag?" he said.

"I love you," I said.

"Yeah," he said. "Just don't go faggot on me."

"Go," I said, and I put my arm around his shoulder and walked him toward his new wife and took her in the other arm, she swinging a beer bottle still and I walked them toward their honeymoon rig, a fancy '58 Caddy someone had set up for the occasion, baby blue and sparkling and beautiful, an ice chest full of beer in the back seat and a Raiders bobbing-head doll in the back window, Ben Davidson. I opened the door for him. His new wife got in on the passenger side.

"You're not my son," Pop said, "but you're a good son."

"And you're not my father," I said, "but you're a son of a bitch." And Pop smiled.

The fight was getting pretty bad. Grandpop Murphy's wife had nudged Grandpop Murphy and he'd tipped over and she tried to get him back into a sitting position but he tipped over again and I couldn't hear her but I saw her calling his name, at first softly and with love and then frantic with despair mixed with terror. If her eyes hadn't been milked with rheum they would have been wild. Lots of other people were down, even some of the kids. Someone had tied tin cans to the bumper of the Caddy and they clanged and sparked as Pop drove off.

I weaved my way through the fight to Rhonda, who stood untouched and smiling at me. She took my hand. I caught Father Camozzi's eye and waved at him and he came toward us and I turned to Rhonda and I said, "Marry me."

Rhonda smiled and she took my hand.

Father Camozzi clubbed someone and stepped over a wrangling pair of newly pronounced in-laws. "Marry me," I said, and I don't know what I said next, but what I should have said, and what I tell people I said, is this: Rhonda, marry me. Marry me now, here, here amongst and before my people, your people, these asshole warriors of shame and courage and despair and endurance—endurance, Rhonda, the thing we do, endure. Marry me now, here and in their sight and with or without their approval or even knowledge, Rhonda, now and here and know this, Rhonda, that though I am of them and though Oakland will never leave me, my blood and flesh spilled into countless construction sites and playgrounds, blood mixed with concrete and mortar and asphalt and skin now powder inhaled by all my fellow Oaklanders, though the smell of the dumps at which I live will never leave my memory if perhaps my pores, though, Rhonda, my scars roadmap the courses of both adversaries and friends and chart the hanging rebar and wire and cable of sewer and basement and jail-cell window-wire (yes, Rhonda, I've been there and seen men weep and soil themselves in abject fear and I was repulsed, not by my own act or my possible fate but by their cowardice and lack of understanding that all can be taken away any instant but their souls, which remain, which, intact, continue in sewer and dump and jail-cell), Rhonda, though I am of them and of this place and will never leave either, would not abandon either even were I able, I am not like them. I'm not like them, Rhonda. Rhonda, I'm not like them. I'm not. Marry me. I'm not like them. Really, I'm not.

Eric Miles Williamson's first novel, *East Bay Grease*, was a PEN Hemingway finalist and listed by both the *San Francisco Chronicle* and the *Los Angeles Times* as one of the best books of 1999. His second novel, *Two-Up*, was listed by the *Kansas City Star* and the *San Jose Mercury News* as one of the Best Books of Fiction published in 2006. The *Atlantic Monthly* said his 2007 book of criti-

photo by Jean-Luc Bertini

cism, *Oakland, Jack London, and Me*, is "one of the least politically correct texts of our time." He is an editor of *American Book Review, Boulevard*, and *The Texas Review*. Winner of fellowships from the National Endowment for the Arts and the Christopher Isherwood Foundation, after many years as a laborer Williamson went to college and now works at the University of Texas, Pan American. He lives with his wife, Judy, and their sons, Guthrie and Turner.

LaVergne, TN USA
30 September 2009
159509LV00002B/1/P